FINDERS KEEPERS, COWBOY

Rachelle Paige Campbell

© COPYRIGHT 2024 by Rachelle Campbell Dio
All rights reserved. No part of this book may be used or reproduced in any manner whatsoever without written permission of the publisher except in the case of brief quotations embodied in critical articles or reviews.

Warning: Not intended for persons under the age of 18. May contain coarse language and mature content that may disturb some readers. Reader discretion advised.

Cover Art Design by: Kelly Moran/Rowan Prose Publishing
Photo Credit: Adobe Images
First Printing
ISBN: 9781961967267
Rowan Prose Publishing, LLC
www.RowanProsePublishing.com
Published in the United States of America

PRAISE FOR
RACHELLE PAIGE CAMPBELL:

"A clean wholesome read romance fans will enjoy."
-In'd Tale Magazine

"I love Rachelle Paige Campbell's writing style."
-Long & Short Reviews

"A sweet story."
-Paranormal Romance Guild

Acknowledgments

First and foremost, I want to thank the late Dawn Dowdle of Blue Ridge Literary Agency. Dawn read an early version of this book (about twenty thousand words less than it is today) and signed me as a client. For a little over two years, she was my agent. Her kindness and patience came at the right moment of my career. She believed in me and my books, and I'll be forever grateful for the time we worked together.

A huge thank you to Kelly Moran at Rowan Prose Publishing for picking up the entire trilogy and to my fabulous editor, Katie O'Connor, for making this story shine. As always, I am grateful to my husband, my kids, and my parents for their unwavering encouragement.

Last, but not least, the Panera Supper Club supports every idea no matter how wacky. Thank you Kelly, Shannyn, Tammy, Kelly, Julie, and, of course, Miss Pamala for being the best writer friends in the whole world.

CHAPTER 1

R yan Kincaid hated wasting time. Hank, his grandfather, called him impatient. His late grandmother, Susie, used to berate him for twitchy legs. If he had focused more on fixing the flaw at any point in his thirty-eight years, he wouldn't have been in such a rush today. Could he have saved himself from nearly cutting off his finger? *Probably.*

The day went downhill before he even got out of bed.

The phone rang ahead of the alarm.

BRING. BRING. BRING.

The loud ringtone blared.

He stifled the growl building in his throat. The peaceful tones he'd selected for his alarm should gently rouse him. The electronic chime blasted, drawing attention for the caller.

Instead of sitting and reaching for his cell phone, he kept his head on the pillow and fumbled for the device on the nightstand. He swatted the phone off the smooth surface, it landed with a thud on the wooden floor.

The phone stopped ringing. He turned his head to the cool side of the pillow. Good, maybe he could get another few minutes of sleep.

Under his four-post bed, the cell rang again, louder than before.

Grumbling, he rolled out of bed and knelt on the floor. With his cheek pressed against the boards, he groped, his fingers connecting with the device near the back corner. Reaching, he caught the cell and tweaked his shoulder. Grunting, he retrieved the device and frowned at the screen. Two missed calls from his ranch hand, Ted.

In a rush, he pulled on his jeans and work shirt, groaning as his aching shoulder stretched. Downstairs in the kitchen, he operated on autopilot, brewing coffee without too much thought. He tapped a quick text message to Ted, grabbed a travel mug, and reached for the glass pot. He grabbed the carafe off the coffee maker too early. Hot coffee scalded his hand and spilled onto the floor. With paper towels, he soaked up the mess but couldn't rid the room of the lingering stench of burnt coffee.

He rinsed his hands with cold water. The icy chill did the caffeine's job, jolting him to full alertness. He wasn't sure he'd survive his next slip-up.

He didn't wait to greet his grandfather to review the day's plans. Striding from the house, he was out the front door as the sun rose. With the opening day approaching and guests arriving soon, he didn't have time for pleasantries. His grandfather, a dyed in the wool cowboy, would understand.

Missing those moments with his grandfather, however, nagged Ryan for hours. Since losing Grandma, he never wanted to take a moment for granted. Their time together was too precious to let a single second slip past unremarked or a beautiful morning go unnoticed.

The Kincaids had been ranching outside Herd, Montana since the nineteenth century. As one of the three founding families, their legacy was awash with intrigue and backstabbing. Eventually, they'd found stability and mutual respect with their only remaining neighbors, the Hawkes. Over the past decade, however, the Kincaids had been the last ranchers standing. And then Ryan had sold off the cattle and chased after an unexpected idea. High-end tourism.

Hopping into his truck, he drove out to the former Hawke property and the site of the newest lodging for the ranch's guests. Grass stretched toward the horizon, unbroken and abundant in every direction. The ground rose and fell in gentle undulations. His property had been claimed by his forebears for its pond and the creek that ran through the eastern boundary, believing a false claim of gold. But this stretch of landscape had been coveted by many a Kincaid for its seeming infinity.

He met up with Ted and the rest of the crew at the yurts. The traditional canvas tent home for nomadic tribes had been a unique choice for additional accommodation. Circular in shape, the structures both stuck out and blended into the rolling grass landscape. Set back from the new property line, he couldn't see his annoying neighbor Megan's house nor could she see his. He didn't want to encroach on anyone's privacy, legal right or no.

Sniggering, he shook his head. The woman would talk to his guests until they cried uncle and ran away, but he was steering clear. He wasn't some selfless neighbor, but a man looking out for his best interests. Since childhood, Megan had been an incessant chatterbox. Had she ever had a moment of quiet contemplation? Could she keep a thought or opinion to herself without blurting every idea to any passer-by? Didn't she have friends for girl-talk? He hated feeling cornered at every encounter.

Of course, Hank didn't care. She was thick as thieves with his grandfather. Always had been. In his youth, their bond stuck in Ryan's craw. Couldn't she spend her summer vacation with her family and leave his alone?

Grandma had understood. She was quiet like Ryan. To his chagrin, Grandma, his staunchest ally, had found Meg charming in the sort of head-scratching, bewildering way he reasoned everyone must like her. He wanted peace. Meg craved chaos. Even now, when she wasn't physically close, she was stirring up his mind.

He parked the truck, leaving the keys in the ignition and hopping out of the cab. He scanned the worksite. Cupping hands around his mouth, he whistled.

His lead ranch hand, Ted, and the two men hired for the summer turned their heads. Standing near the first of three yurts, they circled the erected frame.

"How's it going?" Ryan called, strolling toward the group.

Ted turned away from the men and strode toward the boss. "Glad to catch you. I haven't had luck finding a replacement yoga instructor with such short notice. Most of our back-ups have accepted other roles."

Ryan nodded. He wasn't surprised. Before he'd turned the ranch into a resort, he wouldn't have imagined many in town had ever heard of the exercise discipline. Their corner of the world wasn't awash with yogis. "I asked Joe to put the word out at school. One of the teachers might have a hidden talent."

Ted stroked his jaw.

Joe was a middle school teacher and, in the summers, tour guide. His knowledge of the history of the ranches and Herd was unparalleled. With a love for meeting new people, he was a natural for the part-time role.

"Or you could fill in?"

Ted grunted.

Ryan chuckled and clapped a hand on the cowboy's shoulder. "Never say never, right?"

"Sure, learned that since I started here."

Dropping his hand, Ryan scrubbed his face. While he employed a few additional cowboys in the summer season to mend fences, maintain the property, and separate wildlife from guests, he mostly employed spa staff. The old bunk house was now co-ed, and Ted managed people more than animals.

Life had definitely changed in ways unimaginable even a generation earlier when this land had been devoted to grazing cattle. "Never mind that problem. If someone doesn't turn up, I'll issue refunds for the classes already booked. I'll come up with something else to add to the schedule. You could teach meditation."

Ted chuckled.

"How's the progress out here?"

"Good. We're almost ready to stretch the canvas over the frames," Ted said.

Ryan grinned and rubbed his palms together. "I'm right on time."

"You sure about this?" Ted tipped his head to the side.

The question was fair. Ryan's latest venture wasn't a guaranteed success. When he'd first considered the idea of adding more campsites to the property, he'd hesitated.

For a while, he'd been in discussion with several wildlife groups about reintroducing a bison herd to the town named for the grouping. If the environmental impact and ecological study was approved by Herd's town council at their meeting in the fall, the first bison would be introduced in the spring.

The needs of the bison would take precedence on his land. He had no intention of swapping cattle for bison and raising the animals for profit. He wanted to restore the balance of nature to the ecosystem, and he'd be glad to let the animals take over the grass. Too much time and money had been spent on mowing and maintenance that the bison would handle for free.

The yurts might last one season. Ryan understood and accepted the risk. When he decided to make reparations, he was prepared for the potentially expensive and short-term chance. He profited off a complicated family legacy of arrogance that settled the land and placed man's will above nature. His family had been at least partially responsible for the devastation of bison herds.

The animals had been eradicated from the environment by force. Their treatment was only one in a long list of historic misdeeds. He was glad to do his small part to correct past wrongs. But he couldn't let fear of tomorrow's failure hold him back today. The ranch's lodging expansion was happening. "I'm ready. Show me what to do."

He listened, without comment, to Ted's instructions on completing the yurts. While the tents were Ryan's idea, he had tasked Ted with deployment. Construction could be tricky and dangerous. Withing a few minutes, Ryan proved his point.

In the process of stretching the canvas over the first frame, he reached for his knife to slice the material. In a second, he lost his grip and plunged the blade too far. He yelped and swore. Holding the finger tight, he staunched the bleeding with his shirt.

"You better clean up and find a bandage. I'll finish this," Ted said. "Can't have you bleeding over the yurts or dying of an infection on opening weekend."

With a grumbled, muttered oath, Ryan nodded and retreated to his truck. He drove the rutted road toward the house, cradling his injured hand to his chest and steering with his right. Hitting each bump and dip jarred him, and he winced.

At the fork to the house, he drove around back and slowed on the gravel drive leading to the barn. He kept a first aid kit on a shelf inside the doors for treating guests quickly. He couldn't remember where band-aids might be stashed inside the ranch house. He could ask Hank but would probably bleed out before Hank finished some non-relevant anecdote. His grandfather loved to spin a yarn.

He parked next to the barn and frowned. Motion in his peripheral vision caught his attention. He snapped his head and spotted her. Megan.

"What in the world," he muttered, pocketing his keys, and hopping from the vehicle.

In a few quick strides, he reached the outbuilding Hank had assumed control of years back. The uninsulated, man-cave was not to be entered without express permission of its rightful laird, Hank Kincaid. Not that a person could sneak in. A chain strung through the door handle and an iron ring was secured with a lock.

Ryan had never seen the key. He'd only been inside once with Grandma, and the visit lasted ten seconds. Hank had packed the structure from floor to ceiling. Grandma and Ryan hadn't managed more than three steps inside. The collection didn't allow for a person to take their time and survey the contents. They had retreated, walking backwards to do so, and neither mentioned the shed again. Their determination withered with the reality of the project.

Today, however, some clever person—or rascally Grandfather—found a way inside.

Stained, cardboard boxes surrounded the shed's perimeter.

With each step, he discovered more debris, and the throbbing in his temples increased.

A pile of old magazines was stacked on a broken chair against the side of the shed. The furniture leaned to one side. Another few ounces of weight, the precarious structure would tip and the yellowed pages would scatter.

Breathing in through his nose, he willed a calm he didn't feel. Patience was a virtue he couldn't find. He had enough work to do without adding another project. Cleaning up after Hank's mess wasn't ideal on a good day, let alone when he didn't have the use of both hands and was under a time crunch.

Surely the old man couldn't have gotten himself into this much trouble alone. He was no longer capable of this much physical labor in a relatively short amount of time. Shutting his eyes, Ryan shook his head and breathed deep.

A familiar floral scent tickled his nostrils. High-pitched chatter danced in the air. He swallowed the groan building in his throat. Frustration pounded in his forehead in time to his heartbeat. *Why is Meg the root of all problems?*

"Of course, I had to take the chance. Right? You understand," Meg said.

Who was she talking to? His hand throbbed. Was Hank inside, listening to the inane prattle?

Ryan stepped over the threshold and frowned. "What is going on here?"

A low woof woof responded.

He stood in the doorway, blocked the exit, and squinted into the dark interior. Without power, the outbuilding had no light source making it hard to confirm if she was alone or not. Blinking, his eyes adjusted.

At the back, Meg sat on the floor, a pink skirt floating around her like a gauzy cloud and her arm wrapped around a salt and pepper colored, mid-sized dog. She cooed to the dog, glaring at the entrance. "You scared her."

"What?" He poked his chest with a finger and strode forward. "Me?"

The dog howled.

"Yes, you. Who else? Is someone behind you? Are you hiding Hank?" She turned to the dog. "Shh, shh, Colby. It's okay." She returned her gaze to him. "Hold out your hand."

"Excuse me?" He drew back his chin. She trespassed on his property and had the nerve to dictate orders?

"You heard me." She got to her feet, straightening, and pulling back her shoulders. "Hold out your hand. Colby needs to sniff you. She needs to know you're a friend."

Am I? He frowned. Adding a dog bite to his list of injuries wasn't worth holding his ground against her. The black and white poodle mix was a stray Meg had rescued a few years ago. He'd worried she was getting herself in over her head by owning any dog, let alone one with unknown origins. Instead of telling her, however, he did the next best thing. He told Hank and let the old cowboy warn her off. Not that it had made any difference.

"It's okay, Colby. He's nice." She patted the dog on the top of the head. "To animals." She studied him.

He stared at her until she had the sense to glance away.

The dog trotted forward, sniffing the air, and wagging her tail.

He held out his hand.

She nosed his knuckles.

The cold sensation caught him off-guard, and he tightened his fist, wincing as he added pressure to his fresh wound.

"Oh, no. Are you hurt?"

He sucked in a breath and raised his hand, elevating the finger and holding it to his chest.

She neared, stopping inches away. "Hold out your hand. Can I see?"

"Why?"

"Because I can help." She rolled her eyes. "You don't have to be the macho, tough guy all the time."

Is that what you think? She wanted to fling insults and accuse him of casual misogyny? While destroying his land?

"Oh, stop shaking your head. Just hold out your hand and let me see," she insisted.

You're not dressed for it. She wore some sort of floaty, flimsy pink dress with a jean jacket over top. She always wore the clothes she wanted and not what was suitable to the task. He wouldn't get anywhere arguing against her outfit. He'd tried that too many times over the years.

She reached for him, grazing her fingers along the back of the hand resting near his collarbone.

He'd left the top of his work shirt unbuttoned and revealed an inch of tough, tanned skin on his neck. With the wide brim of his hat, he hadn't worried about overexposure. Until too late.

Her light touch sent shockwaves through him. He stared at her hand. What would happen if he looked at her and acknowledged the strange surge pulsating between them? He didn't have time to ask the question let alone learn the answer.

If he didn't have a second to stop his finger from bleeding, he definitely didn't have another minute for the odd sensation stirred up with her subpar nursing skills. "No, get out," he murmured.

"I'm sorry? Did you say something?" She tilted her head to the side.

Had she not heard him? He wasn't sure if he should laugh or cry. "Leave, Meg. Now," he delivered the words with as much stoicism as he could muster. "I don't know why you're here. Or what possessed you to trash my yard. In five days, the first guests arrive. You have single handedly added hours to my day. I know you don't like me. But why are you sabotaging my ranch? The tourists who stay here spend plenty of their dollars in towns at stores like yours." He kept his voice steady, never raising to any level that might be misconstrued as yelling. But he wanted no misunderstanding about his seriousness.

Red-cheeked, she straightened, flaring her nostrils. "Hank invited me. He asked for my help."

Well, he didn't tell me. If he wasn't annoyed, he'd admire her backbone. Instead of shrinking, she stood tall and held his gaze. He wasn't sure what was worse, the uninvited, stubborn woman on his property or his secretive, rule-breaking grandfather. While running a business together, they'd established one very important rule. Talk to each other. Hank, his grandfather, had not kept Ryan informed today.

"I'm asking you to go." He lifted his injured hand high on his chest, shielding the wound from view but redirecting the blood flow back into the limb.

She pulled back her shoulders and took in a breath.

Here comes the wind-up. He knew her cues and didn't want the fight she was readying for. He wanted so many other things. Top of his list, he sought every ounce of serenity he could muster in the dwindling days of solitude on the ranch.

Once the resort opened for the summer, his house would be a revolving door of guests and staff. No inch of his ten thousand acres would be spared from incessant chatter. For a loner, he chose a shocking new direction for family business. If he righted some past wrongs and saved the land for another generation, every sacrifice would be worth the effort.

"Okay, I'll go." She held up her hands, palms facing out. "You can tell Hank you ran me off. I'll leave the clean-up to you and Ted. Come on, Colby. Let's head to the store. We've got a business to run."

If rumors were to be believed, her words weren't mere segue to escape an uncomfortable situation. He'd never seen much of a crowd at her antique store. Was she struggling? He almost asked. Neighbors helped each other here. But he was too frustrated to form the words.

With the dog at her heels, she strode down the significantly widened center aisle. The shed's very own equator had been transformed from a thin line to several feet wide. For the first time, he spotted the plywood floor, a mismatch of different scraps unified by a dark stain.

If he didn't have junk littering the lawn he wanted to mow, he'd be impressed by her handiwork. She must have been the one to clear the path. Hank couldn't be decisive about his things. She'd moved quick on sorting the items. Hank picked the right person for the job. The man needed to learn how to choose a better moment.

She reached the door.

Her light, lavender perfume wafted on the cool, late spring breeze. He breathed in the scent and studied her.

Her chin trembled, and her hands shook.

She was too delicate for ranch life. Every year, he expected her to cut ties and run. She was slight and pretty. She wasn't a western woman. He'd known that since childhood. The day she finally realized she might find real purpose in her life, somewhere far away, he'd cheer if he didn't fear she'd take that as encouragement to stay. Now, he stepped to the side.

She exited.

The dog sniffed his hand and licked his palm.

The sandpaper tongue tickled his lifeline, and he jumped. He'd have to teach the pet what her owner already knew. He was tough and unyielding. He had to be. He had no room for sweetness or sentimentality. His life dealt in absolutes, and she was all murky grays.

He stared straight ahead, not daring to turn and glance her way. He stayed in place, counting to a thousand. At a thousand and one, he turned and spotted his grandfather strolling down the path.

Hank held up both hands. "You've scared her away?" His tone was incredulous.

Scared? Ryan would laugh if he wasn't so annoyed. Meg Hawke was intimidated by nothing and no one. "You know this is the worst time to start a project. Why send her here? She always gets in the way." He folded his arms over his chest.

"I have my reasons." Hank stopped a few yards away and pointed. "You want to bandage that cut before you start hauling everything back? Or maybe you should apologize to her first. Be mad at me. Not Meg. I called her."

"Why?" He muttered the word like he snuck in a swear. On the best days, Hank was entertaining. At his worst, he was exasperating.

"You've been mad at me about this mess for years. She has a business that could help me out. It's a win-win. You waste your energy searching for any reason to not like that girl. You're about the only person around who doesn't."

If that was true, why does she spend her time alone? Arguing with his stubborn grandfather wouldn't do any good. "Maybe the problem is I see her too clearly."

"Or maybe you're the fool who can't see himself for what and who he is."

Ryan held perfectly still, his injured finger throbbing in time to his pounding heart. If Hank wanted to illuminate who Ryan was, he'd listen. Most days, he kept his head down, racing from one task to the next. Focused on the business and the community, he'd admit he lost himself somewhere along the way.

A road map or instruction manual would be welcome, if Hank had either handy. Meeting his grandfather's steady stare, however, he nearly shuddered. In a single look, Ryan traveled back through time and was again the lost child, alone except for his grandparents. Disappointing his grandfather remained the worst sin.

Hank raised him better than to lash out at a longtime neighbor and accuse her of trespassing without cause. Ryan entered the shed burning from a hundred other frustrations that didn't involve Meg. She hadn't deserved his tirade. He shamed his family with the outburst.

Hank nodded slowly. "Come on, let's get you fixed. Then you can call Ted to help you clean the yard. I'll leave it to you to figure out how to apologize and get her back out here. We don't have all the time in the world for my project."

Don't I know it. "I'm not saying I'm sorry."

"Pardon?" Hank narrowed his gaze. "If you don't make time to do the right thing, you'll regret it."

Exhaling a sigh, Ryan sagged his shoulders. Why couldn't he have one exchange with Meg that didn't end in total frustration? He couldn't shake off Hank's words. For no reason, he'd been mean. Hank was right. Ryan owed her an apology. "I'm not running over there today. I'm too busy."

"Maybe you can't go tonight. Fine. You've got chores. But you need to make amends sooner than later." Hank strode away.

Ryan studied the ground. He wouldn't pretend he wanted a friendship with the girl who'd always gotten under his skin. For the honor of his family name, he'd admit he'd been wrong. First time for everything since he was always right.

CHAPTER 2

Kneeling behind the front window display of her antique store, half-hidden from passersbys on Main Street courtesy of the Frontier Days poster taped to the glass, Meg sprayed furniture polish directly on the water-stained floorboard and rubbed with a rag. With the fading daylight, she wasn't making any progress. Improving the decades old spot from a long since repaired window leak hadn't been a task she could cross of her to-do list. Which was exactly the point.

If she suffered frustration about something she couldn't change, she'd rather deal directly with an immovable object. The spot couldn't calmly berate her and, in a few seconds, send her back to her youthful misdeeds and every idea that ended in disaster. Under the steady, disappointed gaze of her childhood nemesis and neighbor, a rational defense had abandoned her. In the heat of the moment, she'd flinched at his words.

She sat back on her heels and dropped the rag, circling her aching wrists. Of course, her current location, wasn't exactly proof that she'd matured and changed.

Finders Keepers, her store for the past five years, struggled. When she had floated the idea of moving into her late grandmother's ranch house and using her savings from years of gallery work and living with her mom in their Chicago home, Meg had a champion in her mom. She'd been happy to know the ranch house would be lived in and cared for and even more thrilled that Meg would use her education and love of antiques to establish herself somewhere that had always felt like home.

Her savings funded her lifestyle. With the money dwindling, however, she needed the store to cover overhead costs and then some. If she couldn't turn a profit, she'd do what she should have done years ago and head back to Chicago. Mom wanted Meg to stay and succeed. But building a life in a small town in Montana wasn't easy.

For some, like unstoppable force Ryan Kincaid, sheer determination and willpower carried dreams from thoughts to reality. Meg admired him for what he'd done in transforming his ranch and revitalizing an entire community. Without him, the town would have disappeared from most maps. And his purchase of her family's land, leaving the ranch house untouched, set Mom up for the rest of her days.

Meg was grateful to him but wanted more. In her entire life, she had never revised Ryan Kincaid's opinion of her. Why grant him the power to upset her again? He had made his annoyance known more times than she could count. *The definition of insanity....*

Heaving a huge sigh, she sat back on her heels. Her issue was she sort of liked him. Sad as it was, he was her only age-appropriate, friendly acquaintance within a hundred miles. She wasn't oblivious enough to claim friendship. She'd like to though and had tried for years.

He was quiet and calm. While she'd never admit such a thing out loud, she appreciated his subdued personality. She was well aware others considered her a handful, overhearing the description a few times in town over the years. In his stoic company, she relaxed.

During every encounter, she vowed to do better. With advance warning, she gave herself a pep talk to listen and pause before speaking. At some point in each meeting, however, she slipped. She'd ask a question or make a comment. Instead of an immediate reply, he'd shoot her a look or tilt his head. She'd be so concerned about what he wasn't saying she'd blurt out anything to fill the silence with nervous chatter. If he couldn't remember why he shot her a stern expression, he'd stop judging her. Or so she had convinced herself.

The morning's encounter ruined everything. In her experience, she wasn't always met with his best manners, but he was unfailingly kind. In the grand scheme, she valued the latter more. Nice was about keeping up polite appearances. Kind was real depth and caring for other people. She had been so flustered by the whole encounter that she'd left with hurt feelings. Now she didn't know how to proceed without more awkwardness between them. She promised Hank, and she couldn't renege.

Their impromptu interaction in the shed kept replaying in her mind. With cool fierceness, he asked her to leave. His tone burned her skin like a sharp, biting, winter wind. She'd been shocked at his raised tone.

Red-cheeked and sputtering, she bolted and spent the rest of the day berating herself for both showing up without his permission and kowtowing to him, abandoning Hank and the project. She couldn't be righteously indignant when she accepted an equal share of the blame. In the past, she'd been guilty of machinations to involve him in her goals against his will.

A paw reached out, stroking the long-sleeve of her jean jacket.

"Sorry, Colby. You're right." She dropped the cloth and turned to the dog lying next to her, belly up. "I'm making no progress on my work. I might as well be useful to someone."

Petting the dog in long strokes, she fell into the rhythm of the motion, but the repetitive action wasn't enough to stop her whirring brain. She had thought she was being useful to Hank. Regardless of Ryan's opinion and whether or not she cared, she genuinely liked Hank.

With no memories of her grandfather, she gravitated toward Ryan's. Hank was quick-witted with a twinkle in his eye. After losing Susie, he dimmed. One bad joke at a time, he bounced back. She'd been happy to be part of the resurgence. She wasn't ready to lose him.

She had her suspicions the consignment idea wasn't pulled out of thin air. The only way she could be sure, however, was a call straight to the source. She leaned forward, pulling her cell from her back pocket and hit speed-dial.

"Hello? Meggie?" her mom greeted.

She smiled. Mom's voice was sing-song and bright, a perfect fit for her occupation as an elementary school art teacher. "Hi, Mom. Sorry I haven't called."

"It's okay, sweetie. I figured you were getting ready for your busy summer season. Besides, I've been following along on your blog."

Meg turned, resting her back against the wall. She pulled Colby into her lap. *Not much to follow at the moment.* "You and Hank are the only subscribers. I see the updates every time you *like* something."

Her blog was her first attempt at modernization, combining her love of history and storytelling. She couldn't stop herself from creating a backstory for every item that came into her shop. While the craze for blogging had faded in favor of other social media sites, she kept sharing entries on her website. If she spent less time on the not at all profitable venture and more time learning to code, she wouldn't be at her make-or-break moment now. "Speaking of Hank. Have you called him recently?"

"Old Mr. Kincaid? Your neighbor?"

Meg would like to witness Mom call him *old* to his mischievous, grinning face. "Yes, that's the one."

"Sweetie, why would I do that?"

Dragging in a shaky breath, Meg focused on the dog in her lap. At fifty pounds, Colby wasn't small enough to comfortably curl up on a human. At least not in the opinion of the human. Meg rested the dog's ribs and shoulders on her lap, stroking the dog's chest. With her legs losing feeling, she shifted the dog and stretched her limbs one at a time.

"Honey, are you there? Did I lose you?"

"Sorry, Mom. I was adjusting. The dog is on my lap."

Mom chuckled. "You mean the moose is on your lap."

"Colby is a show-quality doodle of murky pedigree and perfectly sized for a watchdog."

"No arguments about her size. She'd have to stay awake long enough to be qualified for a security role. What's going on with Hank? Why did you ask if I've talked to him? Any problems with the house?"

Meg exhaled a heavy sigh. "Did you call Hank and tell him the business is struggling and I might have to move back in with you in Chicago?"

"Umm ... I didn't call *him*."

"Oh, Mom." Meg groaned.

"Sweetie, I'm sorry. You know we care about you and want the best. Grandma loved Herd as much as you do. I want you to stay. If you need help, you can reach out to others. Dreams don't happen without help."

"I know." She wasn't the first to head west with a grand plan that never reached fruition. The pioneer spirit lived deep inside her. Grandma stoked her sense of purpose and adventure with tales of their ancestors.

Every summer of her childhood, she had relaxed here in a place she belonged. Spending her days roaming the land, she never had to adapt to please anyone else. Free to be herself for a few months, she recharged in time to return to life in Chicago with her single mom in a thousand-square-foot, two-bedroom condo. Mom grew up on the ranch in Montana and left the moment she could, preferring high rises and crowded streets.

Not Meg.

Growing up, she'd cherished the close-knit community and dreamed of moving here. After college, Meg had worked various gallery jobs, wishing for the chance to open her own store. Antiquing was a hobby born from visiting Grandma and loving history. Her family had owned their ranch since the nineteenth century. Meg loved the stories passed down from generations, often through objects, and absorbed everyone.

When the opportunity had arisen—a store for sale in town around the time Mom sold the land to the Kincaids—Meg jumped at the miraculous chance. At the start, she hadn't minded being an outsider. Five years later, she remained an out-of-towner to the locals. She wanted to belong.

Mom never made her feel ridiculous for wanting to head in the opposite direction. She encouraged the move. Had she anticipated the difficulties? She'd known the land and people with better insight. Meg hated to give up. Her choices dwindled. "I need a better plan."

"Did Hank help you find one?"

Not much of one. "No, but that's okay. It's not his problem, and it's not yours. I'm thirty-five, you can't keep rescuing me."

"I'll always help. You're my daughter."

Her mom encouraged every dream, promising a safe landing if she fell. She was both a safety net and a cheerleader. Meg found strength from her mom's love. "Within the first month of the summer, I should know if I can make a profit. It's not fair for you to miss out on the prime rental season." Her voice cracked. "I won't stay. I'll be out before the Fourth of July."

"Honey, please don't. I don't need to rent the house. I'm fine, and I'd hate for you to leave."

Meg knew the response she'd get. But she also was determined. "I have to face facts."

"I'll support whatever decision you make."

"Thanks, Mom." While Meg hated emotionally unloading over the phone, she appreciated the results. Without the weight of her potential failure, she held her head a little higher and pulled back her shoulders. She could admit the truth. "I'm hoping for a miracle."

"Which would be?"

"A consignment worth enough to garner attention and cover costs for the next year." The statement was hardly the sort of actionable goal she'd learned about during her years in business.

"You never know. Funny things happen in Herd. It's a special place full of possibilities."

The front door opened jingling bell over the entrance. A pair of boots clicked against the floor in a rhythm too familiar to ignore. Colby jumped to her feet and padded to greet the visitor.

Meg stood and spotted the last person she expected to see.

Ryan shut the door behind him and held his palms out.

With a wagging tail, Colby sniffed and licked his hands.

Meg hated the flutter low in her belly. Ryan didn't want her friendship. The awful truth was she'd always craved his. "Mom, I have to go."

"Of course. Bye, sweetie. Love you."

Hanging up the call, Meg stuffed the phone into her back pocket, dusted her hands on her jeans, and stared at him. For once, she had nothing to say.

Ryan pulled the ten-gallon hat off his head, holding it against his chest.

He wore dark jeans and a pressed black Western shirt. The outfit was one of the dressier options in his closet and something he typically only donned for his guests. Most often, he sported worn jeans and faded flannels. He'd gone to some trouble. For her? Her heart skipped a beat. She wouldn't read into his appearance. More likely than not, she wasn't the reason.

"Hi, Meg. Do you have a second to speak?"

Now he wanted her to talk? She traced the ridges on the roof of her mouth with her tongue, fighting the urge to reply.

Shifting his weight from foot to foot, his gaze darted around the room. He was uncomfortable. She nearly cheered. Only her desire to prolong the moment kept her quiet.

"Yep, okay, probably deserve the silent treatment." He sighed and ran a bandaged hand over his flattened hair.

"Oh no, you are really hurt?" She clapped a hand over her mouth, hiding her frown. In a second, she'd relinquished the upper ground. She couldn't be silent about an injury and didn't regret caring. As she accused him of putting on airs, he had suffered? Her stomach twisted.

He smiled. "Nothing that excuses my behavior yesterday but maybe helps make sense of it."

She nodded and frowned. How oblivious was she to the extent of his pain? While she was busy with a lifetime of frustration, what else had she missed?

Ryan held his hat over his heart, muffling the sound of his pounding chest. In the antique store, he was too much. If he lifted his arms, he was liable to knock something off a shelf. When he spoke, his voice was too loud and shook the baubles hanging off the chandelier. He didn't fit.

Wide open spaces suited him best. He preferred the outdoors with no obstructions. He didn't have to be mindful of anything more than his task.

Meg stood a few feet away, narrowing her gaze. Her focus rested solely on him.

He felt warm and sticky like he'd gone for a long ride at midday. Now he regretted changing into his best outfit. He'd have to wash it as soon as he got home. With any luck, she'd appreciate the effort.

"It's a clean cut. Ted poured antiseptic into the wound as he bandaged me." The memory of the burning in his finger during Ted's first aid session snapped Ryan back to the present. "I'll be fine."

She nodded. "Better safe than sorry. You don't want to contract an infection."

His throat squeezed shut. Now she was saying his tired, clichéd lines. He scanned the room, looking for hazards. If he slammed into something fragile, he'd add to his mounting debt.

She strode toward the register. Her hair swung with every step. She was as pretty as anything else in the room.

Her store was her domain. Every spare surface, from shelves to dresser tops to mantles, held a variety of objects from delicate vases to tiny figurines. Furniture scattered throughout the space in groups of twos and threes. She'd crammed thousands of items into her store. The room should feel crowded and cluttered. Somehow, her overdecorating worked. *Controlled chaos like her.*

He followed, grateful to reach an open space he could stand in. And then he dropped his gaze. Every time he noticed the tiny details that made her *her*, he berated himself a little more. She wasn't the enemy. She looked out for his grandfather, including setting vermin traps under the porch. She was kind.

And she wasn't a child anymore. Neither of them were.

"Let me see, please?" she asked.

Dropping his hat to the counter, he rested his hands in the center of the glass case. Inside, shiny, pretty things lined a velvet shelf.

She inched her fingers toward his injured digit.

With every tiny motion forward, he tensed. She wouldn't hurt him anymore than he'd already accomplished. He fisted his other hand.

She brushed her fingertips over his calloused palm.

The whisper soft touch of her silky, smooth skin over his work-hardened hands sent a jolt through him. "I'm fine."

With a mental growl, he drew back his hands. Every time she touched him, she activated some sort of response he couldn't define or explain. If he hadn't moved, he'd have cracked the display. He dropped his arms to his sides and breathed deep, inhaling lemon furniture polish and lavender.

Woof woof woof.

The dog trotted toward him, sniffing his boots and bandaged hand. Nails clicked against the hardwood as the dog circled him. Finally, she sat next to him, leaning against his leg.

He smiled and stroked behind the dog's ears. The mutt tilted her head, exuding a goofy exuberance. If he was out of place in the store of fragile things, he wasn't alone. The dog didn't let it impact her. Neither should he.

"Meg, I'm fine. Really. Don't waste your time worrying about me." *I don't deserve your goodwill.*

She crossed her arms over her chest.

He couldn't get out of speaking today. He'd come to eat crow, and he barely swallowed the first bite. "I am sorry about earlier. I was rude." The words were stiff and halting. He trudged ahead. "You've given me no cause for my poor behavior." *At least not recently.*

She nodded.

The dog woofed and trotted around the glass case to her owner. She plopped onto Meg's feet.

Loyalty was admirable no matter the species. He liked seeing the black and white dog so trusting. Meg had rescued the stray from a pound several years earlier. At the time, she had asked if they had any spare supplies. He had found an old kennel. Hank had vetoed the artifact and told Ryan to buy something. When he had dropped off the brand-new bed, he had been introduced to a terrified mass of fur.

The mutt's even temper was a credit to Meg's handling. She must have convinced the pup some humans were decent and worthy of love and respect. *When you know, you know.*

He wished he had such clarity. As the hours ticked past, he didn't have the luxury of getting lost in his thoughts. If he didn't keep the ranch in top-shape, meeting, and exceeding guests' expectations, he'd lose the business. In a few more years, he'd have the financial security he needed. Every morning, he focused on what was required to save the future. He had little to spare for the present and even less for the past.

Lifting his gaze, he met her steady stare. He shrugged. "If you're not talking, I'd better go."

"You want me to talk?"

"I'd like an acknowledgment of my apology. You can be mad. I don't want bad feelings between us." *We've weathered worse.*

She frowned.

A soft *tick tock tick* echoed in the silence.

In the glass case, he spotted a gold pocket watch resting on a pillow. He could mark every second as she absorbed his words. Fixing their perceptions of each other was a two-person job. Preferably, he'd wait until the summer was a success and the plans for the bison were officially underway before inviting her to tackle the shed. Waiting created another, bigger problem. Only a fool would give his neighbor and his grandfather three months for stewing and plotting. Reaching for his hat, he slid it over the glass.

She grabbed his wrist, curling her thin fingers over his joint. "No, wait, please?"

Her voice was muffled and subdued. He glanced at her. He never thought of her as anything less than a force of nature. He'd swear the weather changed on her arrival and departure every summer of their childhoods. The year she stopped coming, the air hung heavy and stagnant.

"I'm sorry, too." She swallowed. "I should have waited for your permission. I definitely shouldn't have accused you of toxic masculinity. You're always respectful."

"I appreciate your apology. As far as an invitation, don't worry about it. It's Hank's ranch. He has every right to do as he sees fit." *I wish I knew his motivation.* Hank never did anything without a purpose, hating to waste his two most valuable resources of energy and time. If his goal involved Ryan, Hank wouldn't rest until a conclusion was reached. Ryan shuddered.

She pursed her lips.

He raised a hand to smooth the hairs on the back of his neck. "You know what I mean."

"I do. Hank might own the ranch. Without you, he'd have sold years ago."

With one finger, Ryan traced the brim of his hat. Her words were high praise. His lips twitched as he attempted to hid a smile, schooling his features into an expressionless mask.

"I know your opinion of me. I knew what I risked."

He lifted his gaze. They'd circled this conversation for years. He avoided putting out his thoughts for her thorough inspection. Had she done her own analysis while he was pre-occupied with work?

"I shouldn't have stepped onto your property. You hadn't invited me." She held up both hands. "Believe me, it won't happen again."

Was she offering surrender? He wasn't prepared for her to capitulate. The stubborn girl he'd known would never have admitted defeat. And he didn't like her waving the white flag now. But he couldn't focus on that comment. Instead, he circled back to the most critical statement on her list. He shifted his weight from one foot to the other. "My opinion of you?"

"You think I'm a nuisance." She dropped her hands to her sides. "You barely hold yourself back from rolling your eyes every time I talk."

"I've never said that." He wouldn't correct the latter opinion. Every now and then, he struggled to keep his gaze straight ahead. On occasion, he'd press his fingers against the vein twitching in his temples.

She shrugged. "You don't have to say it out loud."

He gritted his molars. She was wrong. More often than not, he stilled his features best he could, unable to stop both his cheek and eye from trembling as he stifled laughter. She was the funniest, boldest person he'd ever met. She was candid and free. He appreciated silence and calm. He liked to consider his words. Typically, before he could reply, she'd said something wry or self-deprecating, and he had to stop himself from responding with a chuckle. "I'm sorry if I've given you that impression."

"Don't worry about it. I appreciate the apology." She grabbed a cloth and rubbed a nonexistent spot of dust on the metal edge of the counter. "Tell Hank I'll be back tomorrow. I know you have guests coming this weekend and want the lawn clear before then. And I know you hate things disorganized and messy."

Pot meet kettle. She claimed in-depth knowledge, but would she listen to the truth? Was she content to persist in projecting her opinions of him onto him? He stared hard at her half-averted profile willing her to face him. "It's not strictly about tidiness. If you leave the junk from the shed scattered over the lawn, you'll kill the grass."

"Can't you buy sod or something?"

He narrowed his gaze. "Sure, if I have enough lead time. A few days isn't adequate. The guests like to stroll the lawn in the evenings. If the grass is dead, and I can't get new turf fast enough, and it rains, I have a muddy mess."

She tipped her head to the side. "Again, not that big of a deal."

Everything is a big deal. "Time isn't infinite, and my minutes are stretched thin as it is. Once the tourists arrive, I won't have energy for unnecessary chores. It's wasteful to my resources."

"You mean expensive?"

"Well sure if we're talking finances. I've got a lot at stake this summer." He ran a hand through his hair. Didn't she understand cost was comprised of many factors? With a quick glance around her empty store, he dragged his gaze back and studied her.

Hunched and quiet, she looked defeated. Since she moved to town, she kept to her land and her store. He'd never caught her in his house but her light scent lingered in the air some days. On those occasions, he guessed from Hank's pleased expression she'd visited.

He didn't want to fight. They'd made some progress toward mutual respect and understanding. He hated to risk the tenuous truce but couldn't let her misconceptions persist unchecked. "We've moved ahead with the new yurts on your old property, but we haven't booked every weekend. I held off on corporate retreats until the end of the season. I need to at least break-even this year. To do that, I have to sell-out a minimum of four weeks in the next three months."

Or I can't take my next big gamble. If the town didn't believe in him, he'd be out of luck. He needed the full backing and support of the community to successfully reintroduce the bison to the area.

Unlike his ancestors, he wouldn't assume his was the only opinion that mattered. His neighbors relied on him and vice versa. He vowed to change the legacy from winning by force to shared success for all.

She dropped the cloth and huffed. "Is it always about money? Is that your stress?"

At his sides, he clenched and unclenched his fingers. The circular conversation trapped him in a loop. "No, of course not. Dollars aren't the only resource. Don't discount someone's time, too. I'm lucky if I can sleep five hours a night. I'm needed everywhere. I'm coming home, eating dinner, and heading back to work. I am grateful for your friendship with my grandfather. He'd be lonely if you didn't look in on him so often."

"Hank has always been good to me," she said. "So was Susie."

"Like when she was helping you trick me at Frontier Days?" He probably should have kept the thought to himself, like he usually did. Nothing good came from being open and easy for others to read. But sometimes he couldn't fight the urge to tease her. Provoking her was second nature.

She sucked all the air in the room into her open mouth, her cheeks flushing.

He wouldn't smile, but he was glad she suffered guilt from her involvement in the most embarrassing moment of his life. Growing up, he danced with Grandma in the kitchen. He couldn't remember a time before waltzing and two-stepping across the slate tile floor.

When a thirteen-year-old Meg had wanted to participate in the talent show, she had recruited their grandmas to lure him onto the stage. Once he had gazed at the crowd, he had wanted to run. He had never liked a trick or a prank. Her forehead had beaded with sweat and her eyes had grown round. She had looked petrified and had punished herself with the thoughtless plan. He couldn't leave her alone to her fate and had joined her act, spinning her around the stage. The moment he had finished his bow, however, he had vowed never to dance with her again. *Promise kept.*

He sighed. "Your grandma was good to me, too. All I'm asking is that you and Hank don't make more trouble for me right now. Stop and consider what impact your actions have on those around you. Specifically, on me."

She clasped her hands in front and released a heavy breath. Her entire body shook.

Should he prepare for impact? As a kid, he'd swear he heard the crack of thunder before she launched into one of her tirades. He'd endured plenty of them over the years. What if he used a different tactic?

He leaned close and reached out, grazing her elbow with his palm. "I don't want to fight or rehash the past. I came to say I'm sorry. I was injured and frustrated. I lashed out, and I was wrong."

Her hot breath tickled his neck. Near enough to breathe in her exhale, he watched her eyelashes flutter as she looked to the ground. The air sizzled. Instead of her bluster and thunder, lightning threatened to strike. His new plan might not be the better choice. He neither wanted nor needed another complication in his life and especially not a romance with the neighbor who drove him crazy. "I repeat. I'm sorry. You'll come back?"

"Yes."

"Good." He stepped back, breaking contact and dragging his burning palm over his jeans. "I'll get out of your way." He grabbed the hat off the counter and pulled the brim low over his forehead. "I'll see you around." In a few long strides, he reached the front of the store.

The bell jingled as he stepped over the threshold and shut the door behind him.

Outside, the temperature dropped ten degrees and chilled his skin. Whatever just happened wouldn't be repeated. Meg was all sorts of trouble both good and bad. He had no intention of engaging in either.

CHAPTER 3

Meg shivered, tugging the sleeves of her oversized sweatshirt, and covering her hands with the threadbare cuffs. She knew better than to bring only a worn sweatshirt as an additional layer. Never leaving home without at least three pieces of outerwear was fundamental for life on the ranch no matter the season. While sipping her coffee at the kitchen window, she had studied the dark sky and reasoned the temperate weather pattern would hold. Besides, she would be indoors. At the last minute, she had decided against a skirt. Thankfully.

Hours later, the morning had never quite dawned.

Spring was unpredictable. A day could start bright and clear but erupt with hail before lunch. Overcast skies were blown off-course with strong winds. Although, today, she'd welcome a change in the weather. Gloomy, gray skies that hung around all day weren't her favorite.

In her rush to the ranch, she had forgotten to factor in the uninsulated shed. The breeze whistled through the gaps in the wooden boards. With no windows, the chill couldn't be blasted with sunlight. The thin rays breaking through the clouds didn't promise much warmth.

Her priority had been getting to the ranch before Ryan changed his mind. She wasn't quite sure what to think about yesterday evening's encounter. While the morning run-in had been a heightened version of status quo, the second meeting was a marked change. For the first time ever, she had held her tongue in his presence, and he had spoken more than three words.

With every replay, she couldn't think of a better word to define his speech than an oratory. He had never shared his thoughts or his feelings or his concerns with her. It was easy to imagine the man robotic.

He proceeded through life with quiet efficiency, moving from one success to the next with no hiccup in any plan. When he had purchased the bulk of the Hawke ranch, enabling her mom to retain the house, he had done so with his typical few words and stepped aside as the lawyers handled the details. Over the past five years, she had often wondered why he took action. Was the transaction only to grow his business or to help her family? Or both?

She fisted her hands and raised both to her mouth, blowing hot air on her icy digits. Until yesterday, she had no idea he had feelings. Had she ever given him the chance to speak and explain? Or did she cut him off before he could say what she feared?

She based her assumptions about him on her experience and interpretation. Was she wrong? Another shudder racked her body, and she lifted her gaze studying the lone, uncluttered corner of the shed.

Hank sat on a nineteenth century side chair, the walnut frame creaking under his weight. In his lap, he held a box. Rifling through the contents, he focused on his task.

She navigated through the maze of boxes, picking her feet up and stepping over the variety of crates and cartons. The shed had taken years to fill. At various moments, some attempts at preservation had been made.

Analyzing the layers was like studying the strata in the earth's crust. Labeled cardboard levels separated rows of plastic bins on top of wooden crates. If she had to guess, she'd identify the organizational attempt as Susie's handiwork.

Her grandmother's friend had been a strong, stoic woman, much like her grandson. Unlike Ryan, her silence wasn't threatening but comforting. When she did speak, she made every syllable count. She had the best voice, kind and warm, and loved to read stories aloud to others.

Meg had spent many years in Susie's kitchen, seated at the oak table too mesmerized to speak. While her grandma gossiped, Susie baked, her fluid movements like a dance as she whipped up everything from biscuits to croissants. Grandma's voice droned in the background like a classical score for a ballet. The warm air hung heavy with yeast and sugar. *And love.* She couldn't pass a bakery without entering and breathing in the aroma, transporting herself back to a cherished memory for a precious second.

She missed both women with a fierce, sharp pain she doubted would ever ease. Did Hank miss the calm peace of the house from the women's combined presence? He often dropped in to kiss Susie on the cheek and share an enticing tidbit with Grandma. He'd chuckle and head out the back door. Spending time with the Kincaid men wasn't a substitute but at least something of a consolation. She wasn't alone. If Ryan wasn't her friend, he had her back anyway.

Had he grown even more stoic after losing his grandma? In the immediate aftermath, she hadn't noticed. She hadn't made more of an effort to act like a good neighbor. Instead, she restricted her visits to avoiding Ryan altogether. Was she oblivious or self-absorbed? *If you want a friend, be a friend.* She'd do better.

"Hank?" She called. "What did you find?" She stopped in the center. With the shed door propped open, light spilled into the room along the aisle. She crossed her arms, tucking her hands against her armpits and lowering her trembling chin into her collar.

"I'm not quite sure. I reckon I need to take this box and that one," he pointed to the large cardboard rectangle on the ground next to Colby, "inside for a better study. It's getting cold out here. We earned a break."

She nibbled her bottom lip. She doubted Ryan would agree. When she had arrived, she listened to the rules Hank established for the sake of harmony on the ranch. The items that had been removed already were handled. Ryan had loaded the donation pile into his truck and driven to the next town. With Ted's help, Hank had stored his keepers in the barn attic.

While the first efforts hadn't produced anything worthy of consignment at the antique store, she wouldn't be disappointed. The initial disruption created enough space to work inside the shed and a small pile of goods was stacked outside the shed to be loaded into her SUV at the end of the day.

Finishing the project before the ranch opened for the season was unlikely. If she could continue inside the shed and out of view, she hoped Ryan wouldn't mind her presence, and he'd let her keep working while guests roamed the property.

He was changing. Without a big discovery inside the shed, she wouldn't be around long enough to witness the full transformation. She didn't want to leave now. She loved her life in Herd.

Hank set the box on the ground. He stood, his joints cracking.

Colby howled.

"I'm fine. Don't you get started, too." Hank scowled at the dog.

Colby got to her feet and pressed her nose against the cowboy's knee.

Hank reached down and scratched the dog behind the ears. "Want to come inside and rest for a spell?"

Thump thump thump. The wagging tail slapped against the chair's legs.

"Calm down, or you'll hurt yourself. Sprained tail is no joke," Hank said.

Meg froze, pressing her lips together and swallowing her reaction. What happened to his claims her made when she adopted Colby that the animal should be treated like a dog and not a human? The pair was adapting to each other's cues. Hank spoke in the same tone and cadence as his usual voice, indicating he conversed with an equal and not an inferior.

Hank bent and groaned.

She rushed forward, extending both hands and lightly touching his shoulders. "Let me carry the boxes, please?"

He wrinkled his brow.

"It's for my sake, okay?" She bent and grabbed the boxes, stacking one on top of the other. She'd ask for forgiveness and not permission. Yesterday, she had regretted letting him do too much. The old cowboy's ways weren't likely to change, and he never let her do anything he thought he ought to handle. She had to try.

"If you insist," he muttered and shuffled forward.

Colby followed on his heels.

She tightened her grip on the boxes, her chin resting on top creating a wedge with her arms. The boxes were awkward and heavy, her cold hands slipped. She couldn't show the struggle. The bigger than life cowboy in front of her, leading the way to the house, would jump in and hurt himself.

Growing old was a gift and a curse. She understood his frustrations at not being able to bound in and keep pace. Her entire life, he'd been the quintessential western man, rugged, tough, and strong. She wouldn't let him feel his age if she could help it. As long as she remained in Herd…

She stumbled, catching herself in time. Frowning, she glanced at the rock in the otherwise clear path. She'd focus on the present and leave worrying about the future to the side. For one day.

"Hey, can I help?"

She turned in a slow circle.

Coming around the side of the house, Ryan waved and jogged toward her.

Dressed in his usual flannel and jeans, he wasn't as formal as the last time she'd seen him. She wasn't sure she had a preference. Today's light gray buffalo check shirt looked soft and warm. She'd love to cuddle up in it. *Not appropriate*.

Colby raced to him, jumping up and catching him mid-chest with both paws.

He chuckled, petting the dog. "Okay, Colby, down. You're a good girl."

Colby obediently dropped to the ground. Her whole body shook from the excited pump of her tail.

"Good to see you. We were about to take a break," Hank said.

Ryan strode forward and grabbed the boxes from Meg.

He stood close, his hot breath tickling her cheeks. Through her thin sweatshirt, she absorbed warmth from his palms. Would his rough, calloused hands scrape her skin if she pushed up her sweatshirt sleeves to her elbows brushed? Her cheeks heated. Better not to think about it.

He arched a brow and smiled. "You okay?"

She nodded, pursing her lips.

"Speechless, again?" He tipped his head to the side. "Did you lose a bet?"

She rolled her eyes. His tease snapping her out of the moment. "I'm fine. Hank and Colby are taking a break. I thought I'd keep going."

"No, you should take a break, too." Ryan frowned. "I've got something I want to show you. Wait here, I'll get Hank and Colby settled."

She widened her eyes but didn't reply.

He passed Hank and the dog, striding up the path and into the house. The back door swung shut, the slap of the screen into the frame echoing in the otherwise quiet air. When the trio disappeared, she pressed cold fingers to blazing cheeks.

Why was he suddenly so different? Had Hank read him the riot act and demanded politeness? Had *he* lost a bet? Or maybe his total personality shift was an indication that anything was possible, including her chance at staying in Herd and mattering to the community—and people—she loved.

Turning on his heel, Ryan pounded the path under his boots, his heavy steps echoing as he climbed the steps behind Hank and the dog. He slipped inside the screen door before it shut and slid across the slate tile. Behind him, the screen slammed against the frame, bouncing twice.

Usually, the sound made him jump. Living in a hundred plus year home, he learned early to never test the limits of a hinge. He eased every door and drawer closed with care. Today, he didn't flinch. Slowly, he scanned the room, his gaze unseeing.

He was too aware of what had happened moments earlier. When he had reached to grab the burden, he brushed her arms, and the air charged with electricity. Again.

He gritted his molars and crossed the room, setting the boxes on the table. She was his longtime neighbor. If he judged her by her dedication to her grandma and her attentive friendship with Hank, he supposed she was nice enough. She didn't need more of his time or his admiration.

Clearly, he needed to right the balance of the world. His axis was leaning wildly to the left, and he'd be knocked to the ground. The answer was simple and elementary. He'd keep his hands to himself. He groaned.

"You all right, boy?" Hank asked.

Ryan glanced at the old man settled at the head of the table.

Colby circled, her nails clicking against the floor, and laid down at the old cowboy's feet. With a sigh, she rested her head on her paws.

Hank leaned forward, scratching the dog behind the ears. "Well? Are you?"

Ryan narrowed his gaze, crossing his arms over his chest. "Are you?"

Hank shrugged. "She's a good dog. Not many out there this calm. I like her company." He met Ryan's gaze, wrinkling his brow. "Don't tell, Meg."

Ryan smiled and shook his head. He had his own share of secrets to keep from the neighbor. "I'm taking her over to the yurt to show her the progress."

"Riding?"

Ryan caught his breath. Meg could only handle one horse, Grandma's Cupcake. Ryan hadn't saddled the horse in a long time, letting Ted take care of the dear animal. He stopped by with sugar cubes but couldn't bring himself to spend any time in the horse's company. Missing Grandma knocked him sideways some days. "No, not today, but maybe another time."

Hank sighed. "Whatever you think is best." He pulled a box to his lap and focused on his work.

Why are you doing this? What's your motivation? The questions tickled the end of Ryan's tongue. Hank hadn't been so devoted to a task in years. He approached the shed clean-out with focus and resolute determination. The timing of the project wasn't the biggest issue. Ryan had the nagging doubt some deeper purpose propelled the effort.

Besides the annoyance of having one more person poking around the house on the last few days of peace, he couldn't have his ranch hand, Ted, tied up in helping Meg either. The bulk of summer employees wouldn't arrive until the second week in June. The first few weekends operated with a reduced crew, each person shouldering a huge amount of work. Ryan opened his mouth, but nothing came out. Maybe he was better off not knowing the answer. "I'll be back in a bit."

Hank waved but didn't raise his head.

Stuffing his hands in his pockets, Ryan strode to the door. He spent all morning trying to show he regretted his bad behavior.

He believed in doing and not talking. Rising early, he drove the three hours round-trip to drop off the donations from Hank's shed to the nearest city. Sitting behind the wheel, he waited as the staff insisted on unloading the pickup and returned with a receipt. All told, he was at the facility for fifteen minutes. The flat, monotonous landscape of his drive gave his mind too much time to wander.

On the drive home yesterday, he had replayed that weird charge in the air at Finders-Keepers. It was only because he caught her by surprise, and she was silent. The change between them wasn't his concern. He couldn't afford to expend any energy or time on a distraction.

After making up his mind to ignore her, he had parked his truck and hopped out of the cab. Her voice floated past. Following, he decided his best path forward was to help. With actions, he'd prove he wasn't mean and cruel. When he stood close enough to breathe in the hint of lavender clinging to her clothes, his heart skipped a beat.

Pulling back his shoulders, he strode through the open doorway and headed back outside and down the path. He understood his next course of action. With a little more time together, she'd start yammering again, falling into their old patterns. He'd remember he didn't like her because he couldn't think when she was around as she filled every moment with a random stream of consciousness. He needed her constant chatter to annoy him so he could stop wondering if she drove him crazy or if he was crazy about her.

He jogged down the steps toward her. His palms itched, but he kept his hands in place in his pockets. No fast motions or he'd do something stupid. Like reach for her. "Hey." He called.

She turned her head.

A shaft of light broke through a cloud, beaming on her brown hair. Streaks of gold shimmered. No, not gold as much as red, like copper. *What? Huh?* Why waste his time comparing her to precious metals? She had brown hair, like dirt. "Do you want to go for a drive? Give Hank a moment to sort through his boxes? You've earned a break."

"I'm not sure." She nibbled her lip. "We haven't made much progress."

"I bet you have. You're a hard worker." Why couldn't he stop talking? He crossed his arms over his chest and gripped his biceps until he twisted and burned the skin through his jacket. He sounded like a fool.

"You really don't mind if I take a break?"

"Of course not." He frowned. Was he that much of an ogre? Had he made her feel unwelcome? He'd raised his voice before, and she'd never been scared away. What changed? *I don't want to know.* "Come on. I want to show you something. We'll take my truck."

Strolling at his side, her head reached the top of his shoulder. She swung her arm wildly at her side like the thin limb could propel her. *But she isn't talking.* He had to stop picking at every little thing. He wanted silence. He got it. At thirty-eight, if he didn't know his own mind by now, he never would. Rounding the side of the house, he strode toward his vehicle and opened the passenger door on his truck.

She climbed inside.

He caught himself reaching forward, his fingers almost to her elbow. He pulled his hand back and shut the door. Crunching the gravel under his boots, he strode around the bumper, wrenched open the door too hard, and hopped in behind the wheel. He turned over the engine and reversed out of his spot, depending on the mirrors. He would not reach behind the passenger seat and turn. He'd be too close.

Pulling out of the drive, he steered onto the dirt road toward her property. From the corner of his gaze, he studied her.

She looked straight ahead through the windshield.

Her expression was blank. Was she mad? He searched for flaring nostrils, a sweaty brow, or her pinched lips. He found nothing.

Her silence was unnerving. Was she waiting for him to yell? Processing the surge of pulsating energy between them? Nope, he was not going there and couldn't let her confuse the quiet either. "I wanted to give you a look at what's happened on your family's land."

"It's your land now."

His chest squeezed tight. He'd always think of it as hers. His earliest memory was riding in the saddle with the grandfathers and learning the boundaries between the properties.

The men had a cordial relationship based on respect for the other's domain and authority. Of course, shortly after, her grandfather suddenly passed from a massive heart attack. Her grandmother relied on his family for help whenever necessary and offered the same in reverse. She hadn't been a burden. Miss Betty was a sweet chatterbox with a compliment for every person she met. Helping her was a gift.

When he had the chance to preserve her land, he claimed it. For years, he had not developed the acreage. He hadn't done so for her sake. He'd indulged his own nostalgia for keeping the area as pristine as he could. With increased demand and more overhead costs from the purchase, however, he had to find a way to cover the costs. He hoped his plan was a decent compromise.

The additional acreage also secured the ability to partner with the bison foundation. The situation was one win after another.

He never asked if she regretted selling. *I would.* "The yurts are set back from view. I had to run infrastructure out here. Otherwise, the land is undisturbed. If it doesn't work, I can pull the tents down and break up the slabs. I'll restore the prairie. I don't think you can see the new lodgings from your house?"

She shrugged. "I haven't noticed any changes."

"Good. I didn't want to disrupt your life." *Or maybe I do.* A lump stuck on his Adam's apple. He coughed. "I mean I don't want my guests to wander over and bug you. I know you appreciate your privacy."

"You can do what you need." She turned in her seat and faced him. "I trust you."

Why? Was her faith in him based on being a good neighbor or something more? Did she feel the sudden shift in their world?

Why now? He'd never been swamped with doubts or questions. His life suited him. He worked to maintain his legacy for at least another generation. While he understood the world in black and white, he accepted she believed in the murky grays somewhere in the middle of his perception. She was decent and a perfect neighbor. Why must everything change and why the bad timing?

People aren't preserves. They don't keep.

Grandma's words weren't a comfort. He understood he couldn't wait forever. If he could get through the summer first, focusing on his business and paying off the mortgage on the Hawke land, then he'd reevaluate his personal life in the autumn. He promised.

CHAPTER 4

Adjusting the seat belt across her chest, Meg leaned forward. Hot air blasted from the vents onto her icy hands. The moment of sunshine was too brief to stave the chill in the air. Although, his smile had warmed her.

Through the windshield, she surveyed the passing landscape. To some, the grassy land might be boring. A seemingly endless expanse stretching to the horizon. But to her? She'd never seen a more beautiful sight than the sea of green rippling in the wind like waves in the ocean.

She hadn't ridden inside Ryan's truck in years and never alone. On her last trip, during her first Christmas living in Herd full-time, he had fussed over helping cart the trees she and Hank got from the sale on Main Street. While he wasn't berating her this time for tracking needles and sap into the carpeted interior, he hadn't made his vehicle any more comfortable for passengers during the past five years.

The cab was clean and empty. No paper receipt, food wrapper, forgotten tool or other item littered the interior. She sniffed, breathing in only the faint hint of musky aftershave. How was it possible to use a vehicle as much as he did and leave behind no clue about the owner?

Did he clean up after himself constantly? He never carried anything extra like a toolbox or a fanny pack. By comparison, her SUV was a neatly organized garage on wheels. She was prepared for any situation. *Except sitting close to him.* Her senses heightened to a painful degree with the close proximity.

"Hey, are you, okay?" Ryan asked.

"Why wouldn't I be?" She focused on the dashboard.

"I don't know. Why would you sniff my truck?"

Heat crept from her hands straight up her neck and across her cheeks. Had she been loud? *Better out than in.* Hank loved that expression. His meaning was slightly different, but she'd follow the spirit of the directive. "Why doesn't your truck smell?"

He chuckled.

"It's...unusual. There isn't any sort of scent. Not even a hint of your aftershave lingering in the upholstery."

"I guess I don't spend enough time to notice. Is the lack of scent a good thing or a bad thing?"

His tone was soft, thoughtful. From the corner of her eye, she glanced at him. "I'm not sure."

"What does your SUV smell like?"

"If I don't use air freshener, it smells like dog."

"Hmm."

She turned her head. A loud crack snapped the crick above her spine.

"Yikes." He winced. "Seriously, are you okay? What's wrong?"

She straightened, tucking her hands under her legs. "I'm fine. I'm a little sore from the physical labor."

"I can understand." He rolled his shoulders. "I don't know how Hank dragged you in to this. I never thought he'd go through that shed." He smiled. "It's why Grandma put the lock on it in the first place. To stop him from adding more."

She liked how the corners of his eyes crinkled when he grinned. She liked being included in his jokes. She liked belonging. "But she gave him a key?"

He shook his head. "No. He found it."

She chuckled, shaking with the belly laugh. She covered her mouth with both hands. "Sorry, I shouldn't laugh."

Grinning even broader, he kept his face forward, looking out the windshield. "No apologies necessary." He tapped the steering wheel. "The cold snap is supposed to let up soon. By the time the tourists arrive, it'll be mid-sixties and perfect during the day."

"Twenty degrees warmer in a few days?"

"I'm only repeating the forecast."

"I believe you," she said. "If for no other reason than your business needs good weather, and your family has always had good luck."

"Not always, but we're an optimistic sort. We've never wasted an opportunity. When it comes to nature, however, we're all at the mercy of the elements. Here we are."

She turned away, reluctantly. When was the last time she'd seen him smile? When had she ever been the cause in a good way?

He parked the truck at the top of a hill.

From the shotgun seat, she couldn't see much. Unbuckling her seat belt, she opened the door and hopped to the ground.

Set in a small valley, she spotted three large yurts. The short, white cylinders should have stuck out against the landscape. Instead, the dwellings suited the setting. Tall prairie grass rippled in the wind surrounding the buildings. Like they'd always belonged.

Sunlight broke through the clouds, and a shaft of light brightened the property. She held her breath. The setting was magical and peaceful. She exhaled a deep breath and relaxed her shoulders. She sort of liked not talking and listening. Being quiet was peaceful. Maybe she didn't have to fill in every moment. She could let someone else take the lead. *If it's Ryan.*

With a shake of her head, she faced him.

He dragged a hand through his hair, frowning. "What? You don't like it?"

She shook her head. "I haven't been here in years."

"It's nice land." He covered his mouth with a fist and coughed. "The yurts aren't permanent. We take them down and store them before the winter. We'll give the land time to rest and heal."

I wouldn't think you would. First and foremost, he was a caretaker. "I'm glad you bought the land. Selfishly, of course." She faced the yurts again. "Thank you."

"You don't owe me any gratitude."

His sharp tone grated on her nerves, scraping her cheek with the bit out sentence. Did it strain him to be nice and accept her thanks?

She opened her mouth to reply and stopped. Knee-jerk reactions were their default mode of communication. The past few days showed her a chance at something different. She wanted better for both of them. Instead of assuming his mood, she should stop projecting and ask. She could be wrong and her initial assessment correct, but how would she know for certain? She faced him.

He stepped forward and reached a hand out, hovering near her shoulder.

She frowned at his fingers. Why didn't he touch her? Was he afraid she'd bite him? She met his gaze. "What about weddings?"

He drew back his hand and frowned. "Not sure I follow your train of thought."

She didn't either. The words burst out of her without any planning. She could think on her feet and hid her wariness of any change in their relationship status. "I guess not only weddings. Big events, too. Why not expand the resort offerings? You've already made Herd a destination. Isn't this the next step?"

"It's a major industry within the hospitality world." He turned toward the valley. "I guess I never really had marriage on the mind."

She nibbled the inside of her cheek, unsure whether she should be heartened or discouraged by the statement.

"Do you think anyone would want to get married on this lonely stretch of grass?" His tone was teasing and a gentle curve lifted the corner of his mouth.

I would. Her grandparents had married in the exact spot. With wildflowers blooming, Grandma had carried a freshly picked bouquet.

Growing up, Meg spent so much time studying the photos she created fake memories including herself in the event. Her mind supplied the warm feel of the sun, the smell of sweet grass in summer, and the sound of happy laughter as her grandfather dipped her grandmother before the pastor following the vows.

With a hand, she shielded her gaze and considered the spot for a modern audience with no tie to the land. She scrunched her nose. "Sure, the spot might not be ideal especially if you're dealing with high-maintenance bridezillas." She sighed. "You'd need parking and bathrooms. Building permanent structures would change the landscape here forever. This patch of prairie is perfect as is. What about an expansion at the barn?"

He scoffed. "Oh sure. Leave your house alone but give up my backyard?"

She heard the tease in his tone. "Not necessarily. The barn is plenty big enough as is. You could build a deck with an open pergola overhead. String up lights across the beams. You'd have plenty of space for ceremonies on the back deck and cocktail hour inside."

"You've given this some thought."

Not really. She spoke as the ideas formed but could picture the entire setup. Getting married on the ranch would be magical. Could she convince him to both expand and let her be involved?

"You sure you don't have a secret admirer, stoking bridal visions?" He narrowed his gaze.

His question was delivered like an accusation. Under his direct stare, she flushed and glanced away. Of course, she didn't. The small town of barely two thousand residents didn't provide a range of romantic options, and secrets were nonexistent.

"I'm kidding." He sighed. "I like the idea, but you're talking about a major expansion. Catered events and weddings have a lot of pressure and high expectations. The enterprise is very stressful."

"You could focus on smaller events in the beginning."

"True, but I'd need to do a test to be sure everything ran smoothly for my customers. To rent the whole ranch in my busiest season, I'd charge a lot."

"I'm sure you'll find interested guests. Even at an exorbitant rate in the shoulder seasons."

"Do we have those?" He arched a brow. "Seems like the snow falls earlier every year."

She widened her gaze, clapping a hand over her mouth. A sudden, inspired thought sprouted. Would Ryan go for it?

"What?" He uttered the word with his weary, put-upon tone. The same one he'd used since childhood.

"I know the perfect test run. Hank's ninetieth birthday. What could be better? He would love a huge, town-wide affair."

Ryan shook his head. "Please, don't give him the idea. I'm begging."

"Will you... consider it?" She scrunched her nose. *Please, please, please.* When the shed project with Hank wrapped up she wasn't sure she'd be content to being respectful but distant neighbors again. She wanted a legitimate reason to be here. To be near Ryan. Working together could be that opportunity.

"Yes, it's a good thought. I'm always interested in diversification. I'm looking for every opportunity I can. The old-time photography studio could become an official vendor."

"I'm sure they'd appreciate the business. Everyone does. You've done a lot for the community."

"I can't sit around and wait for my chance at success. In this life, we have no guarantees."

The breeze whipped past. The environment shook her as her thoughts threatened to do the same on the inside. Her tie to town wasn't a strong rope but a thin ribbon. Without her last name, she wouldn't belong. If she didn't fit here, could she find home anywhere?

"I better get back to work."

She nodded and lifted her gaze, but she didn't move away.

Neither did he.

They stood closer to each other than ever. Nearer than the weird moment at her store yesterday afternoon when her skin electrified. She'd been convinced if she touched anything she'd be jolted by a static shock.

Today, she was sure the spark in their touch would cause a wildfire on the dry prairie. If she inched closer, would he step back? Better not to risk the land she loved. She sighed and turned to gaze over the grass again. "I probably should return, too. We're making progress on the shed."

"It won't be done by the weekend though."

She pressed together her lips, stifling her smile. She didn't hear the usual admonishment today. "No, it's a long project. I promise I won't be in the way."

"You aren't," he murmured. "Thank you for coming."

She caught her bottom lip. In a moment, she trespassed on unknown territory. She struggled to process the words of someone she'd known—and never understood—almost her entire life. Warmth spread through her from head to toe.

"Let's get back." He stepped away, turning toward the truck.

He saved her from a response she wasn't sure she was ready to think let alone verbalize. Following, she grabbed the door handle and pulled herself into the truck, buckling her seat belt.

He turned the keys in the ignition and circled the vehicle onto the road.

"How's the store faring?"

Her stomach twisted. She sucked in a sharp breath, breathing through the stitch in her sides. He'd rescued her once already. If he knew how bad things were, would he try to swoop in again? Why?

"Oh. Do you need he—"

"Stop, please." She held up a hand. "I'm working on a plan. You don't need to get involved. You owe me nothing." *I don't want to be an obligation.*

"I don't mean to offend you." He scowled, gripping the steering wheel tight.

"You didn't." She sighed and focused on the dashboard. Now she was being flippant and unkind. Pride was no excuse to cut him off. "I need to improve business for the rest of the year after the tourists leave." She kept the true depths of her problem to herself. If he knew, would he help her? Would he feel forced to ride to her rescue? He'd purchased her family's ranch and thus enabled her to move here. He didn't owe her more.

"Do you have any ideas?"

"Some," she murmured.

"If you're modernizing, I can help," he said. "I had to establish our website and e-commerce system. I didn't want to pay someone to set us up initially or charge us every time I need to change a tiny detail. I can teach you."

"Thanks." She turned toward him and smiled. Sharing her burden was both harder and easier than she'd imagined. She was glad to have someone to take her job seriously enough to ask. How strange to consider him a confidant. "If I get to that point, I'll take you up on the offer."

He turned his head and arched a brow. "Promise?"

She nibbled her bottom lip. He studied her so earnestly. What was happening? She nodded.

Sliding his gaze back to the road, he pulled the truck in front of the house and braked. The engine idled.

She unbuckled her seat belt. "Are you coming inside?"

He shook his head, wrinkling his brow with deep lines. "No. I've got some work to do. I'll see you later."

She shivered. Reaching for the door, she opened her side and hopped to the ground. Without glancing back, she rounded the house to the shed. She'd thought they were thawing. Had she been wrong? Again?

One hundred forty-eight, one hundred forty-nine, one hundred fifty.

Ryan halted. He'd reached the corner of the barn. Swiveling on his heel, he strode back to the approximate center of the building.

He hadn't intended to spend his evening pacing his property. After dinner, however, he couldn't stop thinking about his conversation with Meg. The sun didn't set until nearly nine in late May. While chill lingered in the air, he wouldn't waste the extra daylight. He had time, and he preferred action to sitting around.

He also couldn't ignore a good idea, no matter how unlikely the source. A cool breeze stirred. He raised the collar on his jacket and stared across the rolling prairie of swaying tall grass.

She'd looked so wistful as she discussed the idea. When she had mentioned her grandparents, she almost glowed. She'd lost her beloved grandmother, too. They had an unspoken understanding of each other's grief because of the gift of knowing each other's family.

Her grandmother, Betty, had talked nonstop, making Meg seem restrained by comparison. He couldn't remember a time in his youth Betty's deep voice didn't echo from the kitchen.

She had loved jokes. She wasn't always skilled in the delivery, but her contagious good humor was impossible to ignore. Everyone laughed with her. She had an instinct about people and never pushed. Several times, she came to his defense with a smile and an off-topic story, distracting Susie and Hank from reprimanding him.

Since his apology to Meg, he recognized the fundamental shift in his opinion of her and vice versa. After years brushing her aside as an annoyance, he couldn't label her so simply anymore. She had thoughtful ideas and depth he never suspected. Whatever came next, he couldn't return to their previous status. He didn't want to.

"Hey, boss. You need help or something?"

Only two people called him boss. It was a nice change from answering to *boy*. He didn't need to face his companion to know Ted stood behind him.

California born and bred, the ska-music loving cowboy listened to his tunes almost constantly while working on the open range. The low sound of a horn line from a late nineties hit filtered out from the headphones dangling from Ted's neck in the seconds before he hit pause.

Hank had hired him years ago. At the time, Ryan had been annoyed his grandfather made a major decision without asking for any input. In the years since, Ryan was forever grateful for his grandfather's gut instinct about the quiet. Ted's positive pragmatism and hard work encouraged Ryan through the tough times.

"Good evening," Ryan said. "I'm finishing up. Sorry if I disturbed your rounds."

Ted approached with his heavy-footed strides.

Ryan glanced again at the red painted boards. The barn was painted every three years. The southern-facing side faded quick.

"It's no bother, boss. Everything is in order. The first wave of staff is settled in at the bunk house. We'll have our orientation in the morning."

"Good, good. I'll be sure to drop in," Ryan said over his shoulder. He pointed at the wall. "Since you're here, you can give me your opinion. Do you think we could build a deck here? Add French doors off the backside of the barn?"

"For a cost, anything is possible." Ted stroked his chin. "You'd have a short window to build during the fall and spring so guests aren't disturbed. Why? What are you thinking?"

"I'd like the deck in a semi-circle shape extending out from the barn. I don't want it covered but a retractable roof might be a nice addition if it's too sunny or a little drizzly. No one could be out here in a full-blown storm. I'd want a clear view of the stars overhead." Ryan glanced up, shielding his gaze with a hand.

In big sky country, the night was a display not to be missed. Overhead, the constellations burned brighter than a planetarium. He'd hate for guests to lose an opportunity for stargazing. Joe, middle school history teacher and ranch tour guide, might be keen to give talks. He'd probably have to do some research first. Luckily, Joe loved learning more than anything else.

Years ago, Hank had taken Ryan and Meg cowboy camping. The plan was to sleep under the stars without a tent. Once Meg started talking about how bright the stars shone, she never stopped. The next morning, she remained chipper and chatty. He and Hank dragged with exhaustion. The experience was never repeated.

"Sounds expensive." Ted folded his arms over his chest.

"I know." Ryan sighed. "Everything is."

"I can't see the upside. Why invest so much without a way to add revenue?"

Ryan shrugged. "Maybe we expand into weddings and events."

Ted whistled. "Welp. Now I've heard everything. I wouldn't have thought you'd turn your focus to romance."

"I haven't. I'm not." Ryan frowned. "It wasn't my idea."

"Meg's?"

Ryan nodded.

Ted looked across the landscape. "It's a good plan. We're busy enough but always smart to have another revenue stream."

"Yep. If we host events, we can extend the season on either side. The guests' focus would be the wedding. We wouldn't have to worry if Joe can't take off time from school for excursions. The guests would be otherwise engaged."

"Gives Abby a chance to extend her season, too. Running a food truck in the winter is a non-starter."

Ryan nodded. Abby Whit operated a barbeque food truck on par with the best restaurants he'd ever visited. In two years, she established herself in town as the best chef and accomplished the remarkable feat of keeping her personal life and history secret. She'd arrived in Herd with a fully-fledged business and never offered much in the way of relatable anecdotes or childhood story.

He didn't mind. She approached him about catering, and he'd been happy to sign the contract. Questions were Hank's forte and not his. The more he considered Meg's plan, the more he liked it. He only observed potential and no pitfalls. His blind spot made him apprehensive. What was he missing? Where was the hiccup? "Any change needs Hank's approval. Retrofitting the building, again, wasn't my plan." Ryan turned and considered the paint-chipped boards on the side of the barn. "We've already patched and pieced so much together. Wouldn't mind the chance to build from scratch."

"Losing the building and a big piece of history would be a shame. The roaming bison might change how we operate," Ted said. "Perhaps we need time to co-exist with the new herd before pouring footings."

Ryan studied the prairie. After selling the cattle, he adjusted to the absolute silence at night. He hadn't understood how much noise the animals made until they were gone. He'd also grown lax about watching his step for cow patties.

The new herd would disrupt the environment for a time until everyone acclimated. *Sort of like living with Meg's chaos*. He agreed with his cowboy's assessment.

How often had Ryan reconsidered a plan lately? Reintroducing the bison would heal old wounds from generations past. He couldn't overlook someone in the present either. Ted hadn't watched Meg's face light up as she discussed the idea. As much as Ryan found her presence complicating, he couldn't imagine living here without her. "I doubt the bison would get this close to the house. But you're right. A lot to consider."

"Sure, have seen a lot of her lately."

Ryan wouldn't insult either of them by pretending he didn't know which *her* Ted mentioned. "If Hank's happy, who am I to complain?" Ryan shrugged. "Did you need me? Were you looking for me?"

"Yes, I have a couple things. Number one is do you have any leads on a new yoga instructor?"

Ryan shook his head. "No word yet from Joe but I'll reach out and touch base with him. See where he's at with it."

"He hasn't mentioned any names?"

At the quizzical look, Ryan paused. Did Ted know Joe's colleagues? Was he worried about someone in particular? Ted and Joe were Ryan's closest friends. He couldn't easily transition from his role and responsibilities to the town into a carefree guy having fun on a night out. The same couldn't—and shouldn't—be said of the cowboy. Ted and Joe probably socialized with a wider group. Ted had a whole other life including a sister and niece. Ryan didn't know everything about his employee's personal life.

"Never mind."

"Sorry for my distraction lately." Ryan scrubbed a hand over his face. "I wouldn't make a hire without your involvement. You're a great manager of people and livestock."

"I enjoy the people more than I imagined. I've met a lot of different folks from all sorts of places since the spa opened. I've learned a lot from listening to their stories."

Ryan envied him. He couldn't admit as much because too many depended on him for their livelihoods. He was always the boss. No one ever opened up to him and vice versa. *Except for Meg.* "You mentioned two items to discuss?"

"Heads up, the vet is coming tomorrow to check on the horses and to re-shoe Cupcake."

Cupcake was Grandma's mare. The sweet old horse only got ornery when she spotted the vet. It took a lot of sugar cubes and Hank's soothing voice to calm her down for any procedure. "Thanks, I'll be sure to tell Hank so he can be there."

Ted turned toward him. "For the record, I like the event idea. You don't pay me enough to be your yes-man. I have to find the flaws."

Ryan chuckled. Ted was a good friend. He'd started as a cowboy during the final year of cattle ranching. Ryan changed the rules by transforming the property into a travel destination. Luckily, Ted continued in a new role. They kept each other on their toes and helped the other through grief for Ted's late wife and Ryan's grandma.

"Do you need me to keep an eye on the shed project? Make sure those two stay on task?"

Ryan studied the cowboy. History meant reading between the lies from a hundred paces off. Ted sensed something was different between Ryan and Meg. Ryan read it on his friend's face. Unless Ryan screwed up, he was assured of Ted's silence on the matter. For his discretion, Ted was more valuable than gold. "I'll manage them. Have a good night."

Ted reached for the brim of his hat, tipping his head.

Ryan strode around the barn and toward his house, passing the shed. Progress happened everywhere at different paces. The middle of nowhere wasn't immune to life surging forward in leaps or tiny tiptoe steps.

He'd focus on the positives and leave the worries about the changing nature of long-held acquaintances. But that wouldn't stop him from replaying what they'd said. Or spend the rest of the night debating the best excuse for another meeting.

CHAPTER 5

At the desk in Grandma's front parlor, Meg rubbed her weary eyes and leaned forward. Squinting at the screen, she clicked on the toolbar and enhanced the resolution of the nineteenth century, black and white cards again. She should go to bed. In the lower corner, she spotted the time. Almost midnight. She hadn't stayed awake so late in a decade. Her vision blurred.

Until she accomplished one task, she wouldn't be able to sleep. Working on the best chance at hidden treasure was a better prospect than dragging herself for what she did and did not say to Ryan. Did he like her event space idea, or was he humoring her? She hated not knowing if he laughed at or with her.

Grandma never had that problem. *As long as the person's smiling, I'll take it as a win.* Not for the first time, Meg wished she possessed more of the woman's moxie.

She leaned back in the chair and tapped her fingers against the edge of the walnut secretary desk. Her initial excitement at the potentially valuable discovery was quickly tempered by the process. Much like the rest of her day, she wasn't certain if she was better off than when she started. One step forward and two miles back.

She hadn't seen Ryan again after he dropped her off at the house. He had plenty of work to do with guests arriving soon. She understood but couldn't ignore the odd twinge in her gut. She didn't miss him. The idea was preposterous, but she had the weird sense she had never spent time with him before today. Would she get another chance at a relaxed, friendly conversation?

What about expanding into events? She had no experience, and nothing to offer besides her willingness to help. Would he take her seriously enough to consider?

This newly talkative, attentive man was the opposite of the neighbor she'd known. His company was enjoyable, and he tempted her with his offer to help with her store. Proficiency in social media wasn't quite the same as extensive html knowledge. She couldn't claim knowledge in either sphere. Shortly after moving to the ranch, she'd given up sharing updates and photos of her personal life in favor of blog posts highlighting her business. She didn't want to open her home to public scrutiny and speculation and finally understood Mom's constant railing against over-exposure. She gave her head a shake and focused on the screen, moving the cursor to adjust settings and click start.

The scanner whirred, and a bright light flashed under the lid.

She jumped, startled by the sudden burst of blue. She blinked and rubbed her tired eyes. Swiveling the chair, she looked for her supposed companion.

On her back on the velvet couch against the wall, Colby was unaffected. Her paws moved, her tail thumped the cushions, and she snarled. In her dreams, the sweet shadow must have imagined herself a fierce huntress.

The dog might not be alone in personal misconceptions. How wrong was Meg about herself? Was she the friendly neighbor? Or a nuisance? Or both?

The scanned image flashed on the screen.

With higher pixel count, she had a clearer view of the faces than with the naked eye. She leaned close and squinted. Her gut instinct, based on memories from school textbooks, told her she knew the bearded man in the cowboy hat and the Native American man seated beside him. Seeing wasn't always believing. The card wasn't an original photograph and could be one of thousands of reproductions.

She zoomed in again on the signature, studying the bleeding ink. The likelihood of Hank planting a signed fake in the shed, stoking her hopes, were slim. She couldn't shake her skepticism of the sudden good fortune if the card was authentic.

She uploaded the image to the facial recognition database she found after a quick internet search, tapping her foot against the desk chair leg. If today held one miracle, friendship with Ryan, why couldn't she hope for more?

After the expedition to the yurts, she had spent the rest of her day in the shed. Sorting through crumbling boxes and broken furniture, she'd created three piles for Hank's assessment. Once again, the consignment stash was the smallest with only a handful of salable items. Why bother Ryan and ask for help creating on online store for nothing?

Working alone, she had made better progress, but the process was lonely. She had especially missed Colby. While the dog only made noise in her sleep, she had a presence that relaxed Meg.

Keeping her head down, Meg had focused on one task at a time and had only stopped at the knock on the shed door.

"I reckon it's quitting time," Hank had said.

She turned toward the door and stared past him into the twilight sky. "Already?"

"We made good progress today." He reached to his side.

Seated, Colby pressed against the man's legs and lifted her furry face to gaze at him.

The dog adored the cowboy. Meg bit the inside of her cheek. Over the past few days, she'd appreciated the renewed companionship, too. She wasn't as independent as she wanted to believe.

"How come you haven't updated your blog this week?" he asked.

She wasn't sure her best response. Because she was using her free time on his property or because she had nothing to say. Should she tease or answer truthfully?

"Guess I set you up to fail with that question." He chuckled. "I like the stories you tell. Sometimes I worry you spend too much time observing and not enough living."

She stared, slack-jawed. He'd picked that up from a few paragraphs here and there? "I'm not sure I always..." *belong*. If she admitted as much, she knew her concerns would be brushed aside. Hank had always been the heart of the community. How could he relate to her troubles? "Not every item has a story worth sharing. Besides, if I posted about the shed, all your business would be shared with the whole world. Do you want that?"

"Hmm. Maybe not." He smiled. "I've got something for you inside the house. Might be worthy of a tall tale."

She frowned. "You do?" Her chest squeezed tight. If he was about to offer her something of Miss Susie's, he'd be disappointed by her response. She would not stoop to selling his memories, no matter how desperate her business was for income. The shed was turning into a bust. With her head held high, she'd help a neighbor who always did the same in return. She didn't need payment.

"Remember those boxes from this morning?"

She remembered too much from this morning. When he grabbed the boxes, he'd flashed her a lopsided grin and electrified her every nerve ending from her fingers to her toes. Her heartbeat pounded, and her throat closed. She nodded.

"I found a bunch of old photographs and signed cards," Hank said. "I think some are from the Wild West Show."

That snapped her back. "You mean Buffalo Bill Cody and Annie Oakley?"

"One and the same. I don't know if they are old souvenirs or originals. They don't mean anything to me. I think they could be valuable."

He was probably right. Western art remained a hot niche of the fine arts market. On the rare occasions she got a print or statue, she couldn't keep them in stock. Would photographs be the same? She could be out of her depth. If she was honest, she'd admit to handling smaller items worth, at most, several hundred dollars. She'd never sold something worth five figures or more. She couldn't let him down with her lack of connections. "Should I call an expert? Like a museum or an auction house or something?"

He shook his head side to side. "A deal is a deal. I want you to sell these for me."

"I don't know if I can." She exhaled a heavy breath and hung her head. "The first step is authentication. Whether real or not, I want to get you top dollar. As collectibles, the set is desirable. I'm not sure how to price the collection."

"You're clever. You'll figure something out. Come on, let me show you."

She'd followed him inside. Spread across the kitchen table were black-and-white images of bearded men in over-the-top western wear. Fringe along every seam of velvet buckskins, the too much persona was Buffalo Bill's signature. The collection of images included one with an older Native American man in feathered headdress seated next to the buckskin clad, bearded figure. Could it be Sitting Bull and Buffalo Bill? She'd seen a few pictures of each man individually but didn't recognize this shot.

Hank had helped her pack up the photos and load her SUV. With reluctance, Colby had jumped into the vehicle. Driving away, Meg had banished her thoughts of Ryan for a time. She considered the various paths she could take to sell Hank's goods for top dollar. Central to any plan, however, was identification.

Ryan provided the answer. Their talk about modernization sparked an idea and an internet search. Couldn't facial identification software spot a well-known historical figure? Buffalo Bill and Sitting Bull were famous since their time. With hundreds of images available, A.I. would be able to tell her definitively right away. She'd have one problem solved.

Seated behind the computer at midnight, she curled her toes and grinned as the results popped up on the screen. She had a reason, and now she had a path to stay.

Ryan woke early the next morning. Or, more accurately, he had left his bed an hour ahead of schedule. He couldn't wake up when he'd never quite fallen asleep. After their visit to the yurts, he had dropped Meg at the house, he had vowed to focus.

Almost immediately, he had broken the oath. The rest of his day—and night—was plagued with thoughts about her.

He took up every chore he could, staying away from the house as long as possible. Because he didn't know what would happen when he ran into her again. He wasn't scared. He wouldn't deign to empower the change with an emotion.

The situation was absolute madness. For the time being, he couldn't start thinking about her as anything other than someone to manage. In the future, when he finished paying off the mortgage on her ranch and saved enough of a nest egg to feel in control of his future, he could maybe indulge these new thoughts.

She implied concerns about her future. How could anyone live for the moment when they were terrified about tomorrow? He knew Hank didn't understand. Every issue in his grandfather's life resolved itself almost by magic.

Ryan didn't begrudge anyone their good fortune. His path wasn't one of faith but focus. Approaching any new situation, he learned the variables and navigated to safety. He wasn't spontaneous. He was steady.

When she spoke of her worries, she couldn't have guessed how she spoke to what weighed so heavily on his heart. Somehow, she was different. Since the apology, she wasn't the girl she'd always been. Or maybe he'd changed and was no longer so set in his opinion of her that she surprised him. The moment at the store hadn't been a fluke. Unfortunately.

Something shifted, and he understood her in an entirely new way. Instead of the electricity in her company, threatening him with a bolt of lightning, yesterday he found peace. She knew him. He didn't have to explain every thought. He wanted to correct her misunderstanding but didn't want to upset the calm of the momentary ceasefire.

Standing on the hill, looking across the building site, she had looked serene like an angel on a Christmas Tree. She was contemplative and content with pretty features and lustrous hair.

He swallowed a groan. The hair thing bugged him. Couldn't he reset their relationship and avoid the painful, hyperawareness? Shouldn't people have a factory setting mode so he could meet her again for the first time without any of the past mistakes?

Tightening the belt on his robe, he jogged down the stairs and through the hall, pushing the swinging door to the kitchen. He only had a few more days of leisurely wandering through his own house in his pajamas. The one downside to the business was utilizing the main house as the lobby. He did his best to separate his personal and professional lives. He'd installed the door at the end of the hall to block the kitchen from view. Growing up in the house, he often forgot the changes. More often than not, he smacked his forehead into the panel door, remembering what had been and forgetting the present.

In a couple years, with enough capital, he'd build a special lobby away from the house. If he raised a family, he wanted to give his wife and children the privacy and freedom he had loved as a kid. He frowned. Again, with the family talk. He had to get himself under control.

At the sink, he filled the coffeepot reservoir, added grounds to the filter, and started the much-needed brewing cycle. Spending time together should have summoned a return to old habits. Familiarity should breed contempt. He'd been counting on her talking too much.

She hadn't fallen into her old patterns. During the last few encounters, every word she uttered was a devastating blow to walls he hadn't realized he had erected. Each touch stirred up more feelings than he ever remembered. Lately, she forced him to operate in the moment with heightened awareness of how fleeting time was. He longed for peace but worried their former status quo equaled a resumption of mixed signals. Couldn't the revelations wait a few weeks, or months, for a more convenient time?

Loud knocking echoed in the quiet room.

Spinning on his heel, he frowned at the panel door. Had he imagined the sound? The sun hadn't risen. Who would be on his property so early?

If Ted had a problem, he'd call. Or let himself in. Ryan must have imagined the noise and turned away.

The pounding resumed.

"Coming." He strode across the slate tiles, his slippers gliding over the floor. Reaching for the doorknob, he twisted and pulled open the unlocked door.

Meg stood on the other side, bouncing from foot to foot. Colby sat at her feet. "Hi, Ryan. Sorry about the early call."

She's here? He shut his gaping mouth. "No, no, it's umm... Fine." He opened the door wider. "Please come in. It's cold in the dark."

"Thanks." She passed inside, her steps muffled.

Colby's nails clicked with each step.

He shut the door and stuffed his hands in his robe pockets. Maybe he should have started dressing for the day to get ready for the visitors. Or prepared for the possibility she had almost total access to the ranch. He couldn't kick her out without ending in the same sort of trouble that demanded his hat-in-hand apology and free-access to the ranch. "Can I get you a coffee?"

She lifted on tiptoe, glancing around him toward the stairs. She dropped to her heels. "Hmm? What did you say?"

He frowned. He hadn't mumbled. Was she distracted? He wanted her focus. "Can I get you a coffee? I'm brewing a pot."

"Oh, sure." She smoothed a strand of hair behind her ear. "I probably need it." She chuckled. "Sorry to drop by so early and unannounced. I have something big to share. I barely slept last night."

Her cheek-to-cheek smile warmed him. It was like standing outside at midday on a cloudless summer day. Except better. Her cheer worked from the inside out, without threat of sun burn. He didn't need his hat for protection or shielding. He had a clear view. "What is the good news?"

"Well, I..." She rubbed together her palms. "I really ought to share my discovery with Hank first." She scanned him from head to toe, and her cheeks pinked. "Don't let me get in your way. I'm sure you're ready to start your day."

He liked her embarrassed. It was almost like old days. Dropping his hands to his sides, he leaned back against the stairwell. "I've got plenty of time. Like I said. I woke up early."

"We got company?" Hank's voice bellowed from the second floor.

Ryan frowned, turning toward the stairs. Had they been loud enough to wake the notoriously heavy sleeping Hank?

Trudging steps sounded from the second floor.

A low "woof woof" echoed.

Meg spun in a circle. "Oh, not again," she murmured. "That dog is stealth."

Ryan faced her. "Not again?"

"She's passionate about mattresses. She sneaks upstairs every chance she gets. Even at a stranger's house."

And we're strangers? The thought stung.

Meg stepped around him to the foot of the stairs and cupped her hands around her mouth. "Colby Woofington Hawke, get down here this instant."

"Your dog has both a middle and last name?" He tipped his head to the side.

"Of course." She narrowed her gaze.

Her incredulous stare knocked him off-balance. "Of course?"

She shrugged. "How else does she know when she's in trouble?"

With his tongue pressed to the roof of his mouth, he held back his retort. He could think of any number of other methods for a dog to know it misbehaved. Every scenario he conjured required a firm differentiation in the pack roles. He suspected neither woman nor animal would understand.

Arguing wasn't earning him points. He didn't want to get shooed away before the big reveal. He was curious. Why was she visiting early in the morning? "If that dog is on my bed, you're washing the sheets."

She turned and glared, pulling back her shoulders.

Nails clicked on the hardwood steps. Colby trotted down the stairs, tail wagging.

Not far behind, Hank descended. He'd thrown on jeans and a shirt. He had advance warning about their guests.

The thick white stubble highlighted the deep grooves of his wrinkled skin. Ryan dropped his gaze. In the mornings, his grandfather looked like an eighty-eight-year-old man. Ryan hated the reminder.

"Morning, Meg. Ryan, you want to put on something decent?" Hank asked.

Crossing his arms over his chest, Ryan locked his knees. He was acceptable for surprise company. He wasn't moving.

"Hank, great news. I got a hit on the photos. You're right. It is Buffalo Bill," Meg said. "Velvet clad and all."

"Like Cody?" Ryan asked.

"Is the man next to him Chief Sitting Bull?" Hank asked.

Ryan dropped his hands to his sides, twisting his neck to study one and the other. What on earth were the pair talking about? Why were they ignoring him?

"I emailed an expert on Native American art and photographs from an auction house in San Francisco. With luck, we'll find out the next steps for evaluating and pricing the collection," Meg said.

"You'll handle the sale, right? I don't want anyone else involved." Hank frowned.

She held up her hands. "I promise I'll be involved in helping you get the right experts on board. I will ensure the property is handled correctly."

Hank grunted.

Ryan darted his gaze between the pair. He was definitely the odd man out of the conversation. His interjection wouldn't be appreciated.

"It's a long shot," she said. "If the expert gets back to me quickly and wants a meeting, that has to mean something, right?"

Too many maybes. Ryan wanted to interject and interrupt. The pair of dreamers needed caution. One of them had to stay on the ground, or they'd both float away into the heavens.

If he was honest, he'd admit he hated being left out. Of course, he didn't have time to involve himself in their business. His exclusion was for the best. He wasn't part of their project, and the sooner he removed himself from their business the better. He had real work.

"What about other options?" Hank asked.

"I'm searching for museums and private collectors. While I sort out what we have uncovered and run my store, I won't be able to help in the shed. I hope you understand. I can resume the project again after the photos are resolved." She glanced at Ryan. "I know you wanted the project finished before the guests arrive on Friday. We should have enough space to pick up our work inside the building. I won't disturb the yard again."

"Sounds like you have your hands full. We understand. We do, too. I'll get out of your way." With a nod, he spun on his heel and continued to the kitchen. Everything was working out. He wouldn't have to worry about bumping into her anymore. He could focus on his business.

Back to normal was exactly his goal. He wasn't a child. The sooner he got the future settled, the faster he could lean into what was happening. He was unhappy about being pushed out of the project. For everyone's best interests, he'd hit pause here and revisit their discussion later.

As long as she did the same.

CHAPTER 6

As Meg stood in line at the grocery store, holding a basket full of microwave meals for one, she mentally drafted a post on the blog about the shed discovery. She wanted to share the thrill of finding documentation tying the present to the past. Did the sentiment sound a little sad?

She'd never worried about the perception of her words but she'd clearly underestimated her audience. She swallowed the sigh building in her throat and unloaded her groceries on the moving belt. She hadn't received a response from the auction house yet. The big company was probably busier than she could imagine. Shouldn't she have, at least, received a confirmation email?

"Dear?"

Meg glanced over her shoulder.

A petite, white-haired lady in pearls and a sweater set stood behind her in line. "Do you mind grabbing the plastic divider?

If I'm not quick, my grandson will wander into the ice cream aisle."

Meg smiled at the hushed, conspiratorial tone. "Of course." She unloaded her groceries on the belt, set the divider behind her order, and slid the plastic basket into the holder.

"Nana?" a deep voice called.

"Over here." The lady waved a hand above her head.

Will Buck, owner of the General Store, approached.

Meg did a double-take. She'd pictured a teenager loading up the lady's cart with pints of rocky road, not a man.

"Hi, Meg," Will said.

"Do you know this young lady?" Will's nana unloaded her groceries onto the belt.

"I do. Meg owns the antique store," Will said. "Meg Hawke, this is my grandmother, Lana Buck."

"Pleasure to meet you, Miss Hawke" Lana extended a hand. "I'm surprised I haven't seen you around before."

Meg shook Lana's hand. "I guess my store fills a niche role. Not like the General Store. Anyone in search of a good cup of coffee has to stop by and order a cup of coffee from your grandson."

"I'll have to look for you at Frontier Days," Lana said.

"It's not really her scene, Nana," Will said.

It's not? Meg thought.

At the same time, Lana replied. "Isn't it?"

"Do you like line dancing, Meg? Carnival games? I've never seen you in town after working hours," Will said.

He had a point. Meg liked to get home. She hadn't realized she'd been such a loner in the town's eyes. Making friends as an adult was more involved than during childhood.

"Paper or plastic?" the cashier asked.

Meg faced the woman behind the register, grateful for the excuse to get out of the conversation. "Paper, please." She inserted her credit card into the checkout terminal and glanced at Lana once more. "It was nice to meet you."

"You as well."

The cashier quickly scanned the stack of frozen food. "Here's your receipt."

Meg accepted the paper slip and pulled her credit card out of the terminal, tucked both into her purse, and grabbed her groceries. With a paper bag in her arms, she pushed out the revolving front door of the grocery store and turned left on Main.

Herd embraced their Wild West heritage, and nowhere was that more visible than downtown. False front architecture dotted the one- and two-story buildings on either side of the road. Painted vivid shades like red, blue, and green, the stores stood out against the otherwise flat landscape. Most of the buildings were wooden. A few stone structures had been erected at great cost not long after the town's founding.

The bag she carried did nothing to ease the weighed-down feel in her limbs. No one had entered her store. She'd spent the day entirely alone. All she needed was a plan to get people inside. With a shake, she shrugged off her doldrums. She'd head home, make dinner, and distract herself with a good book.

She shivered when a cloud blocked the sun, and a chilly breeze blew past.

A hot meal and a cozy cuddle with a warm dog would soothe her. As she stepped off the sidewalk at the next block, another shudder racked her body. She turned her face to the dark sky and gulped. Overdue for rain, she hated to wish away the clouds.

When the weather changed on the plains, it was with dramatic rapidity. A sunny morning could transform into thunderstorms in less than a few minutes. Three blocks away from her vehicle, she didn't like her chances for staying dry.

She glanced across the street at the wooden false-fronts and pitched roofs extending over the plank walkway opposite. She was, of course, in front of the post office at the middle of the block of stone and brick buildings without awnings.

She could go inside and wait out the storm. Standing in the elements was dangerous.

Hail was always a possibility during the tail end of spring.

A late in the day rain could last anywhere from ten minutes to ten hours. Colby waited at home. The dog hadn't been out in hours and would demand dinner soon. If Meg didn't hurry, she worried what she would find. Meg had to reach her vehicle and get to her dog before Colby took matters into her own paws.

In Meg's thirty seconds of indecision, the sky darkened to pitch black. Rain poured down like an upended bucket. She tightened her grip on the bag, climbed the steps onto the next section of walkway, and tucked her chin against her chest.

She couldn't raise her face to follow her progress, or she'd be pelted in the eyes by the fat drops. She trusted her memory of town to guide her. With each passing moment, her clothes became wetter and clung to her body. She focused on warm thoughts like the hot cocoa packets in her pantry. She could manage. She'd dealt with worse.

A truck rolled past, hit the pothole in front of The Golden Crown Saloon, and splashed water like a wave, thoroughly drenching her.

She lifted her gaze at the idling vehicle, her mouth forming a circle and freezing on the gasp.

The truck's passenger side window rolled down.

"Meg?" Ryan asked. "Hop in, warm up," he commanded.

The door unlocked with a loud click.

In normal circumstances, she wasn't one to be bossed around and especially not by him. He always thought he knew best. Arguing was pointless as she shivered in the rain. This one time, he was right.

She hopped into the cab, sliding her groceries onto the floor mat. "Thanks." Her teeth chattered.

With a frown, he turned up the heater. "I'm sorry I added to your misery."

"I should have known better." Keeping her hands on the vents, she turned toward him. "If I'd been thinking, I would have driven to the grocery store instead of leaving my car in the municipal lot. I wanted some fresh air and a little exercise."

"The temperature will improve by the weekend. You've lived here long enough to know one truth." He lifted the corner of his mouth. "Nice weather never lasts."

Nothing good does. She stared into his amber eyes. The amusement in his gaze invited her into a private joke. She didn't want to lose the new connection. Once she finished at the shed, she wouldn't have any reason to seek his company. Worse, she could end up back in Chicago if she didn't make progress on her online store or those cards failed to pan out.

She had to find contentment one day at a time in the present, ignoring her inclination to race ahead. Her tomorrows might not include him so she couldn't squander her todays.

She pointed at a clip on one of the vents. "You bought air freshener?"

"Hank had some in a drawer." Ryan shrugged. "I can't tell a difference."

Shutting her eyes, she breathed deep. "It smells like cedar." She turned her head and met his gaze with a smile.

A car honked.

He broke away from her gaze, raised a hand to the driver passing him, and pulled into traffic. "Can I get you dinner by way of apology?"

She shook her head. "I've got to get home to Colby. A ride to my car would be more than enough."

He nodded and turned at the next intersection, driving onto the side streets and backtracking to the lot on the edge of downtown, a few blocks past her store. "You left the dog at home? Doesn't she accompany you everywhere?"

He keeps tabs on me? The thought was cheering and a little jarring. She wasn't sure she wanted to be so predictable and boring. Or maybe he knew her that well. "Typically, she does." Meg pushed her limp, wet hair behind her ears. "She's in time out for behavior unbecoming of a lady this morning at the ranch."

Ryan chuckled.

Her heart lifted at the deep, rumbling sound. "Why are you in town? Aren't you too swamped to leave your property? Only a few more days until the first guests arrive."

He exhaled a heavy breath. "Believe me, I know. Cupcake was reshoed today, and I spent the rest of the day with the spa staff. My brain is counting down the seconds. Occasionally, a meeting pops up that can't be rescheduled and is easier handled in person." He paused.

Oh. She swallowed hard. Was she a fool for wanting him to seek her company? Their fledging friendship might be endangered if he did. She shouldn't expect more than either of them could give.

He lifted his shoulders. "I was serious about my offer. I'm heading over to Church Street. Joe and I have business to discuss, and I'd like to review the catering orders for the first few cowboy dinners with Abby Whit. She'll have everything handled, of course. But two big events in less than a week is a lot. I figured we might as well grab dinner from her food truck while we're there. Really, it's a good excuse to do just that."

Meg licked her lips. She loved Abby's pulled pork sandwich with mustard coleslaw on a pretzel roll. Eating out was a luxury she couldn't afford at the moment. His offer was tempting. With Joe there, no one could accuse Meg and Ryan of a date. Her cheeks burned. She wasn't sure she'd mind the assumption.

"You want to reconsider now that you know my plan?" He arched a brow and shot her a quick glance before refocusing on the road.

"Don't tempt me."

He pulled into the public parking lot behind Main Street and turned down the first row. All alone, her white SUV waited for her. He parked next to her vehicle and turned toward her.

"Hey, before you go. I want to tell you how much I appreciate your work with Hank. It's a lot to deal with and sort. You helping means a lot."

His sincerity scrambled her brain. How could she form an appropriate response when he was so earnest? She nodded.

"I also wanted to tell you the event space idea is a good one. I am looking into it. Not sure how feasible it will be with some other projects in the mix, but I am considering it."

"Wow. That's great. I'm... glad." He took her seriously. She would have expected him to brush off her idea and never mention it again. He surprised her in the best way.

"I do want to urge caution about the stuff you found in the shed. Might turn out to be nothing, and I'd hate to get Hank's hopes raised only to dash them."

Irritated by his lack of faith, she found her footing. Sitting up straight, she faced him. "You are good at your job. I'm good at mine. Trust me. I would never deceive or hurt Hank." *Or you.*

Ryan scrubbed a hand over his face. "I never accused you of treachery. I'm saying be careful."

She didn't want to fight. How quickly any comment could be filtered through their history and misconstrued. She was overreacting, but she couldn't shake off the foul mood with continued company. "Okay." She reached for the handle and opened the door. Hopping to the ground, she grabbed her sodden bag of groceries. "Thanks for the lift."

With a foot, she kicked the door closed and walked around her bumper to the other side of her SUV, away from his piercing gaze. She had dropped her guard only to have him grab her by the shoulders and shake. Metaphorically speaking.

He probably didn't intend his words as a challenge. Regardless, she'd fight and prove him wrong. She wasn't toying with Hank's emotions or hers.

As Ryan rolled through town, he imagined the community's collective sigh. In addition to much-needed rain during an unusually dry year, the sudden storm encouraged tourists to seek shelter.

The General Store would be hopping with folks looking for souvenirs or hungry for a piece of fudge. Olden Time Portraits would be packed with customers in costumes, snapping sepia-tinted photos. The Golden Crown would be stuffed to the rafters with the supper crowd.

Too bad Meg closed up for the evening. She might have had her best sales yet this year. He couldn't worry about her. She made it clear that she didn't welcome his concern.

On the opposite side of town, he reached his original destination. The rain stopped as soon as he pulled out of the parking lot. *So much for a grand, gallant gesture.* Meg could have waited inside the saloon and avoided him altogether. She would have been better off than after their impromptu encounter. As he said the words about Hank, her hackles visibly rose.

He hadn't intended a professional attack. After she had left the ranch as suddenly as she had appeared, she stirred up all sorts of talk inside the Kincaid house. Hank was jollier than Christmas morning. Ryan wanted to join in the glee but couldn't. What if it all went wrong? Meg could be mistaken about the value.

Their unexpected encounter in town was the perfect opportunity to speak frankly. She cared about his grandfather and would appreciate the concerns for the older man's heart. Ryan made a huge miscalculation. He forgot who he was dealing with. She was equally as determined and stubborn as him.

He wouldn't have responded well to a perceived critique of his work skills and business competency. He hated ruining the otherwise pleasant encounter. Under no circumstances, however, would he retract the sentiment behind the statement.

Hank was larger than life but not immortal. Any big upset in either direction could overwhelm him. Ryan couldn't see the future without his grandfather's presence. He didn't want to be left on his own. If he continued to antagonize, however, he'd scare Meg away. His future looked very lonely without her in it.

He parked and turned the key in the ignition, cutting the engine. The large, open parking lot behind the historic, Presbyterian church faced the town's cemetery. Many people swore the hallowed grounds were haunted. He brushed off the comments. Any old graveyard looked spooky as the iron fences surrounding family plots rusted, the stones discolored from age and acid rain, and the ground uneven due to erosion.

Wrenching open the truck door, hinges squealing, he pocketed his keys and strode toward the food truck parked on the other end. Abby chose the location due to its size and access downtown, successfully petitioning the town for permission. As a member of the council, he supported the enterprise. The spookiness of the location didn't detract from customers. Diners flocked to the spot for the best barbeque for a hundred miles in any direction.

He joined the back of the queue and breathed deep, savoring the mingled smells of damp earth and smoked meat. He'd overstepped with Meg by being too harsh. What he meant as a tease wasn't properly conveyed. One step at a time, he'd fix it. Not tonight. He had to focus on the business at hand and worry about Meg later.

"Hey, boss."

Ryan turned and waved.

Joe jogged across the wet pavement.

"Hey, Joe. Thanks for meeting me. I know you're swamped with end of school stuff."

"It's fine." Joe stuffed his hands into his coat pockets. "To be honest, I'm surprised you had time to leave the ranch."

A popular opinion. If he had phoned, he wouldn't have had the unfortunate run-in with Meg. He couldn't regret riding into her rescue. She would never be a damsel in distress, making an opportunity to help rare.

But his dwindling hours were stretched thin. He'd spent most of the day onboarding the new spa employees and greeting those who'd become summertime fixtures.

"I like to review the order for the first cowboy dinners of the season in person. Two in one week is a big ask. Figured I might as well grab supper, too. Thanks for stopping by on such short notice."

"Of course." Joe sniffed, twisting his neck side to side. "Is it just me or does it smell like a sauna around here?"

Ryan pressed together his lips, resisting the urge to sniff his collar and draw attention to himself. If Meg's face hadn't lit up when she noticed he took her advice, he'd toss the clip-on air freshener.

"Never mind." Joe shook his head. "You mentioned you wanted to follow-up about potential yoga teachers?"

Ryan nodded, holding his breath. He needed every staff position filled as soon as possible.

"I put the word out at the school teacher's lounge. No luck upstairs with the middle school wing. But I struck gold in the kindergarten through fifth grade portion of the building. Stephanie Patricks expressed interest. She isn't just a kinder-garten teacher. Turns out she is a certified yoga instructor, too."

The line moved forward.

If only every problem was so easily solved. Ryan shuffled a few paces ahead, staring at the ground. "Great news."

"You okay?" Joe asked. "You're sort of radiating nervous en-ergy."

Ryan let out a bark of laughter. "I am? Sorry."

"It's okay. Opening week stress, I get it." Joe darted his eyes side to side and shifted his weight. "This is a weird place for a food truck. Don't you think?"

Ryan met Joe's gaze and frowned. Was he trying to deflect Ryan's attention? "It's the biggest parking lot in town with good proximity to Main Street. Makes sense to me. Besides, the benches are on the unclaimed land. Good to see it put to use."

Joe rocked back on his heels. "I hate waiting around for the hundred years to pass. Can't we get a lawyer involved and speed up the process?"

Ryan had no response to the bitter tone. In less than eighteen months, the land the parking lot sat on—formerly owned by the Whittier family—would be absorbed back into Herd. No one ever stepped forward to state they possessed the deed. Why pursue unnecessary litigation? "I don't want to put the money and time into it. Have you uncovered anything in your research that makes you think it should be pursued?"

Joe shook his head. "No, the genealogy records stop with Hoss. I can't find any mention of him owning property or getting married. I haven't located his death certificate. He can't be alive, or he'd be well over a hundred."

"He probably didn't last long after leaving town," Ryan said. "He struggled with his demons."

"I've run into Abby at the library several times."

The words were almost a hiss. Ryan couldn't understand his friend. Something was off in Joe's mood. With the end of the school year and the start of tourist season, he was busy, too. In addition, he toiled on his history of Herd, a project he'd dedicated all of his free time to for the past decade. Ryan gave him a pass on his attitude today.

"We don't have to get dinner."

Ryan would readily admit his own inner turmoil and distraction. He guessed he wasn't alone in the sensation. "No, I promised, and I'm starving. Join me. We won't linger. I know you're busy wrapping up your school year."

Joe nodded. "I have a lot on my mind."

"Next," Abby called.

With a wave, Ryan stepped up to the window. "Good evening, Abby. We'd like a couple three meat samplers, pork, brisket, and sausage with the works. I'm wondering if you got the order I emailed?"

"Hey, Ryan. Good to see you. Hi, Joe."

Joe raised a hand to his shoulder and dropped it to his side.

Weird greeting for an effusive person. Ryan couldn't get distracted by other people's problems. He had enough of his own, and he wasn't Hank. Ryan didn't try to insert himself—by force, if necessary—into other people's personal lives.

"I got the email," Abby said. "I've already reached out to my suppliers. We should be set for both events. If there is an issue, I have plenty of time to find a solution for Friday. Monday will be taken care of, no matter what."

"Good, thank you." Ryan nodded. "Catering twice in one week is a lot to ask."

"Nothing I can't handle. Have you had a chance to think about my proposal to park on-site once a week?"

Joe snorted.

Ryan snapped his head toward the sound in time to catch a corresponding eyeroll. He glared at Joe.

"Sorry. Allergies," Joe said. "I'll get a seat." He strode around the truck toward the grass on the other side and the row of wooden picnic tables.

He moved too quick for a reprimand of his out of character behavior. He wasn't exactly rude, but neither was he nice. "Sorry about him. Allergies." Ryan rolled his eyes.

Abby chuckled and waved a hand.

At least she was good natured enough to brush off Joe. Ryan wouldn't take advantage of her kindness. "I have to run the idea by Hank and Ted. I'll be honest, something popped up recently and has me totally sidetracked. I'll get you an answer soon."

Abby nodded. "No worries. Steve has your order ready at the other window."

Ryan smiled and followed Joe's path. As Ryan cleared the front of the truck, he spotted Joe claiming their meals.

Ryan continued to an empty table and sat down. Pulling his cell out of his back pocket, he shot a quick text to Ted and Hank before he forgot again. Hitting send, he placed the phone face-down on the weathered plank top.

Joe slid a metal platter in front of him and handed a cup of water.

"You feeling okay?" Ryan asked, studying his friend.

Joe stepped over the bench seat opposite and sat in front of his tray. "Ever get the sense you're not being lied to but you don't know the full scope of a person or situation?"

As far as cryptic statements went, Joe was an unrivaled master. Ryan ran a hand along his jaw. "Am I supposed to understand your meaning?"

"I'm glad if you don't." Joe shook his head and speared a slice of brisket. "Should I have Stephanie call and set up an interview?"

"I can call her if you'll send me her phone number." Ryan raised his plastic cup. "Let's toast to a good season." *Including resolving issues with as little disruption as possible.*

Joe set his fork down and grabbed his water, touching his plastic cup to Ryan's before taking a sip.

Ryan drank a large gulp. After a dry, dusty day on the ranch, nothing was as satisfying as water. Maybe Meg wouldn't agree today after he drenched her. If she was warm and toasty at home, perhaps she'd reconsider the encounter and realize his words weren't meant as a taunt or a test.

If she was upset, then she had misread the charge in the air between them. A sense of anticipation collided with fate. He wasn't sure if he loved or hated the new and different feelings. He hoped she welcomed the change.

CHAPTER 7

With her laptop open on the antique store's front counter, Meg refreshed her inbox. Since sending the email late on Tuesday night, she'd spent too much of her time on Wednesday and Thursday staring at her computer screen. Finally, Friday dawned and with it the promise of tourists. She hadn't seen one in the hour since she'd opened.

Propping her chin in her elbow, she sighed at the empty email account. She didn't even have an update from a mailing list about a limited time sale. Had she been wrong to raise Hank's hopes about potential interest?

Ryan was right. Her indignation had been in vain. She should head to the ranch and apologize. Spending more time with him—even to say she was sorry—threatened their status quo. She didn't mind the provocation. Did he?

Instead, she'd focus on the photographs and cards. She pulled up her blog, hit compose, and stared at the flashing cursor on the blank page. The discovery was exciting but unknown.

Could she share anything without jinxing herself? Or worse, revealing too much? Hank had guessed at her feeling like an outsider through her entries. She was guilty of waiting on the sidelines as life happened.

What if she put herself out there? If she joined the knitting club that met at The Golden Crown or directly asked Stephanie about helping with Frontier Days, what was the worst possible outcome? Being told no?

Her neighbors weren't rude or unwelcoming. She hadn't attempted to befriend anyone besides Hank and Ryan. She had to do better or she'd never belong.

In her back pocket, her cell phone vibrated. She pulled out the phone and smiled at the screen. She answered the call, pressing the cell to her ear. "Hi, Mom."

"Well? How's it going on your treasure hunt at the ranch? Anything to report? The blog hasn't been updated all week."

Meg chuckled. Her loyal—and top—follower would know. "I doubt I'll have much that I'll be allowed to share." She nibbled the inside of her cheek.

"Oh? Really? Why?" Mom's voice pitched high.

Had Hank called Mom? She'd grown up with Hank's son, Ryan's dad. Mom talked to Hank every so often. Were they in cahoots about saving the store? *Probably.* "We found a box of old photographs and souvenir cards from the nineteenth century. I can't say much more at the moment. The discovery could be valuable." *Although, now I have my doubts.*

The bell over the door jingled.

She straightened and smiled, meeting the gaze of a teenager.

The ponytailed girl blushed and backed out, shutting the door.

The glass rattled in the frame.

"Is someone there?" Mom asked.

"No, just the wind." Meg sighed. "I'll keep you posted about any new developments. In the meantime, don't expect much on the blog. I am focusing on the website."

"You should. Couldn't Ryan help you? Didn't he have to build one for the ranch?"

Meg nibbled her lip. Hank and Mom played the same tune. They were wrong. Two people of the same generation—like Meg and Ryan—weren't automatically friends. With their occasionally acrimonious history, Meg and Ryan should be well past any sort of clunky *setup*. Too bad their respective families didn't understand the definition of futility, and informing Mom of Ryan's offer of help wouldn't win Meg's argument. "I'm not sure what he does on his ranch. I'll ask Hank. I better go, Mom. Don't want to discourage customers with a phone plastered to my ear." She forced a chuckle.

"Bye, sweetie. Good luck! I'm rooting for you." Mom ended the call.

Rolling her shoulders, Meg shut the laptop and tucked the computer and phone into her purse on the floor. She needed to dust off her customer skills, or she'd scare everyone away on the first day of the busy season.

Herd was in a celebratory mood. Every store was open. Flowers filled planters. Flags hung on lampposts, and banners strung over the street. A few wandering cowboys strutted down the sidewalk, playing up the Wild West for tourists.

She loved the small town in every season but especially during the contagious cheer of summer courtesy of outsiders. Her sleep deprivation shouldn't dampen her spirit. A heart heavy with questions and concerns slowed her. Grabbing the feather duster from under the counter, she stood and started cleaning.

The mindless motion gave the appearance of activity while her brain drifted to a ranch not so very far away. When she'd been splashed by Ryan's truck last night, she hadn't shared the details she and Hank had worked out in the morning. Over coffee in the kitchen, she had devised a plan, and Hank agreed with a condition. She didn't want Hank to miss out on a big payday.

He'd use the money to help the ranch. No doubt, he'd pay off the mortgage on the land Ryan bought from her. She'd feel a lot less guilty about the Kincaids riding to her rescue. Without the stress, Ryan could slow down and enjoy himself.

Had he ever?

She snorted and dusted the first row of shelves at the back of the store. Hank had insisted she take a cut of the final sale price of the photographs. She had no intention of doing so but would save the disagreement for another day. First, she needed contact from the auction house.

Jingle jingle jingle.

With a smile on her face, she turned slowly toward the door. "Hello, welcome to Finders-Keepers." She used the brightest, cheeriest tone she could muster.

A man strode over the threshold and shut the door. He turned.

Each quarter inch of action happened in slow motion. Dressed in a slim cut, light blue dress shirt and tailored, charcoal slacks, he stood out from the usual jeans and T-shirts crowd of locals and tourists alike. He was instantly the most interestingly out of place stranger she'd ever seen. When he connected his gaze with her, he smiled.

He looked like an old movie star. With dark hair and dark eyes, she couldn't quite tell the color of either. A cleft in his strong jaw deepened with his grin.

Ryan's more handsome because he's real. The thought slipped into her mind and she couldn't shake it. This stranger's beauty was undeniable. But she was drawn to the inside of a person.

The man tipped his head and approached.

With each step, he came into focus. He wasn't quite five ten, but his trim figure gave a lanky impression. *He's going to change my life.* The complete thought was like a bolt of lightning surging through her veins. She wished she understood the how and why of her certainty as much as she instinctively knew the what.

If such a thing were possible, she'd throw the idea to the ground and crush it under her heel. She wasn't ready. She wanted everything to stay the same for as long as she could hold on. Or, if she could have a hand in manipulating fate, she longed for Ryan to be the one to spark change.

"Hello, are you Megan Hawke?"

His voice was smooth and deep, lower than she expected. She coughed, raising a fist to her mouth. The feather duster tickled her nostrils. She dropped her hands behind her back. "Yes, hello. Thank you for stopping in." Her voice cracked. "Are you looking for anything in particular?"

He stopped a few feet away. "I'm Eric York, from Campbell and Company Auctioneers in San Francisco." He arched a brow.

"Oh, wow. You came?" She clapped a hand over her mouth, her cheeks burning.

He grinned again. "I did. Your photographs are worth an examination in person." He extended a hand.

She reached forward, batting him with the duster. "Oh, sorry." She tucked the duster into her back pocket and tried again. "Thank you for coming so quickly."

"My pleasure."

A loud yawn echoed in the room.

"Is someone here?" he asked.

Colby trotted out from behind the front counter, tail wagging and nose sniffing the air.

"This is my coworker, Colby."

The dog stopped at her side and sat.

Eric kneeled on the floor. "Pleased to meet you, Colby."

When's the last time I mopped? He'd ruin his pristine slacks to greet her mutt. She couldn't offer to pay for dry cleaning. The town didn't have such a service. She remained motionless, fighting to keep her cringe internal.

The dog lifted a paw.

Eric shook and reached forward, scratching behind Colby's ears before straightening to his full height. "Very polite."

"We try." Meg shrugged.

He reached into his pocket and retrieved a business card. "A first-hand examination is paramount before we go any further."

She grabbed the extended card and held it in between both thumbs and index fingers. The heavy weight of the smooth card hinted at a company with means. Her business cards felt shabby and rough by comparison.

She drew in a shaky breath. Had she overcorrected? Maybe the find wasn't worth his time. What did she know? Running a small-town antique store was hardly equivalent to his experience, she squinted at the card, as lead expert in Western and Native American artifacts.

"I wanted to stop by and see if we could set a time to review the collection in person."

"Oh, yeah, of course." She scrunched her nose.

"Is there a problem?"

She lifted her gaze. "I think I explained in the email that I'm helping a friend? I'm not the owner. I would like to coordinate with that person before moving ahead."

He nodded. "Absolutely. I'm sorry I stopped by unannounced." He rested a hand on his heart. "I found an opening at a nearby resort and wanted to jump at the chance. I'd like the opportunity to do some research in town, and lodging was booked until mid-July after this weekend."

She smiled. "Herd is a popular destination."

"I can see. I wanted to introduce myself before I check-in at the resort."

"I'm glad you did." Dropping her shoulders, she relaxed. He was direct and not pushy. She could handle straight-forward, business interactions. She had no doubt he'd put Hank at ease. Hank's feelings mattered, not hers. "I'll speak with the owner today."

"Great. I'll be staying at the Kincaid ranch. Do you know it?"

"I do." She smiled. He made her job much easier. "In fact, the photographs are at the ranch."

He rubbed together his palms. "Better and better. Perhaps I can do some on-site research as well."

As long as you don't get in Ryan's way. The thought was unkind. Her experience shouldn't color a stranger's. Especially since she wasn't sure how to categorize the state of her interactions with her neighbor. He wasn't a close friend, but neither was he an enemy.

She shook her head. "If you want, you can follow me to the ranch. I'll speak to the owner while you check-in."

"Are you sure you want to close?"

She shrugged. "I'll only be gone for a little bit. I'll leave you to settle in. With any luck, I can introduce you to the owner, and he might have more information to share to get you started."

"That sounds wonderful. Please, lead the way, Miss Hawke." He waved a hand in front of him, turning toward the door.

"Please call me, Meg." She smoothed her hair behind her ears, brushing her hot cheeks with her fingers. "Everyone does."

"As long as you call me, Eric."

Her stomach dropped at his smooth delivery. Was he flirting? She wasn't looking for love and especially not with someone who wasn't from Herd. She dried her clammy palms against her sides.

I might not be a resident much longer, either. Not sure anyone will notice. She couldn't think like that. If she wanted a friend, she had to be one first. With the stranger's arrival, she might soon have enough capital to buy time and try.

"Let me grab my bag." She returned to the front counter and grabbed her purse off the floor. Greater concerns than romance waited her. She wouldn't read anything into the stranger's physical tics. She had a hard enough time deciphering the actions of someone she'd known her whole life. One more man was too much trouble.

"You're all set," Ryan said. With a smile, he pushed back his chair from the folding, banquet table and stood. Reaching over the table, he handed a set of keys to the guests, a couple celebrating their twentieth anniversary in cabin five near the fishing pond.

"Thank you." The wife turned to her husband.

With silver streaks running through her dark hair, she didn't look young, the cheeky smile she shot her companion was youthful. The couple exited through the ranch house's propped open front door.

Stretching his arms over head, Ryan twisted one way and then the other. A morning spent seated wasn't his usual modus operandi. His muscles ached, and his stiff back needed a heating pad. He'd settle for a little movement instead. Dropping his arms to his side, he glanced at the wall clock. Barely ten a.m., he'd checked in almost all the cabins and two of the three yurts.

"Hey, Ted," he called to the table set up kitty-corner. "I'm putting on another pot of coffee. You want some?"

"Yes, please." Ted widened his eyes and nodded.

With a chuckle, Ryan turned toward the kitchen. He'd set the check-in table to block access to the heart of the home, giving Hank some peace when possible. In the front room, he'd constructed the adventures sign-up table. Helmed by Joe, the middle-school social studies teacher during the school year and ranch guide by summer, a steady stream of guests stopped by to approve their itineraries, change activities, and add more experiences.

At some point, Ryan needed to discuss the bison plans in-depth with the teacher. His summer employee and full-time friend earned a stellar reputation within the community. Joe was well-respected and well-known. Between his work at the school and his years of interviewing older citizens for his book, he'd become a person many in town knew and like. His public approval of the plan could do a lot to ease potential concerns that might arise regarding the introduction of a free-roaming herd.

Ryan pushed through the door to the kitchen, the panel swinging shut behind him, and headed straight to the coffee maker on the counter. If the pace continued all summer, he'd meet his goal quicker than planned. He might need to invest in another coffee maker to properly fuel his staff.

Filling the water reservoir, he found the filters and scooped the grounds into the machine. He hit brew and leaned his hands against the edge of the counter, rolling his neck from one side to the other. Almost every inch of him ached from manual labor. He could stretch for hours and still feel sore. Was town as busy as the ranch? How was business at the antique store?

None of my concern.

He sighed. He was glad for the busy morning. Between final preparations and checking in guests, he didn't have a second to think. Which was good. Because any moment of quiet turned into contemplation. Meg was becoming a nuisance. Again. For an entirely different set of reasons.

As shocking as her appearance yesterday, while he was in pajamas, she somehow belonged. Of course, she should treat the home like she could arrive, unannounced, at any moment. She'd practically grown up inside the four walls.

Less pleasing was the time he spent wondering about her and wanting to see her. After their second encounter, he wanted to apologize again. Would she show up at the ranch today and give him the opportunity?

The house hadn't had any female energy to ease the machismo since Grandma passed. He hadn't understood the loss until the constant presence of Meg. She fit. What did that mean? He liked her?

She drove him crazy. *Or am I crazy about her?* He shook his head. *Get back to work and focus on your job.* Once he secured the future with a successful summer season, paying off the mortgage on her land and ensuring the arrival of the bison, then he could let his mind drift to other thoughts. He needed time.

"Woolgathering, boy?" Hank asked.

Jumping, Ryan pressed the heel of his palm against his beating heart. He squinted and turned, spotting Hank at the head of the table. His grandfather had been so quiet, Ryan assumed he'd gone to the shed. "Didn't realize I had company."

The coffee maker beeped.

He pulled three mugs off the hooks on the wall. "Can I get you a cup?"

"No, I'm fine." Hank sighed.

Ryan frowned, leaving one mug on the counter in case Hank changed his mind. Grunts, growls, and groans were Hank's non-verbal forms of communication. Not silence or heavy exhales. He filled his mug to the brim. "You okay?"

"Feels wrong not to see her."

I know what you mean. Ryan woke up, came downstairs, and started calculating how many hours it had been since seeing her. He couldn't let Hank see this mental quandary, or he'd force Ryan to act. "She can't stop by every day."

"Well, I don't see why she can't. How different is it for her to be there or here?"

Ryan returned the coffeepot to the machine and turned. Leaning back, he blew across the top of her steaming mug. "She has a whole life without us. I'm pretty sure she'd be offended if you implied her day to day was incomplete without a man."

Hank shook his head. "I'd have to disagree. She's missing the ranch as much as the ranch misses her."

Ryan had no response. Why on earth was Hank digging in his heels about Meg? He'd never concerned himself with seeing her before. She'd always been around. If a few days went by without a visit, why not call?

The kitchen door swung inward.

Ryan spun, but he didn't spot an intruder. Did he need to add trapping a ghost to his ever-growing to-do list?

"COLBY!" Hank called with glee.

A flash of black and white raced past.

Shaking his head, Ryan grabbed his mug and turned to watch the pair.

Wagging her tail like a fan blade, the dog approached the old cowboy at top speed. She rested her paws on his legs and stretched, lavishing his face with licks.

Hank chuckled. "Oh, I missed you, too. I was talking to Ryan about you." He pet the dog and grinned broadly.

Oh. Why had Ryan assumed Hank meant Meg? Because Ryan couldn't stop thinking about her?

A knock shook the door.

Without waiting for a response, the door cracked open.

Meg poked her head in. Her gaze met his and then she twisted her neck toward Hank and the dog and back again. "Hi, is it okay that she's here?" She murmured. "Sorry, she didn't wait for permission."

"She doesn't need permission. Neither do you," Hank said. "Come in."

"Umm, well, actually. I can't. I have someone with me," she said.

Who? Ryan frowned. He didn't like the way her voice dropped when she said someone. Holding the mug, he couldn't curl his hands into fists. He lifted the coffee and sipped, grateful for something to do besides question her.

"Whoever you brought is welcome, too," Hank said.

She stepped back, and the door swung shut.

Ryan turned to his grandfather and arched an eyebrow. What was the old cowboy playing at?

Focused on the dog, Hank was too busy for Ryan's pointed look. Or smart enough to avoid the steady stare.

The door swung open.

Meg entered, followed by a man.

Setting his mug on the counter behind him, Ryan pulled his shoulders back and strode forward.

The guy had styled hair and loafers. He looked slim but not strong. Dressed nicer than most Herd grooms on their wedding days, the stranger didn't belong. He couldn't imagine anyone more out of place on the ranch, including the wide variety of guests the Kincaids had welcomed over the years.

Ryan wrinkled his brow. *This pretty guy can't be her type.* Why did that matter? In a few steps, Ryan closed the gap and extended his hand. "Ryan Kincaid."

The man returned the grip with surprising force. "I'm Eric York, from Campbell and Company in San Francisco." He twisted his head back and forth between Hank and Ryan. "I've come to look into the photographs, and I've booked a yurt for the weekend."

A chair scraped the slate floor.

Ryan dropped his hand and turned away. He hated to break first and show any hint of weakness to the new arrival. Letting Hank overexert himself because of Ryan's pride, however, was a non-starter.

Hank got to his feet with Colby at his side. "I'm the man to see about the photographs once you're settled. It's no rush." He chuckled. "I'm not going anywhere." He bent and scratched Colby behind the ears.

"I can get you checked in if you go back out into the hall." Ryan waved to the exit.

Eric turned to Meg and lifted a brow.

She nodded.

Two strangers had an unspoken language? Ryan pressed his lips together. Growling at a guest wasn't top tier customer service.

She walked to the table, brushing past, and sat at Ryan's usual seat.

Hank sank back to his chair.

No hello? No how is the morning going? He turned toward the counter and grabbed his mug. Spinning back around, he met the expert's gaze. "If you'll join me in the front room?"

Eric nodded and strode across the kitchen.

Ryan glanced at the table. Hank, Colby, and Meg made a picture-perfect trio. He wished he could pull up a seat and join them. With a shake, he exited through the door the stranger held open with a hand.

He had guests waiting and a business to run. This pretty boy was probably exactly the right person for Meg. He understood old things and could drop everything to turn up someplace else for a week. She'd like that spontaneity.

The only time Ryan's plans changed were for emergencies. This scenario was the best possible outcome. The surest way to get her out of his thoughts was for her to overtake someone else's.

CHAPTER 8

U nder a bright, still blue sky, Meg turned off the dirt road and steered her SUV onto the gravel drive. With a glance at the clock, she read seven p.m. on the dash. If her cheeks didn't ache from smiling at customers all day, she'd be fooled into thinking she had nothing but time. She snorted. When she wasn't worried about tomorrow, she'd enjoy today. Maybe in a few months. Hopefully not from her mother's condo in Chicago's Logan Square.

The tires crunched over the tiny rocks. In the shotgun seat, Colby sat up. Tail whacking the upholstered seat, she turned toward the windshield. She emitted a low woof.

Meg smiled. At the store, she'd had her biggest sales day in eight months renewing her hope for a future in town. Receiving a call from Eric, asking her to drop by the shed for news, lifted her to new heights. She'd pinpoint her joy on her business and not on the prospect of bumping into Ryan.

She shook her head and narrowed her gaze on the circle drive in front of the house. She hated the tense visit to check-in Eric that morning. If she stopped by to address the subject, she wasn't sure what she would say.

Hi, Ryan, we've been such good friends lately, and I'd hate for you to think I have feelings for some random guy that I showed up with at your ranch when I was trying to help check him in so we could work on the project for Hank. She blew out a sigh. Rambling went nowhere with Ryan, and she hated the defensive twinge in her prepared remarks. She wanted to be friends and had done nothing to owe him an apology.

Tightening her grip on the steering wheel, she navigated as close to the edge of the lawn as she dared. With guests visiting, she knew he liked to keep the front drive clear. Using the house as the check-in meant the gravel path filled up quickly at peak times though she wasn't likely to block any new arrivals arriving this late in the day.

Parking the car, she leaned over to open Colby's door.

In a flash of black and white, the dog bolted to the front of the house.

Meg hopped to the ground and locked the car. "Come on, Colby. Hank is in the shed."

The dog jogged down the steps and raced around the side.

At a subdued pace, Meg followed, looking eager wouldn't earn her any points. *Maybe Ryan's around here somewhere.* She stiffened. She absolutely refused to dwell on him. Instead, she filled her lungs with a deep breath and inhaled the sweet perfume of summer grass.

The clean scent should be bottled. Montana summer promised a few thunderstorms, the occasional hail, and endless, glorious blue-sky days. She'd lived other places but she'd never enjoyed the hottest months of the year so much. The annual childhood escape from her big city hometown recharged her spirit for the rest of the calendar. She'd spent enough Junes, Julys, and Augusts in Chicago as an adult to appreciate fresh air.

The shed door was propped open. Colby pushed it wide and trotted inside, tail swishing.

As she neared the building, she strained to decipher the low voices of the men in conversation drifting through the doorway. If she was a subject of conversation, she wanted a heads up. Inside, she spotted two figures seated at a small table in the back corner. In the center, a battery-powered lantern barely illuminated the surface.

Had Ryan done this? How sweet to make Hank more comfortable. She should have thought about it.

Squinting, she spotted Hank and Eric. Neither turned toward her. She couldn't shake the unsettling feeling the stranger hadn't come with the sole purpose of helping with Hank's project. The unease of déjà vu hyper-charged her senses. Whatever Eric's purpose in her life, she didn't want romance.

Eric was perfectly fine, but she'd never let him be more. Because if she did, she'd move, leaving her heart behind. "He's only visiting. He'll go home," she murmured. "I'll stay."

With a shake, she narrowed her gaze again. Where had her dog gone?

Lying under the table, Colby rested on top of Hank's feet. Her snores echoed in the small space. The dog was the master of sleep.

Meg smiled and knocked on the doorframe. "Hello?"

Chairs scraped the floor.

"Meg, come in, come in." Hank rose and waved a hand. "We've set up shop back here."

She entered; her steps silent on the plywood floor in her soft loafers. "This is very cozy." She pulled out the chair opposite, careful to avoid her sleeping dog's paws.

"Eric's idea." Hank smiled and sat.

Oh. She didn't know why, but she was disappointed. She smiled at Eric.

He was nice, and thoughtful. Wasn't that a positive? Especially if Hank was about to enter into a lucrative business agreement with him? She wasn't upset with Eric as much as letdown that typically thoughtful Ryan hadn't noticed and anticipated the need.

"Thank you for coming so quickly. I hope we didn't cut your workday short." Eric frowned, wrinkling his smooth brow.

"Not at all. I was already closing up for the day," she said. "You have news?"

Eric nodded. "Hank has been gracious enough in assisting with the process today."

"My pleasure." Hank puffed out his chest.

"I can confirm the collection of photographs and signed souvenir cards are authentic including the images of Buffalo Bill Cody and Chief Sitting Bull," Eric said.

Meg sucked in a sharp breath. "Wow. Really?" She twisted her neck, gazing from one to the other and back again. "I mean. I knew they were. The computer software already told us. The confirmation is ... thrilling."

"To be honest," Eric interlaced his hands and leaned forward. "We've had an influx of false identification because of the artificial intelligence software that you utilized."

Heat crept up her cheeks. Her victory was very short-lived. She was little more than an armchair historian? She didn't share his illustrious credentials. Her undergraduate degree was in comparative literature. During her years of handling antiques, first as a hobby and then as a career, she thought she'd gleaned some knowledge.

"You were one hundred percent correct." Eric smiled. "You have a good eye."

She pressed cold hands to her cheeks. Now her skin burned for a completely different reason. "I'm confused about the origins. Why would the Wild West Show perform here? The town wasn't on the railroad, and the population was under a thousand at its peak during the era."

"I don't believe they did stage the show here," Eric said. "With the proximity to the reservation, Buffalo Bill probably came to recruit more native people into the show. Some Lakota were pushed over the South Dakota border and onto Fort Peck along with other tribal nations. Of course, Chief Sitting Bull only participated in the show for a short period. I believe he'd already left the production when these cards were originally acquired."

She drew back her chin. "Would the tribe want to join? Wasn't it sort of pretending to lose their battles all over again?"

Eric nodded. "It was. The pay was good. He offered a chance to send money home to family struggling under difficult conditions on the reservations. The show toured the world, performing for monarchs across Europe."

She crossed her arms over her chest, rubbing her shoulders. She supposed his explanation made sense, but her heart ached for the poor choices Indigenous people faced. She lifted her gaze. "What do you think, Hank?"

"I'm glad something in this shed has value. I've proved Ryan wrong. I'll be crowing over him for the rest of time." Hank grinned and winked.

She chuckled. What would she give for the same chance? Nothing. She'd rather have his friendship. "Are you prepared to sell the collection? You don't want to keep them in the family?"

"I had no idea of their existence." Hank shrugged. "I'd rather see a little good come from your hard work cleaning out this shed to get my grandson off my case. I'll be happy to see you take a nice chunk of money."

She shook her head. "You owe me nothing. This is your property. Besides, finders keepers. Right, cowboy?"

Hank shook his head and waggled a finger. "A deal is a deal, miss, and I'm a man of my word."

She knew better than to imply anything else. In good conscience, she couldn't take a cut of his payday. Arguing in front of a stranger, however, was inappropriate.

"Besides," Hank continued. "Mr. York explained the finder's fee is a percentage of the auction company's cut and not mine."

Could that be true? She wasn't sure how to accept payment for doing nothing. She offered him a discreet nod. Turning, she faced Eric. "What are the next steps? What do you need from us? Are you heading back to the auction house right away?"

"I'd like to stay for a few more days. The auction wouldn't be until the fall. I'm in no rush to catalog and photograph. I would like the opportunity to do research." Eric coughed. "I was hoping you might be able to help."

Why me? She poked her index finger into the center of her collarbone. The physical tap wasn't strong enough to convince her she wasn't dreaming. He'd raised and dashed her hopes several times. She wasn't sure of her footing anymore.

Eric nodded.

"I'm not a historian. I'm not sure how much help I could provide," she murmured.

"You know this place, this land." Hank held her gaze with a steady stare.

His confidence was like a fuzzy blanket, wrapping her in warmth. How soon until he snatched it away again? With Ryan, she always understood he respected her. He didn't always like being around her, but he never made her question her worth or shake her self-confidence.

"Can you help?" Eric asked, leaning forward.

Neither Eric nor Ryan asked for her heart. She was the fool reading too much into the sudden interest of two men. She'd be a fool to miss a professional opportunity. But she didn't have a ton of time. She shrugged. "If you think I can be of assistance, you can find me at the store. You can stop in whenever. I'll be there."

"Good." Hank pushed back his chair and stood. "Don't let me keep you. It's past supper."

Eric got to his feet and slid the chairs into position.

Her stomach growled. *Always classy, Meg.* She bit the inside of her cheek.

Hank laughed and waggled a finger. "See? I know what I'm talking about."

She giggled and pushed back her chair.

Colby followed Hank, tail wagging.

Hank hung an arm at his side, brushing the dog's head every time she neared.

The pair brought a smile to Meg's face with every encounter. The rough cowboy and the lazy mutt were a perfect, opposites attract, couple. She didn't know too many pairings that didn't end in spontaneous combustion. *Like me and Ryan.*

She slung her purse onto her shoulder, exiting the shed. Until Hank's project, she had avoided the younger Kincaid like she was paid for each snubbing. Now she couldn't go more than a few hours without finding herself on his land, hoping for a run-in. He drove her crazy, and she came back for more.

Eric followed her out, shutting the door and walking beside her.

"Thank you," she murmured.

He clasped his hands behind his back and lifted a brow. "For…"

"For taking my call seriously and showing up."

"I'm glad you reached out. It's quite a find." He smiled. "I love solving a good mystery."

She did, too. As long as ghosts were left undisturbed. She stifled a shiver.

"I'm heading in." Hank yelled. "Call your dog, Meg."

She spotted the cowboy at the backdoor. With a wave at Hank, she whistled.

Colby turned, with great reluctance, and trotted toward Meg.

"Would you believe he doesn't like dogs?"

"Not one bit," Eric said.

"It's true." Meg bent, turning a palm toward the dog trotting her way.

Colby kissed the hand and leaned against Meg's legs.

"Some cowboys change their ways," Meg murmured.

"Not most, in your experience?"

Her throat tightened, cutting off a response. The cowboy she cared about wouldn't change.

"Why is Meg's SUV blocking my drive?" Ryan's deep voice boomed in the stagnant air.

Her cheeks burned, and she bit her lip. Did he have to bellow in front of his guests? "I'd better move my vehicle."

Eric nodded. "See you in town tomorrow? Your store?"

"Stop by around one. That's my lunch break. I can close up and get you started at the library."

Heavy steps pounded the ground.

She turned.

Colby, heedless of the glowering expression, ran to greet Ryan.

Meg met his gaze and gulped. She lost track of Eric, her focus solely on the cowboy. With the fading light at his back, Ryan stood with his chiseled face in shadow. He was the definition of tall and dark. *And handsome?* Her memory filled in his hidden expression. How his brow knit and his full lips pursed at every encounter, like he wasn't sure if he should be amused or annoyed. Her heart skipped a beat.

If he didn't care, he wouldn't expend his energy. He was a master of efficiency. Was he missing their friendship, too? Something changed over the past week. He transformed from a man of few words into a poignant conversationalist.

When he showed her the development of her family land, he proved with actions what his words never had. He valued her. She wasn't sure if she was thrilled or terrified.

Ryan shook his head as he glowered at the guest standing too close to Meg on his lawn.

The yard was off-limits to guests. *That's not what I told Meg.* He gritted his molars and narrowed his gaze. The man hovering around Meg lurked somewhere between customer and vendor.

The gray area demanded respect. As long as he stepped away from Meg.

With a nod to her, the man strode down the path toward the barn. Was he walking all the way back to the yurt he rented? Ryan squinted, watching the guest's progress.

Ted intercepted him at the door and lead him to a gator. He'd drive the man where he belonged. *Can the vehicle get good mileage on the highway?* Ted could take the guest all the way back to San Francisco as far as Ryan was concerned.

"Ryan? Hello?" Meg called.

He turned his head to meet her gaze and winced. His whole body ached. He agreed to give Miss Stephanie, the teacher and a colleague of Joe's, a job interview for teaching yoga classes. While he wasn't one for meditation and stretching, he valued the appeal of the exercise to his clientele.

What he hadn't anticipated was participating himself.

In the barn a little over an hour earlier, thankfully with the doors closed, Stephanie, who was only a few years out of college, had insisted on leading Ted and Ryan through a beginner's class. He didn't think she understood how far he was out of his depth. He didn't bend. He wasn't a noodle.

Ted was a natural. The ranch hand twisted and turned like he was a secret gymnast. Or a human pretzel. Stephanie had praised him, and Ted had turned red, offering some random movie reference Ryan hadn't understood.

Judging by Stephanie's sudden silence, she hadn't either.

Witnessing his unflappable employee's embarrassment, Ryan had lost focus. Balancing on one foot, he'd lost control. He had circled his arms but couldn't stop his crash to the ground. A pulled pectoral was almost worth the price to see the rough cowboy blush. Ryan had hired Stephanie on the spot, if only to torture Ted about becoming the assistant teacher.

Colby padded back to him.

Ryan scratched the dog on the head once and then raised the hand to massage his aching chest. "You heading home? Or you plan on blocking my drive for the rest of the evening?" He frowned at Meg.

She rolled her eyes. "I've been here all of ten minutes. Don't blame me for your poor timing."

Or good. "You know, for someone who once accused me of rolling my eyes at her, I can't help but point out you are almost always staring heavenward in my company."

She blushed.

He smiled and scrubbed his hands over his face. When had he pulled behind her little SUV, he whistled an upbeat tune. He wanted a chance to apologize for his poor behavior this morning and fate provided him the opportunity. He dropped his hands to his sides and lifted the corner of his mouth. "You're probably right."

"Excuse me?" She widened her gaze. "Can you please repeat your statement?"

He gritted his molars. This was exactly the reason he never admitted to being wrong on the few occasions the rare occurrence happened. Other people tended to gloat when he needed grace. "I'm sorry."

"Hmm. Not quite what you said, but I'll take it. She smiled and sashayed past him, elbowing him in the sore ribs as she passed. "Walk me to my car, cowboy. I've had a long day."

Up close, he caught a hint of lavender wafting in the air again. He could identify the scent anywhere. He remembered watching Grandma and her best friend work on the little sachets. In the first few months after her passing, Hank had declared himself allergic to the herb. He wanted all trace of the potpourri eliminated from the house.

Ryan hid one heart-shaped packet in the bottom drawer. Try as it might, the little sachet stood no chance against the lingering stench in his socks even after a thorough laundering. If he focused on thinking about his smelly feet, he'd ignore the other sensations racking his body at her hot breath so close to his collar. She made the same lavender scent her own, different from the sachet with a hint of soap he couldn't identify. He tipped his hat and turned. "Ma'am, let me escort you and your dog off my land."

She batted his arm and laughed. "Stop teasing me, and don't be mad. I only came by at Hank's request."

"Oh?" He studied her from the corner of his gaze.

"Eric authenticated the photos. I'm sure Hank wants to tell you the details. I'd hate to spoil his fun." She sighed.

He narrowed his gaze.

"Oh, okay, I'll tell you a little more. Eric wants to do research, so he'll stay a little longer on the ranch. I promised to help, when I can of course. I had a great day at the store. It's a nice first wave of tourists you've brought here. Very deep pockets." She smiled.

Warmth spread through him. He couldn't take any credit for the shoppers but was glad for her good day. He didn't want her to leave. His silence encouraged her old pattern of rambling. Instead of the flare of annoyance as she spoke, he almost smiled. He liked how she couldn't hold herself back from blurting every thought in her head. He only had one issue. "Eric?" He arched a brow.

She turned pink and fumbled with the purse on her arm. She studied the contents with far more interest than him or her path.

Rounding the house, they'd reach her vehicle in another few strides. First, they had to cross the bigger rocks he'd hauled up from the pond to create a boundary so Hank didn't drive the truck into the porch. She wasn't looking. She stepped on a rock, lodging her shoe and flailing her arms.

He reached out and grabbed her, hauling her against his chest as he lifted her over the rock. In his arms, he wrapped an arm around her waist, gripping her slight frame. If he wasn't careful, she'd slip through his grasp. He was so used to her being a force of nature he never considered how small her actual stature was. He set her down on the ground but didn't drop his grip or move back.

Her chest rose and fell with rapid, shallow breaths.

In the light from the porch, her hair glimmered and sparkled again. Her eyes shone bright, more rich mahogany than mud brown. She couldn't hide her surprise or her reaction in his arms.

Eric couldn't do that. Ryan wouldn't give himself the satisfaction of saying out loud what they both knew was true. The expert was a slim, city man. Not rugged and rough, with muscles honed from manual labor instead of trendy gyms. She couldn't leave him for Eric and a new city.

"Ryan?" She croaked.

"Hmm?" He studied her face.

"I'm safe. Can you put me down?"

I can't lose you. With a nod, he dropped his hold and stepped back.

She raised her key fob and unlocked her vehicle. Colby raced to the passenger side.

He followed the dog, opening the door. At least he could be useful while giving them both a chance to catch their breaths.

Her SUV door opened, and she hopped behind the wheel as he shut the passenger door and rounded the car to her side.

She lowered the window.

He rested his hand on the roof of the car, leaning forward. *I could kiss her.* Standing close, he noticed everything about her. The light hint of shampoo and laundry was the best perfume he'd ever inhaled. At the base of her throat, the delicate skin meeting her collarbone fluttered. Once again, her hair glimmered in the fading light, the copper streaks luring him to reach out and smooth the strands to see if he could touch a bit of the magic.

"You're sure it's okay if I visit the shed? I know you have guests all week. I promise I won't be in the way. I want to do my part for the research. To help Hank."

He nodded. Helping Hank. Right. Ryan pushed off the door and stuffed his fists into his jeans' pockets. He winced again, the twinge of pulled muscles in his torso aching. Yoga was rougher than the old days doing cattle drives and sleeping under the stars. "Of course. You're always free to do as you please."

She smiled. "Thanks. I'll be around." She twisted the key in the ignition. The engine turned over.

Lifting a hand, he waved until her vehicle pulled onto the road and disappeared from view. Never let Meg out of his sight was another lesson he'd learned years ago. On her own, she stirred up all sorts of trouble. *Maybe being with her wasn't much better.*

He turned toward the ranch house. Movement around the side of the building caught his attention.

Ted and the guests celebrating their twentieth anniversary, Marcia and Ford Clayton, studied a row of chest-high waders and the lost and found collection of old, mismatched rain boots. As he got closer, the stench of dead fish and rubber permeated the air.

Ryan pinched his nose, unprepared for the sensory assault. "Good evening. What's going on here? Can I help?"

Ted lifted his chin, meeting Ryan's gaze and subtly shook his head side to side.

"Yes, please, Mr. Kincaid," Marcia said.

The tilt of her head and hands on hips posture assured him she'd suffered fools already and would endure no more. He kept his mouth shut and clasped his hands behind his back, leaning forward. "Ryan, please."

"Okay, Ryan. Please call me Marcia and this is Ford." Marcia pointed to her husband. "Tomorrow, we are panning for gold in the creek near our cabin. I'd like to be properly outfitted. Ted thinks we only need boots. I like to be fully prepared."

Ryan nodded. Now he understood. "Marcia, I'm sorry to tell you the gold was only a legend. No one has ever found a fleck." He glanced from wife to husband.

Ford grinned. "Told you."

She rolled her eyes. "I did some reading before we came. One of your ancestors found something and claimed the land for his ranch."

Acquiring the worst plot in the process. Gold in the western portion of the state fueled settlement of the Montana territory in the 1860s. South of the Missouri River along the eastern boundary, however, no one struck it rich near Herd. "I know the book, ma'am. The family wasn't consulted. If my grandfather had been approached, he'd have informed the author of the man's undiagnosed vision problems. The saloon in town is named after his find."

"Golden Crown like a tooth?" Ford asked.

Ryan nodded.

Ford chuckled.

"Still. It's an adventure, and I want to go." Marcia shrugged.

"The creek is less than a foot deep, but the current is strong in some sections, especially near the mouth of the fishing pond,"

Ryan said. "I don't recommend wading into the water no matter the precautions. I'm sorry to say we haven't used these waders in quite a while. They smell like they should be thrown out and not lent to guests. I can't, in good conscience, give you these old things."

She lifted her chin higher. "I'm not squeamish. I'll be fine."

She remained undeterred? Ryan turned to her husband. The man hadn't turned green from the smell. That was a promising sign.

"I'd rather avoid whatever calamity we'll find the in creek," Ford said. "I'm against the plan but pro defensive measures."

Ted stepped forward. "I think they'll be much more comfortable in boots. No need to be restricted."

"I agree with Ted's assessment." Ryan nodded. "The waders can be pungent. Only guests determined to go on one of Joe's all-day, offsite, fly-fishing expeditions wear them. Because they have no choice."

"Fine, I'll stick with boots. I concede." Marcia held up her hands. "I will pan for gold in the creek along the shore."

"Somehow, I know I'll end up in the bottom." Ford winced. "I don't want to be right and muddy."

"Oh, darling. Don't worry. You won't be." Marcia wrapped an arm around her husband's waist and stretched up on tiptoe, kissing his cheek. "You'll have fun."

Ford smiled. "Or else."

Marcia giggled. "You're so smart."

"Please wait until tomorrow. The sun sets soon." Ted extended a pair of boots. "Drop the boots off at the checkout when you leave. If you need anything else, let me know."

"Or me." Ryan reached for the other set. "Have fun."

"If I find anything good…" Marcia accepted the boots from Ryan. "You'll never know."

Ryan chuckled.

The couple waved and turned away, each carrying a pair of boots.

They were a curious pair. The husband and wife had to be in their mid- to late-sixties, judging by the streaks of gray in their hair and firmly established laugh and smile lines. At that stage, a person knew their own mind. Why partner with someone who pushed all your buttons? Was it comfort?

"You good, boss?" Ted asked.

"Tired. You'll keep an eye on their adventure?"

Ted bent and grabbed the waders by the straps. "Of course. I'll put these away before we attract hawks."

"Thanks, Ted." Ryan strode around the house to the front door without another look. Maybe the smell would lure a certain mutt next-door to return. He wasn't sure what to think of the prospect.

After months of quiet, the first day of hosting guests took a lot out of him. He wouldn't let his strain lead him to any rash decisions about his life. I looked like Meg would stay. He didn't need to make a big deal about it.

When life settled down, he could reevaluate how he would like their friendship to proceed. He wasn't in a rush and didn't need to be. He had to focus on the bigger picture before he could worry about minor details. *Like romance.*

CHAPTER 9

Meg tied a bright pink ribbon on the handles of the shopping bag and slid the purchase across the front counter. Smiling, she met the customer's gaze. "Thank you for stopping by today."

The older woman returned the grin, grabbed the package, and strode toward the door.

The bell jingled.

Meg followed the paying customer's progress, ignoring the latest round of selfie-takers near the hats and boots. Should she lock up the valuable goods? For the most part, the accessories were treated with care. If she removed the tempting items to a locked case, she'd eliminate the lure. Today wasn't the day. She appreciated having any company at all.

From the corner of her gaze, she glimpsed the empty dog bed on the ground. Her chest squeezed. While Colby rarely made noise, she had a presence that soothed Meg's soul.

After she had dressed for the day, she had turned toward her companion lying on the bed. "Want to go to the store?"

No response.

"Want to go to town?" She infused her question with as much cheer as she could muster.

The dog sighed and turned the other direction, facing the wall.

Meg didn't need to be a pet psychic to understand. Crawling across the four-poster bed, creasing the quilt, she stroked the dog's belly. "We can't visit today. I promise you'll see him soon."

The dog shifted and licked Meg's palm with one flick of the tongue. Then she laid her head on her paws, shut her eyes, and snored.

Meg could take a hint. On her own, she had opened the store for the day. Within twenty minutes, she greeted her first guest in what became a near constant stream of customers. Busier than she'd been all year, she had no second to spare. Still, she missed her dog.

Was this the future if she had to leave town and return to working for someone else? She hadn't yearned her desk job at someone else's gallery. Would she return to days under florescent lights without Colby's calming presence? She'd worked the same long hours in her previous roles but hadn't been fulfilled. And she'd crave interaction that didn't revolve around her career.

In her pocket, her cell phone chirped.

She jumped and reached for the device, silencing the alarm.

On cue, the front door opened again, and Eric walked in.

Dressed in a V-neck sweater and jeans, Eric was more casually attired today, yet he remained too sophisticated for his setting. Was the navy-blue sweater cashmere? Were the jeans tailored?

He nodded at the two girls posing in the cowboy hats. With bright red cheeks, the girls deposited the hats on the nearby rack and raced out the door. The overhead bell nearly shook off its hook.

Meg chuckled. "That's one way to close up for the afternoon I suppose."

"I get you for the whole afternoon?" Eric approached, each step creating another beat in an even melody against the pine floor.

Now it was her turn to flush. Grabbing the phone, she tucked the cell in the back of her worn out jeans. "You know what I mean. Just my lunch hour."

"I'll savor every second. How's business today?"

She lifted her gaze and met his smiling face.

A couple good days weren't enough to make the store suddenly profitable. The stranger didn't need to know that. Neither did Hank, or he'd insist on her accepting the auction house's proposed finder's fee cut when the signed images sold. "Things have been great all morning. Most people will be eating lunch. We should have the library all to ourselves."

He swept a hand toward the door. "After you, please."

She grabbed her purse, pulling out her keys and lacing her fingers between each one. It was a reflex. Growing up in a big city, she hadn't relinquished her street smarts training in tiny Herd. She doubted she needed to defend herself against Eric. Appearances could be deceiving. *Like Ryan and his constant scowl.*

Last night, for a second, she had sensed a charge in the air. Ryan had leaned in her vehicle window. The tiny hairs on her arm had stood on end. She'd studied the quirk of his lips and wondered what kissing him would be like. The urge had been unsettling and overwhelming. Shaking off the thought, she flipped the sign in the window and opened the door.

Eric stepped out first.

She followed, pulling the old wooden door shut and jimmying the frame as she spun the lock in the dead bolt. She pocketed her keys and tipped her head. "This way."

Eric fell into step beside her, his gait matching hers as they passed the edge of her store.

Herd's downtown consisted of an approximately five block strip of stores and businesses on either side of Main. Wind gusts rolled the occasional tumbleweed through town in late summer, delighting tourists with the visual cliché. The nineteenth century style false fronts played up and romanticized the town's early days.

"Have you ever seen bison roaming in Herd? Or out here on the ranches?" Eric asked.

She nibbled her lip, scrunching her nose. Had she? "I don't think I have."

"With the name, I'd rather assumed you'd be outnumbered." He smiled and scanned the street. "It is charming."

"We aren't much, but we do pack a punch." She grinned.

"It's almost a theme park style Wild West town."

The metallic clang of metal on metal from the blacksmith shop filtered down the street, punctuating his sentence.

He smiled, and his look was genuine bemusement. She wasn't sure if his enjoyment was directed against the town or in its favor. From the saloon to the old-time photo studio, Herd embraced the sanitized version of its past.

"Hard to believe this is original," he said.

She nodded. With wooden sidewalks extending along either side, she studied the timber structures on her side of the road and the stone opposite. "Herd is historic. On this side of the street, the buildings date to the eighteen-eighties when the three families founded the town."

"What about the other side?" He tilted his head across the road to the post office, saloon, and grocery. "Rather interesting to see stone all the way out here. Unusual, isn't it?"

"Rather a sad story." She nibbled her lip. "A little ruthless, I'm afraid." She dropped her chin to her chest, studying her steps. Airing dirty laundry wasn't her style. The town might not consider her one of their own. In her heart, she remained a loyal citizen.

He nudged her with a shoulder. "Now, I'm dying of curiosity."

She reached the alley between the buildings. Stepping off the main sidewalk, she stopped against a wall near a dumpster. "A fire spread from the original saloon in 1894. In 1904, the rest of the block burned from another blaze. The Golden Crown was a fiery pile of ash for the second time in ten years. The townsfolk came together for justice. They demanded that side of the street be rebuilt in stone."

He chuckled. "Can't make this stuff up, can you?"

She gritted her teeth at his ringing laughter. Something about the teasing tone riled her. A local could joke about the foibles of the community but not an outsider, no matter how otherwise polite and charming. Her hackles raised.

"My apologies. I didn't mean to offend you." He turned and pressed a hand to his heart.

His expression was sincere. She shook her head. "It's fine. The townsfolk blamed one man for both incidents, Hoss Whittier. His father was a successful Boston businessman who was one of Herd's founding families."

"Along with the Kincaids and Hawkes?"

"Hoss wasn't the same as his father. He struggled with alcohol and fighting. After the second fire, it was decided by a council that the Whittiers would pay to rebuild the street in stone. To do so, the ranch was sold and split down the middle."

"What happened to Hoss?"

"Run out of town. It's sad to think all the hard work his father did amounted to nothing in the end. The family retained one plot of land in town but left soon after Hoss." She shrugged and strode back to the sidewalk. "I'm sure the families whose livelihoods he impacted twice couldn't handle another disruption."

Passing the next few storefronts, she slipped into silence. How would Ryan have taken the out-of-towner's chuckle? Perhaps with better humor than her. The stoic cowboy had grown accustomed to tourists.

The blasé response irritated her. Of course, the town's founding involved backstabbing and machinations, her ancestors teaming up with the Whittiers to give the Kincaids the worst plot. In a little over a decade, the Hawkes changed allegiance again to run the Whittiers out of town. Until, finally, the Kincaids owned it all.

"We've reached the end of the block. Did I miss the library?"

His question cut through her inner monologue. "Nope. Here we are." She opened the door in the corner entrance of the building at the end of the street. "After you, please."

With a nod, he entered.

The library had been one of the first attempts at historic preservation in the 1970s. While Herd sidestepped much of the destruction of old properties by nature of being so far out of the way, it wasn't until her and Ryan's grandmothers had banded together for a concerted effort to save the town that laws and codes were changed.

Visiting the building brought Meg comfort. She had spent so much of her youth checking out as many books as she could carry under her arms. She'd read until her vision blurred. In the years she hadn't traveled to Montana, she relied on the library for that instant connection. Summer was symbolized by plastic-protected hardbacks.

The main room of the former store housed the checkout counter and shelves devoted to children's books and popular fiction. She nodded at Miriam, head librarian.

"Good afternoon," Meg said.

"Hi, Meg and mister?" Miriam removed her reading glasses, letting the frame dangle on a chain around her neck.

"Eric York." He extended a hand and a warm smile.

Miriam brightened.

"Mr. York wants to look into some history about the ranches. I'll help him settle in upstairs and then head back to my shop," Meg said.

"Certainly. If you need anything, Mr. York, please let me know." Miriam turned toward Meg. "It so nice to see you with a friend."

Miriam meant the words kindly. But the off-hand comment stung like a slap. Meg nodded and strolled past the desk and through the stacks to the spiral staircase. She glanced over her shoulder, readjusting her slipping purse.

Eric nodded.

Her steps clanged on the metal risers. At the top, she stepped to the side and breathed deep. A curious mix of wood and vanilla scented the air from the aging books. In the winter, a small potbelly stove in the corner heated the room and added the smoke to the aroma. She found the scent intoxicating, often losing track of time in the warm room during the long, dark months. "Sorry, I always forget how loud it is on the stairs. But once you're up here, the sounds from downstairs and outside are muffled."

"Is the bulk of the collection up here?" he asked.

She was glad he focused on the task at hand and not her unnecessary apologies. "It's sort of a hodgepodge of nonfiction, public records, and microfiche."

He widened his gaze. "I'm captivated. I love research."

Thank you for not commenting on being declared my only friend. In this moment, he might be. She never found an eager partner for pouring through nonfiction texts. "I can help get you started, and then I want to head back. It's been a busy weekend."

"Say no more." He held up a hand. "I appreciate your time."

She nodded and strode through the windowless room. Along one wall, an empty research desk faced four oak tables with lamps. Pushed together, the tables formed a large rectangle. She crossed to one and flipped on the light, dropping her bag to the table.

He mimicked her actions at the table opposite.

The soft glow of the pair of lamps softened the harsh glare of the overhead lights.

She scanned the room, hoping to spot Joe engaged in his research. He could prove invaluable. His knowledge of the town was unrivaled. *He's leading a tour.* The realization landed in her gut like a heavy stone. She didn't mind being alone with Eric but wasn't entirely comfortable in his company.

Eric shot her an expectant look.

Dusting her hands on her jeans, she pointed behind him. "Those shelves are the nonfiction books. It's a wide range of topics, but the first row is local and state history. I think I know of something that might be interesting to get started."

"Please, you're an excellent guide. I put my faith in you."

At the shelves, she reached for a red, leatherbound book. The cover was stained, the pages dog eared, and the spine cracked. Cradling the book in her arms, she gingerly brought it to the table and opened the front cover. "This book was donated by Susie Kincaid, Hank's wife. She was part of the committee that fought for the library in this location."

"Fought?"

"It was the seventies." She shrugged. "The locals were used to the bookmobile and preferred the convenience." She flipped through the first few pages, running her index finger down each margin as she read the dates handwritten in pencil annotating the text. She stopped. "Oh, my goodness."

He leaned close and squinted at the page and then turned to her with a broad grin. "I didn't think it would be that easy." He chuckled.

This time his mirth lifted her soul. The first book she pulled off the shelf, an old Kincaid ranch ledger, mentioned the auditions at the Kincaid ranch. The calendar marked off the day from typical operation for the special occasion. "I'm sure you'll want to do more research to verify."

"Of course, I will, and I have a date to help pinpoint my study. Maybe this is a good opportunity, since you've shown your exceptional skill, for another piece of business." He paused and studied her. "I'd like to offer you a job."

Her jaw dropped.

"It's not always this fun." He held up his palms. "I deal with a lot more dead ends than hidden treasure. Often, my research time is measured in hours and not weeks." He dropped his arms to his sides. "You have what it takes. You have a good eye."

She shook her head. "I don't know about such praise. Didn't you pretty much say it was a fluke that my software made an accurate hit?"

"I did. What were the odds you would make another instantaneous hit? You have a good memory and an eye for details. I'm always looking for someone to train with those qualities."

She nibbled her bottom lip. Approaching the auction house had not been meant as a job interview, but maybe it was supposed to. Maybe this was her next step.

Her initial impression of him carried an immediate understanding he'd change her life. She'd—wrongly—assumed with a romance and entered every conversation apprehensively anticipating some sort of move on his part.

This job could be fate. She told Mom she would let her know with plenty of time to rent out the old house before the Fourth of July. She had a back-up plan now.

Maybe her success depended on taking herself seriously and not relying on her family name alone. If she applied a little determination and self-belief to running her store, could she stay in Herd? Or would she fail the moment she tried?

She blinked against the sudden sting in her watery eyes and rubbed a hand over her nose. Leaving was her worst-case scenario and most likely option. Could Ryan be her back-up plan? If he moved forward with events, he'd need a coordinator. He told her he liked the idea but would he really do it or had his agreement been lip service?

"Don't give me an answer now," Eric said. "You don't even need to tell me before I leave. Just consider the option."

She nodded and dropped her shoulders. For the first time since meeting Eric, she relaxed. The path he offered—and his importance to her next step—suddenly made sense of what she had felt in the moment they met. She wouldn't choose to totally upend her life, but she was glad for a choice. "I will. I'll leave you to your research."

"I have one more request. If it's not too much trouble?"

"Of course not. How can I help?"

"Come on the ride tomorrow. It's late afternoon. Hank suggested I go. I would feel a bit awkward by myself. I would appreciate some help in asking questions of the adventure guide."

"You mean Joe? He's about the easiest person to talk to."

"I'd appreciate an insider approach." He lifted a shoulder. "Mr. Kincaid suggested you might want to come."

She considered Eric. He dropped his gaze to the ground and shifted his weight from foot to foot. He wasn't being entirely forthcoming.

She wasn't sure what his motivation was. Getting her to agree to the job? She wouldn't mind an excuse to see Ryan. Perhaps she could prod him a little about events and find out if he would hire her. The slow thaw in their relationship heartened her. After a vague sense of childhood animosity, their years of acquaintance mattered. Shared memories were special.

She owed Colby a visit with Hank. What did it mean that Hank put Eric up to asking her? What angle was the old cowboy playing? Matchmaking? She figured it was only a matter of time before the opinionated older man got involved in the personal lives of his friends and family. But she wouldn't have pegged Hank for wanting to pair her off with an outsider. Did he want her to move on? "Yes, thank you. I would love to join you tomorrow."

Eric grinned. "I won't take up anymore of your time today."

She spun on her heel and strode toward the stairs. With each step descending the metal staircase, her steps rang out. While she didn't mind giving him time, she owed her business more attention. Leaving town was her last resort. For her best chance at staying, she had to get to work.

Slowing the pickup in front of the house, Ryan parked and cut the engine. He moved without any hitch and his end of the day lower back tightness was gone. Maybe yoga wasn't so bad. After a full night's rest, his usual aches and pains had disappeared.

When he had stepped out of bed and stretched his arms overhead, he reached a little higher than yesterday morning. Had one class been the magic tonic to boost his flexibility? *If only I'd let her get to the meditation part, I might have peace during my day.*

With a fully booked resort, however, controlled chaos was his best hope. From sunrise to sunset, he'd been on the move. He was grateful he hadn't wasted much time with his thoughts. He was promised nothing but anxiety if his mind strayed to Meg and where she might be. And who might be keeping her company.

Shaking his head, he hopped to the ground from his truck and strode to the front door. The sky finally darkened. A hint of woodsmoke curled in the air. He sniffed again. A vaguely fishy, muddy scent wafted past.

Deep, rumbling laughter floated around the corner of the house.

He turned from the door and jogged down the steps, rounding the side in several long strides.

Drenched and mud-splattered, Marcia and Ford Clayton trudged from the barn and across the lawn in socks.

Ryan winced. Wet socks were the worst thing on earth. He could—and had—assist in a live birth and stitched a gushing wound without flinching. Ask him to do anything that ended in soaking socks squeezing his soles, and he bowed out before his stomach churned. "Good evening. Can I help you two?"

"Good evening, Ryan," Ford said. "We dropped off the boots we borrowed at the barn. Marcia has something to say." He stepped back and motioned for his wife to walk forward.

Marcia grinned broadly and pushed her stringy, soaked hair behind her ears. "You were right. We didn't find gold. My husband was right. We fell into the creek."

"Ah, I never get tired of hearing her say that." Ford chuckled. "Makes every bad idea worthwhile."

"Hey." She swatted her husband's arm. "Don't you have something to say?"

Ford grabbed her hand, raised her fingers to his mouth, and kissed her knuckles. "You were right. I had a lot of fun." He faced Ryan and shrugged. "I always do. I'd never do anything outside my comfort zone if not for my wife. I wouldn't have so many memorable tales."

Ryan smiled and nodded, hiding his confusion. Why had she pushed? If two people hadn't sanded off each other's rough edges with twenty years' together, how was this bliss?

"I learned the hard way," Ford said. "I prefer having her push all my buttons to sitting around in silence."

Marcia kissed her husband's cheek.

Because—in spite of differing points of view—they like the end result.

Meg definitely pushed Ryan into uncomfortable encounters. The talent show was the most prominent in a childhood of awkward, on-the-spot moments. He could write a thousand-word essay for every day spent together. The years she stopped coming were all one giant, boring mass of memories.

He couldn't fill even a single sheet with his recollections from the decade without her.

"Will we be seeing you at the campfire tonight?" Ryan asked.

"Absolutely," Marcia said.

Ford rolled his eyes.

Marica giggled. "See you soon."

Ryan nodded and waved, watching the pair stroll away hand in hand. He dropped his hand to rub against the ache in his chest. If Meg had a decision about what came next, what would she choose?

He couldn't ruminate on Meg. Dropping his hand, he glanced at his watch. The campfire started in thirty minutes. He'd come home to pick up the guest of honor, Hank, and for a break from his public persona.

Saturdays in summer meant smiling nonstop. Opening the front door, he scrubbed a hand over his face and aching cheeks. Faking cheer wasn't his style. If he'd bumped into Meg, he might have a reason to grin.

Or more of a headache. The moment he almost kissed her burned him. He should have leaned forward and pressed his mouth to hers. It would have gotten the whole will-they-or-won't-they dilemma over with. Or created a bigger problem.

Pushing for something to happen was asking for trouble. At the moment, he had enough on his plate without getting involved in *them*. She hadn't stopped by, and he should be glad for the space. He pushed through the swinging door into the kitchen, heading straight to the sink to wash up. With the faucet running, he turned his head and frowned.

At the head of the table, Hank hunched forward over a pile of papers.

His wrinkled, tanned skin highlighted his white hair. The opposites enhanced the other to an unflattering extreme. He looked old.

Ryan shuddered. Shutting the faucet with the back of a hand, he tore off a paper towel and dried his hands. "Hey, Hank. You almost ready for the campfire?"

Hank lifted his head and scowled. His eyes were unfocused and glassy.

Is he confused? Ryan caught his next breath. He'd been grateful his grandparents hadn't suffered from any of the diseases that stole a person away in their later years. Nearing ninety, however, Hank entered unknown territory. He was the longest living member of the family. If he started to lose himself... Ryan shook off the thought. He'd do whatever he could for the man who'd loved him unconditionally.

"Is that tonight?" Hank rubbed the crust from his eyes. "Guess I forgot the time. I've been going through my papers, looking for anything of interest to the expert."

Ryan slid onto the bench at the large oak dining table. The kitchen could serve a crowd, but the pair were often alone. He hadn't missed company. Until she stopped dropping by. *It's one day, and I'm busy.* "What are you looking at there?" Ryan pointed to the pile.

"Susie's papers." Hank waved to the sheets fanned across the table. "She was quite the historian. I reckon you know she gave several boxes of old records and books to the library when it opened." He propped an elbow on the table, resting his chin in his palm. "I'll have to remind Meg, so she can show the expert."

"She probably already did," Ryan muttered.

Hank widened his gaze and leaned forward, peering closely.

"It's nothing. I talked to her while she was leaving yesterday."

"And?" Hank drummed his fingers on the table.

Ryan fought off a flinch, meeting his grandfather's gaze without blinking. "And...what?"

"Did you tell her how you feel?"

Ryan propped his elbows on the table.

"Oh, come on, boy. You are the most frustrating person on this earth."

Ryan rolled his eyes. *Takes one to know one.*

Hank held up both hands. "At least I know I'm trouble. The problem with you is you're always so wrapped up in the future and the big picture you're missing right now."

"If I don't, I won't have a future. Neither would anyone in the town. Living in the moment is a luxury. I have to plan ahead. For all our sakes."

Hank scoffed and leaned back in the chair at the head of the table. Crossing his arms over his chest, he glanced at the ground.

"Fine. You know you're trouble." Ryan sighed. His grandfather's self-awareness had a blaring blind spot. "You accuse me of worrying about tomorrow. What about you? You're trapped in yesterday."

Hank shrugged. "At least I'm trying. Cleaning out the shed isn't easy. I don't want to go through the memories. I've been too focused on what I'm missing. I'm taking my days for granted. I'm here. I don't want to waste another second."

"What's inspired the introspection?"

"I miss Meg and Colby." Hank sighed. "I want them to stay. You know she chose to make her home in Herd even though it's hard. We have some opportunities but not a lot. She's special, and she'd different for most folks."

"I know." Ryan nodded.

"I worry she's lonely. She needs more than work for a good life." Hank shook his head. "She doesn't even have much of that. Now the big city fella is here, and she'll see what she's missing. He'll tell her stories about his life and work. He'll present her with tantalizing tidbits."

And she'll leave? Ryan couldn't imagine Meg running off. She wasn't a grass is greener person. She had a good—if quiet—life here. He'd been glad he could present a solution to the initial problem of her leaving by purchasing the land. In the years since, had she been too scared to fully commit to life in town? Did she have friends besides his grandfather and her dog? He never asked the questions.

Hank held his gaze.

What wasn't the cowboy saying? Did he know more information he wasn't sharing about Meg? Had the auction house expert said something in front of Hank? No, Ryan wouldn't read into everything. He didn't have time. "We all make sacrifices."

Hank snorted and pushed back his chair. "Like my beauty rest. Come on, let's go tell some stories so I can get to bed."

Ryan followed his grandfather to the back door. If he didn't tell Meg how he felt, would she go? Or would his honesty propel her escape? Maybe she didn't share his feelings. Maybe he made her feel uncomfortable in his company and that was why she stayed away today.

He'd focus on what he could control and worry about the rest after the guests left. Could Stephanie walk him through a meditation over the phone? Otherwise, he faced a sleepless night.

CHAPTER
10

Riding horseback on the open range wasn't the place to let a mind wander. Meg knew better. As she followed the tour group across the Kincaid ranch, however, she couldn't seem to focus.

After another successful weekend at the store, Meg had hated to close early on Monday afternoon. Would she jinx her recent string of good luck? If she kept pace with the tourists, she'd cover her overhead costs for the summer by the end of the month. With her immediate costs covered, she could build her internet store and get her business ahead. She could—conceivably—stay without involving Ryan, Eric, or anyone else in her decision.

Her plan depended on too many external factors she couldn't control. She'd hate for Mom to miss out on a lucrative time to rent the ranch house. Mom didn't need the extra income. On several occasions, she assured Meg of that fact. Meg couldn't get it out of her mind, however, that she was taking something away from Mom and providing no benefit.

Meg would like to stick around at least until the Frontier Days at the end of June. Mom had again reiterated that she didn't want Meg to rush into her next move against an arbitrary deadline. If she could somehow earn enough to cover costs through the rest of the year, she'd feel better about staying. Resetting the window display, she'd straightened the sign advertising the event.

In between helping customers, she'd created a tableau featuring the hats and boots, effectively stopping the selfie-takers and luring in new buyers with the merchandise. During the first hour, she had several compliments on the display and sold one of the hats. She was conflicted about leaving but promised both Colby and Eric.

The group of riders ahead of her stopped.

"Whoa." Meg pulled back on the mare's reins. Astride the oldest horse in the Kincaid stables. She didn't have to use much force to convince the horse to stop. Getting Cupcake started, however, was another matter.

She leaned forward, patting the mare's neck with long strokes. "Good girl, Cupcake."

"You are a natural," Eric called and walked his horse over.

Meg snorted. Only city folk thought what she did looked *natural*. She grew up around horses but never caught the bug. At her elementary school, she was the only pre-pubescent girl not obsessed with the creature. She preferred her own feet as mode of transportation.

Whenever she got the chance, she loved to watch Hank and Ryan ride. Both men moved with their animals in perfect harmony. She understood why the Greeks dreamed up a centaur. Some people were born to gallop.

Not Meg. Astride the back of a horse, she was too high off the ground. She didn't move in tandem with the creature but struggled against her. In the old saddle, she hit every bump and jostle, every twig and uneven patch of ground. With her two feet on the dirt, she controlled her motion and center of gravity. If she rode, she wanted the easy-going mare. "Hardly. Cupcake here is pure sugar."

"She looks quite..." He frowned.

"Ancient?"

He nodded.

"She used to be Hank's wife's horse. He's sweet enough to let me ride her. I'll probably have to turn her around and leave the rest of the group soon." She nodded her head to the rest of Joe's morning tour.

A family of four, including two elementary school-aged kids, a retired couple, and a trio of twenty-somethings celebrating a bachelorette made up the motley band of wannabe cowpoke.

Joe stopped the group near the two-foot wide, rocky stream, cutting through the valley.

A couple of the horses bent their heads to drink the clear water.

Pulling up the rear, Meg was content to take things easy. She wasn't in a rush. Scanning the terrain she knew by heart for the possible location of the Wild West Show auditions was like discovering the land for the first time. She could hardly believe the empty prairie had ever seen much excitement. "Do you suppose this is the place?"

He nodded. "It must be. From what I read the show needed lots of land for the fake stampede. This space would have been perfect."

In the beautiful valley, tall grass waved in the slight breeze under a bright blue sky. Sunlight warmed her from the top down. Inside her boots, she curled her toes.

She could almost feel the earth shake as hundreds of hooves pounded the ground. If she shut her eyes, she heard the call of the Lakota feigning a battle as onlookers cheered.

"It was quite unusual. Buffalo Bill didn't often set up large scale tryouts like this. He had scouts do the work for him. After the show got going, people came to him. This situation was different."

She wondered who enjoyed the show more. The city folk glimpsing what they must have assumed was an authentic encapsulation of life past the Mississippi? Or the performers eager to pretend the old days persisted? "How so?"

"My research also uncovered the reason you've never seen any bison," Eric said.

"Really?"

He nodded and shifted on the saddle. "Apparently, the show needed more stock for the stampede. When the auditions came to town, Buffalo Bill put out a call with a price for every bison caught in good condition. In one swoop, the cowboys rounded up every last one. The other ranchers had relocated most of the animals onto Kincaid land years earlier. When the herds from all surrounding areas were gathered, John Kincaid made a fortune."

"The bison were forcibly removed from their environment? Taken from their homes?"

He nodded.

"The babies, too?"

He held her stare.

She turned and gazed at the grass again, blinking back the tears. On the wind, she heard the pained grunts of the animals.

Were the Kincaids solely involved in the round-up? Her family must have participated in some fashion, too. They were neighbors and, when the moment suited, allies. She'd never looked too far into her own past because she worried what she'd find.

Her privilege allowed her to ignore what happened in the nineteenth century and form her own sentiment. Her west wasn't the Old West. She'd grown up with modern amenities in the big city during the school year and absorbed the slower pace of life every summer.

Montana meant spending every second possible outside, picking wildflowers in the morning and catching fireflies at night. Her past held the feel of the warm sun on her skin and the rich earthy smell before the first strike of lightning streaked the sky and the boom of thunder shook the ground. She never questioned her right to the land.

Her heart ached for the bison. Did Ryan know? He benefited from the sale both historically and in the present. The money exchanged over a hundred years ago kept his family around long enough for him to operate his enterprise without the hiccups of wildlife. In the original rancher's position, would he have done the same?

The more worrisome question remained. If her presence in town was only a given because of her family's legacy, what did that mean when the history was bloody and tarnished? Did she belong here?

Eric offered her a way out. His job opportunity was the ultimate chance to prove she could be successful on her own merit. *I'll have no excuse for failure.* Was that unfortunate truth? Was her fear of not being enough her real motivation to stay?

Her unhelpful thoughts weren't fair. The silence stretched on too long. Any uncomfortable history shouldn't be shared with an outsider. She shifted on the saddle. "Do you have everything you need?"

He nodded. "I do. Tonight is the cowboy dinner. I'm sort of looking forward to it."

She lifted the corner of her mouth, forcing a smile. "You're in for a treat. It is a real cowboy hootenanny."

"A rootin', tootin' good time?"

She didn't respond. Another laughing at the town comment? Or teasing her with an exaggerated twist of her words? He delivered the question with a charming smile. She couldn't quite judge the situation.

"I definitely can't miss it. Have you been? Will you join me?" he asked.

What would Ryan think? She froze. Why did her brain immediately go *there*? Perhaps, because, as much as she wanted a minute alone with Ryan to chat, she understood showing up with another guy might send the wrong message.

Or did it? Ryan hadn't made any move that she'd considered romantic. Eric was only a friend and colleague. She hadn't been to one of Ryan's cowboy dinners in years. She had nothing going on. Why not? If she got a minute with Ryan to talk about the collection and her plan to turn down the finder's fee, she'd prove herself more than another of his burdens.

They could meet as equals. Then, the spark between them might have a chance at a real flame.

She met Eric's gaze. "Thank you. I will join you tonight."

He smiled.

"Meg!" A deep voice roared.

She turned her head toward the sound. Racing like a thunder cloud, Ryan strode from his truck parked several yards away.

Good. She unclenched her jaw and relaxed her defensive posture. He was here and could provide answers. She'd gratefully lean into their well-established roles. Ryan was the stoic reasoner, anchoring her mental flights of fancy. He'd reassure her of their legacies' importance.

Stomping down the hill, he moved like a force of nature. He wasn't smooth or refined like Eric. Ryan was rough. From the stubble on his chin that never seemed to be completely shaved in the morning to the simple responses, he didn't put on airs or a façade. He was always real.

Her heart stuck in her throat. Looking at him now, she reconsidered her eagerness to meet him. He glowered. Where was the thoughtful, longtime acquaintance? This Ryan was a version she hadn't encountered before. Red-faced, he practically blew steam from his ears.

"What do you think you're doing?" He glowered, stopping at her side.

Without a hat, his frown was on full display as he stared up at her on Cupcake's back.

Nothing much. Heat crept up her cheeks. What did he imagine she was up to? His scowl could tan a hide without the lye. She gulped.

Raising a hand to shield his gaze against the bright glare of sunshine, Ryan scanned the horizon behind the house. Squinting and frowning simultaneously might be a skill. To him, it was the start of a pounding headache that threatened to rage all day. Spotting no one, he pounded the path to the house and strode in the backdoor.

His hat was gone. Ted or Joe might be playing a trick on him. Ryan wasn't in the mood to be teased. Sunglasses bothered him. He liked being able to see clearly what was in front of him. He scrubbed a hand over his face, tightening the reins in his other. He'd heard enough of Hank's lectures lately to be aware he was almost legally blind in regard to one person in his life.

After several hours under the cloudless sky, he returned to the house. He needed a ball cap or something. When he spotted Colby on the floor of the kitchen, he released the heavy breath he'd been holding. Where there was a dog, the owner wouldn't be too far away. He shut the door and turned. "You got a visitor?"

Hank grinned. "I do. We're heading to the shed in a little bit."

"Are you dog sitting, or is Meg joining you today?"

"I'm sure she'll be around in a little bit. We didn't get into specifics. She dropped off Colby for a visit and headed out. She can't stay here all day. She said she's been doing a lot of sales in town."

"That's good to hear." Ryan sagged his shoulders, relaxing his tense body for a second. If she was busy, she couldn't spend time with that well-dressed guy. Ryan had a shot. *Do I want one?* He wasn't sure.

Before the stranger's arrival, Ryan had sensed the shift between them. After years of avoiding each other, he found every excuse to interact. He wasn't ready to address *them* or face any upset to his status quo. The stranger almost forced his hand. With the pair separated, Ryan had no concerns to plague him. *Except, that's not what Hank said.*

"Wait. Back-up. What do you mean *stay here all day*? Is she here?" *With him?* At his sides, he flattened his hands against his jeans. He would not curl his fingers into fists.

"At the moment, she is on a ride with Joe and the tour group. She earned a break. Sounded like a good opportunity to combine business and pleasure. When I ran into Eric, I suggested he tell her about it."

Ryan's heart pounded in his chest. Hank said the words with nonchalance. The old cowboy was never careless in his speech. Was he warning Ryan? "Oh?" His voice cracked. He winced.

Focused on the dog, Hank scratched Colby behind the ears and smiled.

The grin could have been meant for either of them. Ryan didn't relax, poising for the latest round of the verbal tug of war.

"Eric went, too," Hank said.

"Oh." The word was more grunt than comment. Of course, *Eric* did. Ryan pressed a finger against his throbbing temple. "Why?"

Hank shrugged and dropped his hands from the dog. Leaning back, he folded his arms over his chest. "He's a guest."

"No, why did she go with him?"

"Reckon it's about the photographs and cards." Hank tapped a finger against his bicep. "I'm not sure. I didn't ask specifics. She dropped off Colby a little while ago, and I told her to take Cupcake."

"What?" Ryan gasped; the air sucked from his lungs. The conversation jumped from bad to worse to terrible with every new sentence.

"The horse needs exercise."

"Not that much." Ryan fisted his hands at his sides and dragged in as deep a breath as he could manage.

The mare was twenty-six years old. Losing Cupcake was inevitable. He didn't want to speed up the process. It wasn't like ripping off a bandage. Once gone, he didn't get over the pain after the initial sharp sting. He accepted the ache of missing a loved one and sometimes forgot his loss. The pain never lessened.

Without Cupcake, Hank was the last living link to Susie and childhood. *I'd have Meg.* Would he? He turned and frowned at Hank. "Where did they go?"

"Joe was leading everyone to the creek and then the big valley," Hank said. "I'm sure Cupcake is fine. Meg cares about that horse. She won't push her."

I can't take the chance. Ryan headed outside, pounding the grass to his truck. He turned over the engine and sped off, ditching the road in favor of a short-cut only accessible due to the drier than normal weather. Otherwise, he would have driven into mud too deep for the truck's tires to traverse.

As it was, he ripped up enough prairie grass to be noticeable. Ted wouldn't appreciate his rash actions. *Well, I don't like hers.* She knew what the horse meant to him and Hank. How dare she use Hank's good nature, sweetened up with the re-appearance of his new best friend Colby, to get her way. In another few miles, he reached the crest of the hill and slowed the truck, rolling down the hill. He spotted the group a few yards away. Cutting the engine, he hopped from the truck and strode toward the group.

The horses stood too close. Dangerously close. Apart from the rest of the group, the light brown mare stood almost shoulder to shoulder with Heathcliffe, a young colt with attitude.

Ryan gritted his molars. This was what happened when amateurs played cowboy. Good animals got hurt. "Meg!" he yelled.

She turned her head and frowned.

In three long strides, he reached Cupcake. "What are you doing? Get those horses apart." *And their riders.* He shook his head and grabbed the reins on Cupcake, leading the sweet mare to safety a few feet away. If Meg was a real ranch girl, she'd have had more awareness of the animal. She never quite shook off her city lifestyle.

"Sorry, Ryan. You're right. I didn't realize how close we were." Her cheeks pinked.

He bit the inside of his cheek. She couldn't hide her guilt. Why? Did she have feelings for the stranger?

"I was turning back anyway. I don't want to push Cupcake."

"Or leave Hank to do all the work?" He hated rhetorical questions but couldn't seem to stop himself.

She blanched. "Is he? Oh no. I'm sorry, Ryan. I only came for a quick tour on my lunch. I have to get back to the store. I can stop by tomorrow afternoon."

She didn't deserve his lecture. Hank wasn't in the shed but resting in the kitchen. The only person who earned condemnation was himself. But he couldn't stop his tirade. "Don't apologize to me." He kicked an ant hill. "You sort yourself out with Hank."

"I will." She sighed. "Did you know your family contributed significantly to endangering the world's population of bison? They rounded up and sold every animal they could. They didn't care what happened to the creatures as long as they got paid."

Huh? Why was she talking about this? He turned to her companion.

Eric winced.

"I'm aware," Ryan said. *What game was she playing?* He didn't appreciate her shrill tone or accusatory words. With months of work devoted to the bison conservation project, he didn't deserve a lecture. He was trying. The past couldn't be wiped clean. The Kincaids were part of a larger effort in the nineteenth century to force Indigenous people onto government lands by exterminating a critical part of their culture. Her family wasn't innocent either.

He focused his energy on the future, building a better tomor-row for everyone. Had she wanted to be involved? He dropped the threads of the conversation. She could cling to the past like Hank all she wanted. Without Ryan, however, she would be flung into an unforgiving present alongside Hank.

"Do you have anything to say?" she asked.

I don't like that you're dismissing my hard work based on assumptions. He set his jaw, grinding his molars. Couldn't she pick a better, private moment to argue?

She widened her eyes and flared her nostrils. Preparing for a verbal attack? Ryan scrubbed a hand over his face. He hated explaining himself but especially in front of a stranger. "Save it. Please."

She turned toward her companion but not before Ryan glimpsed her quivering chin. Oh no. Had his words been too sharp? He wanted peace, not to reprimand her in front of her colleague. She hadn't cried in years. At least, not in front of him.

A wave a nausea threatened to knock him off-balance. He hated her tears and especially detested being the source. But he wasn't in the wrong at this moment. He wouldn't cave.

"I'll get going. I've stayed too long," she said. "Bye, Eric."

"Later?" Eric asked.

Ryan didn't want to listen but couldn't walk away. Making plans? While his grandfather pet sat? The pair were supposed to be helping Hank, not cavorting around his property.

She nodded and wrinkled her brow.

Ryan caught her gaze. His throat squeezed shut, cutting off his airway. An apology caught on his Adam's apple. He coughed.

She nudged Cupcake with her heels. The good-natured mare turned toward the stables and trotted, swishing her tail from side to side.

Turning, he caught the outsider's stare. Dressed in fancy jeans and white sneakers, the man was out of place. Yet, he had the nerve to look perfectly comfortable. Ryan grunted. He didn't like the knowing look in the man's gaze.

With a wave, Eric whistled and turned his horse, rejoining Joe's tour group.

Ryan headed back to the truck. He had the cowboy dinner tonight. He couldn't be in a bad mood in front of his guests. Many checked out in the morning. He didn't want his scowl seared into their last memory of the ranch. Could he find a reason to smile? Or at least to stop frowning?

He'd have to track her down and apologize. Keeping her informed was a full-time job. Since he'd taken her input on his business, however, he faced a new reality of sharing his ideas with someone who'd voice an opinion. Hank approved plans without getting into the particulars and his employees never offered a thought. Meg was his equal. His poor treatment of her shamed him. He reverted to pushing her to the side instead of involving her in discussion.

If he kept shoving, he'd push her out of his life completely. *She'd leave for a job with someone who clearly respects her.* With a growl, he hopped into his truck and turned over the ignition.

CHAPTER 11

Once Meg pointed the horse in the right direction, she didn't need to do anything else. Cupcake knew the way home. The mare picked up her pace and trotted. In the saddle, Meg bounced around, but the shaking couldn't snap her out of her reverie.

Ryan was mad at her. Why? His anger rolled off him in waves, and he spoke with such short, curt words. She'd seen him annoyed, frustrated, and indifferent. She could handle those reactions. Him thinking poorly of her? She shuddered and tightened her grip on the reins.

She knew how important Cupcake was to the Kincaid men, on par with Colby to Meg. She trusted Hank with the dog, and Hank returned the favor with the horse.

Ryan was the hitch.

Always.

To drive over, hunt her down, and berate her in front of an audience was clear proof of his low opinion. To do so in front of a professional colleague was even worse. Her ears burned, and her cheeks scalded. She sniffed, scrunching her nose. She would not cry. If asked, she'd blame her red face on wind and sun.

How could she take herself seriously when he didn't? How could she drop the invisible shackles she imposed on herself if she didn't have his support? Would he ever value her as an equal?

She'd never been so embarrassed in her whole life. It was exactly the sort of behavior she might have expected out of the old Ryan, the one she'd grown up with. The one constantly trying to avoid her or blame her for some tiny infraction. Not the Ryan she'd gotten to know since starting the shed clean-out project.

He was right about one thing. She'd left Hank on his own with Colby. She knew the pair would head to the shed to continue the process of clearing through a lifetime's worth of boxes. The old cowboy would overexert himself. If anything happened due to her negligence, Ryan would never forgive her. Nor would she.

Meg lifted her gaze, scanning her surroundings. "Whoa, slow down, Cupcake." Meg pulled on the reins.

The mare stopped and whinnied, shaking her head.

Ted waved and jogged toward the pair. He opened his palm, displaying sugar cubes. "You're back early. Did the old girl give you any trouble?" Ted rubbed the horse's neck, wrinkling his brow. Cupcake gummed his palm.

"No, she's perfect. Like always." She extended the reins to Ted.

He grabbed hold of Cupcake.

Meg swung her leg over the saddle and dropped, her boots hitting the ground. She'd have to sneak into one of Stephanie's yoga classes to loosen up. Straightening, she sighed. "Thanks, Ted."

"Sure thing. I...ugh...don't suppose you've seen Ryan around?"

With his down-turned mouth and shifting gaze, Ted transformed into the physical embodiment of guilty conscience. "Why?" She frowned at the ranch hand.

"I might have grabbed his hat by mistake this morning."

"How? Isn't his head huge?"

Ted shrugged. "I didn't notice until I was on my rounds and the wind blew the thing off my head. I had to chase it down. Took half the morning." He chuckled. "I cleaned it up and put it back on his hook. No harm, no foul."

Speak for yourself. She pressed together her lips. Was she simply collateral damage in a bad day? Ryan's words cut her deep. She needed an apology. *I was accusatory.* Inwardly, she cringed. She didn't want to owe him anything after his treatment, but she owed him an apology.

"Heard about your events and weddings idea," Ted said.

She held perfectly still. *Heard about it* as in Ryan shot down the plan and laughed at the notion? Or *heard about it* as in the concept earned serious consideration from Ryan's most trusted employee?

"Could be a good thing for the future." Ted smiled.

Don't blush. The slow warming crept up her neck. After one confusing interaction, she didn't need another. If Ryan liked the idea, he would have only business reasons at the heart of his acceptance. "Do you mind taking care of Cupcake? I need to check on Hank and Colby."

"Sure thing. He's in the shed. Come on, Cupcake. You've earned a bucket of oats."

Cupcake whinnied and lifted her head and tail.

With a tip of his hat, Ted led the horse into her stall in the stables.

Meg had a half mile walk toward the shed.

With the beautiful weather, guests were scattered throughout the property on different adventures and tours. The lawn behind the house was empty.

She filled her lungs and slowly exhaled, making her way to the shed. Hank had witnessed her grow up. He'd spot any display of emotion, no matter how small, and want an explanation. Until she processed how Ryan hurt her so deeply, she didn't want to talk about her feelings with anyone else.

Strolling to the shed, she rubbed her lashes and dried her clammy palms on her jeans. With her fingertips, she pushed open the door, slipping inside the darkened interior. "Hank? Colby? Hello? Is anyone in here?"

Squinting, her gaze adjusted to the dim light. She walked to the back of the shed. The air was stagnant and heavy, holding the smell of aging paper and old tobacco. The building must have been where he'd stashed his pipe after Susie demanded he stop. There was no smoke in the air, so he hadn't taken it up again. But she was surprised by the changes.

In a few days, the shed had transformed from hazard to cluttered retreat. A roughly ten-by-ten area free of boxes and clutter opened at the back of the shed. On her last visit, she had sat at a small bistro-sized table with three chairs. Now, two card tables were set up along with a battery-powered table lamp. She didn't see either her dog or her friend. "Hank?"

"Over here, Meg."

She turned toward the sound.

A tail and a pair of shoes stuck out from behind a box-shaped igloo.

She'd passed the pair in a cardboard fort and had no clue. "Colby?"

The tail wagged, thumping against the ground.

"Come on out of there, silly dog." She knelt near the opening. Inside, she spotted the cowboy. "Hank, this isn't safe. The boxes could topple on you."

"Hold on. I've just about got it." He grunted, dragging a box.

"Let's give him space, Colby." Meg patted the ground. The dog crawled out.

In another few seconds, Hank followed on his hands and knees, pushing a box. He spotted her and sighed. "What are you doing here? Is Joe cutting his tours short?"

She narrowed her gaze. Something was off. Doubt tickled the back of her neck. What if Eric's invitation hadn't been so spur of the moment? What if a masterful puppeteer lingered in the background, pulling a few strings? "Did you encourage Eric to ask me on the ride to get out of your hair?"

"Why would I do that?" His tone was steady. He stared at the ground.

She pursed her lips. The cowboy was up to something, but she didn't know his motives. She pushed off the ground and reached for the box. "Should we examine this at the table? I'm not much for sitting on the ground."

Hank nodded and slowly got to his feet, his knees cracking as he stood. "I probably shouldn't either. I wanted to grab one more box before that fella leaves tomorrow."

She nodded and walked to the card tables, carefully setting the box on top. "I understand. I wish you had waited for me. Or even let me know you needed to get something specific out of the bottom of the stack. Do you have more to sort through today?"

Wincing, he walked toward her

Her breath caught in her chest. "Are you okay?"

He held up a hand. "Just stiff. I'm fine. Don't start makin' a fuss. That's what I like about you. You don't fuss. You treat me like an adult and not an invalid."

She bit her bottom lip. What she liked about him was he didn't put her in tricky situations between her conscience and her ego. Present circumstances excluded.

He reached the table, pulled out a chair, and sat down. He sighed. Colby trotted to him and rested her head on his lap. He smiled at the dog and scratched behind her ears. "I wasn't alone, if that's what concerns you."

Only partly. She grabbed a chair, scraping the feet against the rough plywood floor and plopped into the seat.

"I have to admit." Hank pulled the box across the top. "I didn't think I would. But I like that city fella. He's nice and knows his business. I appreciate dealing with someone so up-front."

She nodded her commiseration. Once she understood Eric's motives, she'd relaxed. Moving past the odd initial greeting at her store, she had stopped trying to control the situation and focused on her responses. Was seeking domination in their interactions her hiccup with Ryan? She wasn't sure what either of them wanted anymore. *Besides respect.*

"Colby must agree because she didn't bite him," Hank said, his voice scratchy and rough.

Meg frowned and rested her arms on the table. "You sound disappointed."

Hank shrugged. "I guess I'm not used to you having someone with so much in common."

Neither was she. As an adult, she chose Herd. She wanted to belong here. Desperately. Most days, however, she didn't fit. No matter how she smoothed her rough edges, she stuck out.

With Eric, she hadn't needed to explain her passion for history. She enjoyed his company. *But with Ryan, I can be one hundred percent myself.*

"I almost think…" Hank wiggled his bushy brows.

Heat crept up her cheeks. Please let her de facto grandfather never inch closer to discussing romantic attraction. "He's helping us with the project. That's it."

Hank held her gaze.

The cowboy's knowing look rankled. She pressed a cold hand to her hot cheek. "It's nice to talk shop with someone. But that's it."

"Really? I thought he might want to steal you away. You're too smart to stay hidden here."

You guessed? How had he so accurately understood while she'd been so oblivious? She was tempted to ask more of his opinions. With irrefutable proof, however, she couldn't lie to herself. "Leaving isn't my choice, you know that."

He smiled. "Nice way to avoid the conversation."

She shook her head but wouldn't deny his spot-on assessment. "I've got to head back to the store with Colby. Will you promise not to go digging through that pile over there?"

He crossed a finger over his heart.

"Can I grab a particular box for your and bring it inside? You'd be more comfortable at the kitchen table, and I'd feel a lot better."

"Okay. I suppose that's fair. Just pick the one on top."

She pushed back her chair and crossed the room, grabbing the box he indicated. "Come on, Colby. You need to make an appearance at the store. You've been missed."

Tail wagging, the dog licked Hank's palm and trotted to the door.

"Hank? Are you coming?"

"I'll be along in an instant. I promise."

With a nod to Hank, Meg followed the pup outside. Try as she might, she couldn't erase the censure in Ryan's condemnation. He'd been right. Left unsupervised, Hank immediately chose to endanger himself. She hated being at odds with Ryan. Without another confrontation, she couldn't make amends, and the fight wasn't in her.

From his window overlooking the yard, Ryan stood sentry. The second he had opened his mouth; he had understood he was dead-wrong. Back there, standing on the hill, he'd spotted her with that guy and spewed hurtful words. He couldn't stop himself.

As he paused for a breath, however, she took her shot. She gave as good as she got. He was fully aware of the misdeeds that established his family and continued to support him. He just didn't know she knew. He was making amends.

Not fast enough.

He hated arguing in front of a visitor. At least the other guests hadn't noticed or reacted to his poor behavior. Bad customer service and airing dirty laundry in public ratcheted up his frustration until his blood boiled. She had the sense to flee. It wasn't until he returned to his bedroom, spotted his hat suspiciously returned to its hook, he hadn't fully processed his behavior or calmed down.

When he did both, he was smacked in the face with the truth. The other man was her colleague and his guest. In one momentary lapse, Ryan ruined both of their prospects. After giving her a head start, he drove his truck the long way and reached his house in time to spot her talking to Ted.

He'd headed upstairs and straight to his window, overlooking the yard and the shed.

While he couldn't see inside the building, he knew in his heart she was inside. Of course, she'd go straight to his grandfather. She had a heart for him. Ryan had demanded it and heaped on the guilt. The old cowboy wasn't her responsibility. Ryan knew how much each valued the other. Pitting one against the other was a low blow. Adding in Cupcake was petty.

The shed door swung open.

Head down, Meg emerged with a box in her arms and Colby at her side. She moved quickly. No second glance to see if he was around?

His chest tightened. He couldn't blame her for making a quick escape, but he had to intercept her. He strode from the room, raced down the front steps, and flung open the kitchen door, the panel crashing against the siding.

He winced and turned toward her. "Hey, can I help?"

She strode straight towards him and pushed the box against his chest without any comment.

He secured the cardboard in his arms.

And she disappeared from view.

Where had she gone? How had she moved so fast? He set the box on the table and jogged through the house to the main entrance.

She strode toward her SUV, crunching gravel with each determined stride.

He cupped his hands around his mouth. "Meg. Wait, please."
She froze.
He jogged down the path, leaving the door wide open.

With a wagging tail, Colby raced toward him and jumped, nearly knocking him to the ground with her front paws.

I'd deserve it. He widened his stance and petted the dog. "Down, Colby."

The dog dropped and sat.

He raised his gaze to her owner. Meg's cheeks were bright pink. Her lips puckered, like she fought from frowning. Her gaze held steady on the ground.

"Meg, hey, please look at me?" His voice cracked. Raising a fist to his mouth, he coughed. He strode toward her, narrowing the distance from feet to inches.

She ground a rock under her heel. "Why? You want to yell louder? You don't have an audience around to hold back. You ready to really unload your grievances against me?"

"No, listen please?" He reached out a hand, brushing her elbow.

She caught her breath.

Dropping his hand, he tucked both into the pockets of his jeans. He had barely touched her, his fingertips grazing her soft skin. He would never use physical force or presence against another person. "I'm really sorry."

She met his gaze. "For?"

Everything. By virtue of wearing her heart on her sleeve, she was an open book. When she had smiled at the other guy, she looked so happy and free. Tiny creases had formed at the corners of her chocolate brown eyes. Her mouth had lifted. Her skin had almost glowed. She had been prettier than ever.

And he had seen red.

"Bye, Ryan," she bit the words out.

"No, wait." He lunged forward, stepping in front of her path. "I was out of line."

She stiffened. "Because of a hat?" She stared into his eyes.

Who told her? He reached up a hand to the back of his neck, rubbing the sunburned skin. Her blunt statement only added to his feeling of failure. He couldn't hide from the truth.

"Yes, and a lot of other things."

She broke from his gaze.

"I'm sorry. You don't know what I have going on behind-the-scenes, and you didn't deserve poor treatment. What happened back there in front of one of your peer?" He shook his head. "I was wrong. I behaved poorly. I know your work is important to you. I should have treated you with more respect, especially in front of a colleague."

She folded her arms over her chest and popped a leg out, tapping the foot. "And?"

"I am deeply sorry for what I implied about Hank and Cupcake. I know both mean a great deal to you."

"I wouldn't endanger anyone."

"I know. I just..." The words stuck on his tongue. Why was apologizing so hard? "I have to address your accusations."

She lifted her chin.

"When you brought up the bison..." His thoughts jumbled together. He wasn't quick with snappy replies. He needed to think his words through.

The longer the silence stretched, the deeper she frowned. Had his inability to form a speedy retort caused some of the misunderstandings between them? "I fully understand the privilege I have. I stand to inherit a lot of property. Not everything was acquired in ways we'd view as moral with our modern lens. All of this land..." He extended his arms and dropped both to his sides. "The founding families settled the valley. The land was unoccupied because military force cleared it. Doesn't mean it was unclaimed. I can't change history, but I am trying to right a wrong. You hit me with a sensitive subject." He swallowed. "I haven't shared the information with many people off the ranch. Please keep what I'm about to tell you between us."

She arched an eyebrow.

Probably the best encouragement he could expect. "I'm in talks to reintroduce bison to the prairie. If all goes according to plan, we'll have a herd next summer. Properly reestablishing the animals to the environment takes time. It's not a lot. But it's something." He finished before his voice shook with frustration and fear.

With the weight of his small corner of the world on his shoulders, he struggled. He couldn't show his worries to anyone else. He accepted his role as a town leader with all the positives and negatives inherent in the position. But he desperately needed her support and understanding.

Her chin quivered. She scrubbed her face with both hands. "I'm sorry, too. I had no clue about your plans. Of course, you don't owe me an explanation. You have done more for this town and community than anyone else. You shouldn't be accused and interrogated. Least of all by me."

He widened his gaze.

She dug the toe of her boot into the loose gravel. "I shouldn't leave Hank on his own. I caught him and Colby not being as cautious as they should be."

"He's not yours to worry about. I'm supposed to be minding him. I promised..." His throat swelled shut. "I shouldn't have put you on the spot. You have your own business to run. I appreciate how much time you've devoted to us."

"Speaking of my work." She studied him. "I won't be able to help at the shed again until after work on Saturday and Sunday. Think late. Like past nine. It's been quite a busy week. I'm heading to the store now."

We won't see you for four days? Why? His stomach dropped to his boots. The thought was too charged for consideration. He wanted to question her reasoning. Was there a difference between a weekend and a weekday in retail? Was she expecting something—or someone—needing her time after work during the week? "Guess I'd better find some more extension cords and lights."

"Will you do your best to keep Hank out of the shed until the weekend? He's in there now. Eric has everything he needs and is leaving tomorrow."

Is that the real reason? Was she avoiding him or had no more motivation after the other guy left? Ryan coughed. "I can try. I might see if Joe needs his help on any tours this week. I'll put Ted on rotation to check the shed every hour."

"Thanks. Hank means a lot to me."

Do I? Ryan hated this superficial conversation. Everything he wanted to ask and say lurked deep in his mind, beneath the surface of non-controversial pleasantries. *Why was talking to her suddenly so hard? What happened to her nonstop chatter that always left an opening for a reply?* "Can you come to the dinner tonight? It's our first cowboy event of the season. I'd appreciate all the support I can get."

She tilted her head to the side and narrowed her gaze.

Under her study, he didn't shift his weight. He hated the subtext between them. Should he extend a different invitation? Dinner and a movie wasn't an option. If he offered her anything close to a real date, he'd anticipate hearing *no*. "I have something to show you."

He regretted the words as soon as he blurted them. If all he could offer her were professional obligations, he'd do what he needed to keep her here. Without compromising his feelings, he'd offer her a piece of the future. Though he'd been pacing and thinking, he hadn't marked the potential deck event space in any meaningful, physical way. Now, he'd have to.

"Okay, I'll see you tonight." She spun on her heel and stalked to the SUV.

Why had she hesitated? He followed with Colby, helping the dog with the passenger side door. Having thumbs meant he was occasionally useful to the pair of independent women. He owed Meg so much more than an apology, and wouldn't read into what she hadn't said. With any luck, he could formally start his groveling tonight in front of the biggest audience around. He shut the door and backed away from the car, waving as she drove off.

CHAPTER 12

At the open barn doors, Meg stood very still. The sun wouldn't set for another couple hours, and the daylight made the well-lit interior extra enticing. She couldn't go inside yet.

She wasn't sure where, or if, she belonged.

Scanning the crowd, she swayed with the bluegrass music and suppressed the very persistent urge to twirl. In her bedroom, she hadn't been able to resist. She didn't often don her favorite dress, the floral, sleeveless, cotton garment with the full skirt Grandma had made decades ago.

Meg had saved a few of her late grandma's dresses. The quality of the home sewn vintage garments couldn't be matched in modern factories. Every time she wore one, she linked the past in the present. Antiques weren't merely a commercial enterprise but a way of honoring those she loved and lost.

Digging her cowgirl boots out of the back of her closet and applying eyeshadow and dark lipstick, she'd completed the look. She was probably overdressed. When she asked Colby, she barely got a glance. After a few hours at the store, customers cooing over the good girl, the dog was exhausted and happy. Meg hoped Hank was too. Grabbing her jean jacket off the hook, she'd hopped in her SUV and headed back to the Kincaid ranch.

In the entry, she didn't twirl. She didn't watch to catch anyone's eye. She wasn't sure if she'd accepted Ryan or Eric's invitation. Pressing together her lips, she refreshed her lipstick. She had the unnerving sense that it mattered which man she greeted first. Not that she was sure why.

Eric had offered her a job. Ryan had extended a hand for friendship. She wasn't in the middle of a tug of war. She should have told Ryan she had already been invited when he asked her. But he'd flashed such a soft smile. She hadn't wanted to ruin the moment or push him away.

Inside the barn, the cowboy festivities were well underway. Under the hay loft, the seven-piece band performed on the stage. The fiddle dueled with a banjo, whistling through the night air, inviting all to tap their feet to the upbeat rhythm. The entire red painted structure hummed with the buzz of excited conversations and tittering laughter.

Footsteps sounded behind her.

A couple passed, the wife brushing Meg with a shoulder. "Oh, I'm so sorry, dear."

Meg waved off the concern and crossed her arms over her belly, grabbing her elbows. She was at fault, standing awkwardly in the way. She stepped over the threshold, rolling her step from heel to toe in careful consideration. The worn, leather boots had a higher heel than her typical sneakers.

Darting her gaze, she spotted him.

Standing near the buffet, overseeing service, Ryan grinned. The expression brightened his whole face. The rare, genuine look of pleasure warmed her.

I wish he'd smile at me. Following his line of sight, she drew in a shaky breath. If he beamed at another woman, she'd be crushed.

On the other side of the line, guests—a family of four—returned his grin. He chuckled, throwing back his head.

He was natural with kids. Better than when he was a child. He'd always been destined to be a grown up running the ranch. With circumspection, she understood how being young must have been a struggle for someone who needed control.

"You made it."

Eric's voice snapped her to attention. She turned, tugging her jean jacket closed. "Hi, Eric. Yes, I'm here. Ta-da." Why did she say that? She might as well have flashed jazz hands.

He stepped back. "I grabbed us a spot in the corner. Follow me."

She nodded, glad when he turned. She nibbled the bottom of her lip. Where was Hank? Too tired after the long day? She strode behind Eric across the dance floor to the table in the opposite corner from the band.

Passing the buffet line, she met Ted's and Joe's gazes and smiled. Ryan never looked her way. She turned back and focused on Eric.

He reached the table and pulled out a chair.

This isn't a date. She tensed. She appreciated chivalry and compliments but didn't want any confusion. He'd offered her a job. She wasn't planning to accept, but neither was she interested in more. She didn't want to project the wrong idea to him or the community at large. On occasion, small-town living could be claustrophobic.

He walked around the table and sat opposite.

She dropped her shoulders a half inch. At least he wouldn't insist on pushing her chair into the table for her. Or draping her lap with a napkin. She sat and scooted the chair forward.

"I realize this might be..." He raised a fist to his mouth and coughed.

Inappropriate? She wouldn't supply him with his lines. She didn't have a copy of the script.

"Have you had a minute to think about the job offer?"

She nodded, pressing her lips into a straight line. The career change remained top of mind. One good week at her store wasn't enough to salvage the business but could give her time to diversify. She had to get the online store running.

"I'm guessing from your serious face, your answer is no?"

She pursed her lips. Taking him up on his job offer was the sensible choice. Lately, she'd had the urge to leap and try for the big, scary unknown. Ryan had a lot to do with her change of heart. Looking at Eric, *I'm sorry* tickled her tongue. She wouldn't apologize.

"I won't bug you about it. I am disappointed. If you ever reconsider." He reached into his jeans pocket and pulled out a business card, sliding it across the table.

She smiled and pocketed the card. Her tight stomach eased. After Hank's implication, she worried she'd given Eric the wrong impression. "Thank you. I appreciate your time and consideration."

He snorted. "You sound like a formal rejection letter. I understand." He scanned the room, staring past her. "Herd is a special place. Carving out your own path here is almost a throw-back to another time. It's a rare chance."

I wish I knew it was the right one. If she was being honest, which she tended to save for self-reflective nights with Colby, she'd admit she was afraid of failure without any excuse to make herself feel better. She turned in her chair and scanned the room, waving at acquaintances.

Stephanie helped the bluegrass band, moving the mic stands.

Entering through a side door, Abby from the barbeque food truck carried three stacked, covered trays. Ted and Joe grabbed the trays and settled each in respective chafing dishes. Brisket and corn bread scented the air. Meg's stomach rumbled. She lost track of Ryan. Twisting all the way around, she spotted him in the doorway, assisting Hank. *I should help.*

From the corner of her gaze, she spotted Stephanie backing away from the band. Meg couldn't give up on participating in the Frontier Days. At the very least, she could donate a few baskets for the raffle. Everything converged into this moment.

She started to rise from her seat and froze. Where would she go? She would get in the way. She had no role. Wasn't Ryan always frustrated she was underfoot?

Stephanie disappeared from view.

Meg scooted her chair closer to the table. She'd stay put. Five years and a childhood of summers wasn't enough to make her a true resident. The stranger showed her in a handful of days she didn't truly blend in with her surroundings. She might never belong, but she had to try even if she'd always stand out.

Lifting her chin, she faced Eric again. She nodded. "I have to give the store everything I've got. I owe my grandmother and my mother." *And myself.*

With luck, she didn't have to spell out for him what had only—in recent days—become clear to her. She chose Herd.

But she hadn't made a real effort to get to know anyone else. It wasn't too late to try. "Should we get some food while we can? The line is almost empty."

"After you, please." Eric smiled.

She pushed back her chair and strode with her head held high. She might be a temporary member of town, more guest than resident. But she wouldn't give up and walk away. She'd stay and fight. Sometimes, the best course of action was a life well-lived. She'd start by enjoying herself tonight.

Ryan couldn't catch a break. For the past hour, no matter which direction he turned, he glimpsed Meg's smile, inhaled her scent, or bristled at her laugh. He yearned to be included in the joke. Behind the buffet table, he rubbed a palm over his heart. Yearned? He hated even thinking that word, but it was spot-on.

He grabbed the last of the silver frames, holding the chafing dishes, off the table. He looped the empty rectangles over his wrist like a ridiculous oversized bracelet and strode the length of the buffet.

"Hey, Ryan."

Stopping at the end of the table, he turned and met Abby's gaze. In a few steps, he reached her. "Thanks for increasing the order so quickly. I didn't realize we'd have so many plus ones tonight."

She shrugged. "I'm always glad for the work. Thanks for letting me park my truck for lunch during the week. Let me know if you want to do anything for you-know-who." She widened her gaze.

He frowned. For Meg? Was he that obvious? Turning, he spotted her again with Eric.

She was lucky vampires weren't real. She kept throwing back her head and flashing her long, white neck as she chuckled along with what Ryan could only assume were dry, history-related jokes nobody else would understand. Ryan frowned. He'd invited Meg and yet she made no effort to say hi.

Abby snapped her fingers. "Yoo-hoo, earth to Ryan. Ryan, do you copy?"

He shook. "Sorry, you were saying?"

"Hank's birthday?" She lifted a shoulder. "It's not the big nine-oh, but every year is worthy of a celebration."

"You're right." He nodded. He'd totally forgotten. Was getting older the impetus for Hank's clean-out? Was he worried about leaving the project unfinished? Or did he want an excuse to focus on the past and the people long gone? "I'll keep you posted."

She smiled. "Please do. I'll get out of your hair now. Have fun."

He opened his mouth to protest he was working not playing and stopped. Not every comment needed a reply. He used to know that. He smiled, pressing together his lips.

She turned and strode past him toward the exit.

Joe approached, extending both hands. "Need any help?"

"I'm good here. Go check on Abby."

A funny look passed over Joe's face. He puckered his mouth like he bit a lemon and tried to cover it with a smile. Ryan would have to invite the guy around for poker if he made such bizarre facial expressions. He could only imagine the tells. *Another night, when I have time.* "Please?"

"Of course," Joe said.

Ryan reached the end of the table and nodded at the bluegrass band, comprised of more of Joe's colleagues from the kindergarten through eighth grade school. The townsfolk stepped up to the task of putting on a good show for the tourists. He was grateful for everyone's help and willingness to jump in and lend a hand. *Why hadn't Meg joined in?*

He passed the bathrooms, heading into the walk-in closet lined with shelves. When he had converted the barn into the event space, he'd carved a storage space in a slim hall opposite the newly added bathrooms behind the stage. Scanning the contents, he found the correct spot and deposited the frames in position one at a time. The first cowboy dinner of the season always had a few kinks. He couldn't complain about her. He invited her but hadn't specified what the request meant.

The band started another tune. The fiddler taking the lead in kicking off the dancing with a lively number. A cheer erupted.

"Why are you hiding out here?"

Ryan turned toward the open doorway and frowned at Hank.

The old man shuffled through the tight space.

"I'm not hiding. I'm doing my job. What are you doing back here?"

Hank shrugged. "Went to the bathroom and heard a commotion. Figured I'd better make sure you weren't making trouble."

That's your job. Ryan set the last frame on the shelf and strode toward his grandfather. "I'm heading out right now."

Hank held up a hand. "Let me stop you for a second, boy. You have anything to tell me?"

Ryan stared at the older man, unseeing. Had Hank witnessed the almost kiss a few days ago? Ryan slipped a finger under the starched collar of his checkered western shirt. He dressed up for the guests, but the start of the season involved reassessing what shirts no longer worked. This one almost choked him.

"About whatever's happening behind my barn? I spotted the string lights on my way inside. What're you playing at?" Hank narrowed his gaze.

I wanted to take Meg outside and show her I value her input. And her. Ryan unbuttoned the collar and resisted the urge to fan himself. The storage closet was stuffy. He'd add improve building ventilation to the project checklist. "Meg had an idea about expansion. Nothing's been decided. There is no conspiracy or attempted coup here. I'm developing the plan and determining feasibility. I would never move ahead without involving you."

"Oh. Meg?" Hank softened his hard stare. "Puts a different spin on it. Are you taking her outside? Showing her the view? Lots of stars tonight. Nice atmosphere."

I was... Ryan frowned. If, when, and how he acted, he wouldn't follow a dictate from his grandsire. On the flipside, however, following orders took off some of the weight of free will. He clenched his jaw. Back and forth uncertainty wasn't good for his stress levels. "I'd better get back out there."

"Good. You need to start dancing."

"Excuse me?" Ryan frowned.

"You heard me. Why did you invite a pretty girl to a dance if you're not going to twirl her around the floor?"

Ryan gaped. Did Hank have spies everywhere?

"Close your mouth, you look like a fish."

Ryan pinched the bridge of his nose. Getting into a fight with Hank served no purpose. "I don't know. She seems happy with him. Why should I interrupt?"

"You're not going to do anything? You're going to stand by and smile?"

Ryan squeezed his nose tighter, his vision clouding with spots.

"Boy, you need to act. Why have I gone to so much trouble? I never would have encouraged those two to spend time together if I had thought you'd continue to be so obtuse. I was hoping a little jealousy might force your hand. I was wrong. You're too stubborn for that." Hank snorted. "Why don't you admit what everyone else in town already knows?"

Ryan dropped his hands to his sides and stared. After their earlier fight, he'd spent the rest of his day setting up to impress her. Worried he'd lose her; he'd devoted hours to a showy task made the more frustrating because half the string lights were dead. He'd been played by his grandfather the whole time?

Hank exhaled a heavy sigh. "No more games. No more tricks. Just honesty. You two belong together."

"That's not true," Ryan murmured. "No one thinks of us as a couple. Eric has more in common with her. She's always smiling around him."

"Boy, you're a fool. Opposites attract." Hank reached out, dropping a hand on Ryan's shoulder, and squeezing. "Me and your grandma were all the proof you'd ever need for that. Go ask Meg for one dance, and I'll leave it. I've got my sights set on helping out the rest of your sad friends."

"Who? Ted?"

Hank shook his head. "Ted is a tough case. Widower. No, I'll get to him eventually. I'm taking care of all the easy-to-match folks first. Joe is next on my list. I've got someone in mind."

A laugh bubbled up Ryan's throat. With verbal confirmation of his troubling suspicions, he felt lighter than he had in a long time. Should he tell Hank to stay out of his business? Berate the old man for his meddlesome ways?

Ryan stepped forward and embraced his grandfather. If Ryan stopped fighting and took Hank's advice, what would he find? *Happiness*. He hugged the man tight. "Thanks."

Hank kissed his cheek. "Always." He stepped back, reversing to the entrance and tipped his head to the side.

With a nod, Ryan followed. He strode around the corner, pausing at the edge of the dance floor. On the platform, the band performed with vigor. Guests clapped and hollered, but the crowd remained seated. The empty pine planks looked lonely.

Hank was right, again. Ryan rubbed a hand along his slack-jaw. He shouldn't have been surprised, but he was. He continued on to his destination, weaving through the tables until he reached one in the corner. "Excuse me."

Two heads turned in his direction.

She looked at him with a steady, questioning stare.

He swallowed his discomfort. This was his chance. He extended his hand. "Meg, will you help me jumpstart the dancing?"

She stared at his hand.

The second stretched to eternity. Hank was wrong. Ryan shouldn't have done this. He shouldn't have invited her. He could back away and pretend no one saw. The table's prime position, however, ensured the opposite. He was on display for consumption and dissection of the entire town and all the guests.

She put her fingers in his and nodded.

He smiled and helped her to her feet. Once clear of the tables, he lifted his arm and spun her in a circle. Her dress fanned out.

When she returned to her starting position, her gaze widened, and she laughed. "Aren't you the guy who absolutely swore you'd never dance with me *in public again*?"

He lifted a shoulder. She was right. When he wanted to make a grand gesture, he found her steel-trap memory an inconvenience. For the gift of a long relationship, however, he'd pay the small price of having no secrets. "As long as you don't start to shuffle off to Buffalo in the middle of the two-step..."

Knitting her brow, she wrinkled her nose.

He grinned. "Seems a shame to waste such a pretty dress seated behind a table all night." He grabbed her other hand and lifted both, twirling her in the opposite direction.

"It's one of my grandma's. I was happy to have a reason to wear it. I'm not wearing my tap shoes tonight. You're safe from my spontaneous choreography." She bit her lip. "Thank you for inviting me. I didn't get a chance to say hi."

"Are you having a good time?" He reached for her waist and spun around with her, whirling across the floor. With a glance over her head, he nearly sighed.

The couple celebrating their anniversary joined in. As did a young family. Several other tables were getting to their feet and participating in the contagious good spirit.

"I am." She spun back into his arms. "I want to disclose, Eric invited me, too."

"Oh?" He arched a brow. Any other reaction wasn't appropriate. He'd taken too long to realize what she meant to him. He'd had nearly four decades. He couldn't be mad a smarter man wouldn't make the same mistake.

"He offered me a job. I think he wanted another chance to present his case before he leaves in the morning."

"And?"

She held his gaze. "I'm right where I belong." Her smile was soft and sweet. "Herd is my hometown. I'm not leaving."

My place is here with you. Under his palms, he felt her shudder. Was this the moment for truth? Was she staying only for the town? Or was he included in her list of reasons? "Not sure if you caught a glimpse on your way in, but I marked out the proposed deck with spray paint in the corners. I strung up some lights in case you wanted to see."

"You're going forward with it?"

He adjusted his hand on her waist, liking the delight in her response and the feel of her in his arms. If he could keep his grip, he had the illusion of control. "I'm considering it. If I did, I'd need your advice to optimize appeal."

She blushed. "I'm sure I'm not the person to ask."

"You had the initial idea. You see the world differently. You make me ask questions." *You challenge me in the best way possible.* He couldn't tell her how much she scared him. Every encounter left him a little shaken, but he wanted more. If he invited her outside, what would happen?

First and foremost, he had to focus on keeping her in Herd. With enough time, he'd sort through the emotions and fears blocking his way. "I can help with your online platform."

She frowned, scrunching her nose.

Had he overstepped? "We talked about it?"

The day she had smiled and his heart had started beating for the first time in recent memory. She didn't remember? He'd never forget. They'd been standing on her old property talking about weddings. She had looked so beautiful and fragile. A fully formed picture of her in a veil with a sweet grin popped into his mind.

She continued to stare, tilting her head to the side, gliding across the floor with him.

No pressure. "I wasn't sure if you needed any assistance. You've been so generous with your time, clearing out the shed. We owe you." *I owe you.* Why was speaking honestly so hard? He'd known her forever. She must see his struggle. But he didn't want her to give him a way out or to ease away from the difficult part. Until recently, he'd never seen her.

"I was kind of hoping you'd ask me for my than advice," she murmured.

She did? What question did she want him to ask?

She cleared her throat. "Should we discuss plans for Hank's birthday?"

He nodded. "I'm not sure about this year. I don't want to do too much and overtime him. The shed has been taxing." He adjusted his grip on her waist. Under his palm, she was slight and small. He never thought of her as less than a tornado, but she was a woman underneath it all. "If I make any plans, I'll let you know." He lifted his arm and spun her again.

Her dress fluttered around her.

When she returned to his embrace, she frowned for a second. Then she wiped the look off her face like she'd never had a second of hesitation.

Back to business as usual? He hoped so. Why did he feel like he'd dodged a bullet and missed his shot? How many other bad clichés would attack him?

He darted a glance at the doors leading outside. Stringing the lights had been a lot of work. He'd cursed under his breath more than once in the process. What would she think of his handiwork? Would she have ideas for improvement?

He had a niggling sensation he should ask her to join him at the ranch as the lead of the new events department. No one would do the job better or bring more creativity to the role. But then she'd be his employee. A romance would definitely be off the table if she was his subordinate.

Maybe that was for the best. Same with avoiding the proposed deck. Before their dance, he hadn't thought through all the repercussions of leading her to such a cozy, almost intimate spot. It would look like he wanted more than friendship.

If she wasn't going anywhere, she didn't challenge him to change his stance and tell her the truth of his feelings for her. Maybe she didn't want him to. Maybe it wasn't just his foolishness separating them but her clarity that they'd be a disaster. He'd have to follow her lead. He could always count on her to be upfront and honest. Come what may.

CHAPTER 13

On her front porch the next morning, Meg blew across the top of her coffee and snuggled under the afghan Grandma and Susie Kincaid had crocheted decades earlier. The chill lingered from last night's after midnight rainstorm. She'd been home and tucked in bed long before the first drops fell. She should have been asleep.

Instead, she'd tossed and turned. At four am, she gave up on sleep and came outside. The damp morning air refreshed her tired eyes, and, once she'd gone back inside and brewed it, the coffee added a jolt to her system. After two hours of woolgathering, she needed to get ready to head to her store. She couldn't seem to give up the comfort of sitting on a wicker armchair, drinking a hot beverage (her fourth), and tracing the spirals in the hand-made blanket.

She still didn't know what to make of Ryan.

Last night, he had shocked her speechless.

He had approached the table as Eric had relayed a funny story about a recent sale at the auction house. With his eyes shining, Ryan had extended a hand and asked her to dance. Sure, he'd invited her to the dinner, and dancing was part of the evening's festivities, but his request surprised and confused her all the same. When she couldn't catch his gaze for a wave hello, she had contented herself that she misunderstood the intention of his invitation.

On the dance floor, Ryan had twirled her with a deft hand. He'd moved quick and light. The cowboy had a prowess for dance. She liked spinning with him. As he held her tight, her stomach fluttered and her limbs felt fizzy, like her blood was pure champagne. But she hadn't wanted to be anywhere else. In his arms, she was content and safe.

At the first chance, she explained her behavior. If she'd been thinking correctly when he asked, she would have told him on the spot she had already been asked to attend by Eric. She'd been so blown away by Ryan's request that she imagined he had asked her on a proper date. Of course, she'd been wrong to assume. When she had discussed her plans to stay, she'd been hit with disappointment.

He had no response? He wasn't glad? His face turned to unflinching stone and his gaze darkened. She had tensed in his arms but shook it off. She couldn't be mad at him. Only herself. He had offered his help like always. While she appreciated the gesture, she couldn't help but wonder if she was simply another burden. His delivery was automatic, and his tone was emotion-less.

And then she'd almost asked him if she could work for the ranch with the events department.

She took a final sip of her coffee, the rich roast clearing out the sour taste in her mouth at her mishandling of everything.

Setting the mug on the ground, she reached into her pocket for her cell phone. She had no messages or missed calls. While she hadn't expected any, she'd hoped for a valid distraction. She dialed home.

The phone rang and rang.

"Please pick up," she murmured. She wanted a break from her thoughts with a third party unaware of current events.

She couldn't fight the worry that she'd screwed up. Not just about not telling Ryan she had another invitation last night or not seeking him out and greeting him when she arrived. She couldn't shake the gut-clenching certainty that she'd officially brushed off any chance for more to develop between them.

With his hand on her waist, he'd looked into her eyes, and her legs had turned to jelly. She didn't know what came next. And she'd been terrified. What if her feelings weren't reciprocated? Backed into a position of vulnerability, she had given them both an out. She volunteered information instead of making him ask directly. Would they slip back into their old ways? She couldn't go back.

Adjusting on the chair, she tucked the blanket under her legs and held the phone against her ear. It was a Tuesday. Mom had a few more weeks of teaching before her school year ended. But she should be free for a quick phone call before the bell rang in thirty minutes.

The call connected.

"Hello? Meggie?" Mom said.

"Hi, Mom." She exhaled a heavy sigh.

"Sweetie, are you okay? You sound a little off."

Meg scrunched her nose against the tickle in her nostrils. "I'm a little tired. I've been selling a lot at the store. Tons of customers. I'm heading in soon and will be there until late."

"Really? Oh, that's such great news. What happened with the photos? Did the expert leave?"

"He leaves today. He thinks the signatures are real and plans to include the entire collection in the September auction."

"Wow. How wonderful for Hank. Are you blogging about it?"

Meg frowned. She wasn't sure if she should. "I don't think so, Mom." How could she extricate herself from the photographs and souvenirs? The project spurred her toward change, and she couldn't untangle her journey from the discovery. "The expert offered me a job in San Francisco."

"Oh, are you considering it?"

"No. I want to stick around Herd. I'm more determined than ever to get the website going. We still have half the shed to clear out. We might find items for consignment."

"I'm glad you're staying. Did Hank try to get you to sell the photographs yourself?"

Meg smiled. "You know I'd never let him. I can't watch him miss such an important opportunity."

"Your honest, caring heart might be what I love the most about you."

Does Ryan love something about me? Meg hated that she cared.

A red sedan drove down the country lane and turned into the driveway.

"Mom, I think I have a visitor. I'd better let you go."

"Of course, bye, sweetie. I love you."

"Love you too." Frowning, she ended the call and shook off the blanket. She slid the phone into her back pocket. Just in case. She'd never had an unexpected guest. Nor had she ever struggled with the uneasy concern she was too far away from help if she needed it. She got to her feet, shading her gaze with a hand.

The driver's side door opened. Eric exited the car, waving.

She sagged her shoulders.

He shut the door and strode across the gravel. "Hope you don't mind that I dropped by. I remembered you said you lived next-door. It took a little bit of driving, but I figured out what that meant."

She stifled a laugh. Next-door was fifteen miles from the ranch house. "Of course, I don't mind." She strode down the steps. "Can I get you a cup of coffee?"

"No, thank you. I'm headed to the airport. Thought I'd say goodbye and try that job offer once more in person."

She stopped a few feet away. Eric was nice. More than once, she had caught herself sharing in his contagious grins. He shared a love of history and asked questions, eager to listen to the answers. She hated to disappoint him, but she owed herself a chance at her dream. She drew in a deep breath.

He held up a hand. "I get it. You don't owe me another explanation. I've pushed too much. If anything changes, you have my card."

Was he speaking purely in a professional capacity? Or something more? Her answer remained the same. She couldn't force herself to change her feelings into something more convenient. If she had any power of persuasion, she'd utilize her skills to get Ryan to call.

"Goodbye, Meg. I'll be in touch. Maybe you can bring Hank to the sale."

She smiled. "Have a safe trip home."

He nodded and retreated to his car.

She crossed the lawn to Colby, sunning her belly on the damp grass and unconcerned about their visitor. Meg sat on the ground, extending her feet in front of her and holding onto the dog. The red sedan backed out of the drive and turned onto the road, heading toward town.

In her pocket, her phone vibrated. Dropping her hold on Colby, she swiped her finger over the screen and raised the device to her ear. In the bright sunshine, she couldn't read the name on the screen. "Hello? This is Meg."

"Meg? It's Hank. Listen, can you stop by the shed today?"

She scrunched her face. She hated to tell him *no*. While Memorial Day—yesterday—was the unofficial start of summer, tourists didn't descend for another week, after many schools finished for the year. If the past week was any indication, she would be a few very busy months. *With any luck.* But she'd closed the store early too many days lately to take another one off.

"You still there, Meg? Meg?"

"Hi, Hank. Sorry." She heaved a sigh. "I'm not sure if I can make it until later in the week."

"This doesn't have anything to do with the fella leaving?"

"No, of course not," she said without a breath.

"Maybe you don't want to stop by because you're afraid about running into someone else?"

She nibbled her lip. Lying to Hank was impossible. "I had a long day followed by a late night. I'm tired."

"When can you stop by?"

The weekend? She couldn't do that to a friend. "Later? I might have a spare moment after the lunch rush and before the dinner crowd. Downtown has a lull around four. No promises. But if I have time, can I swing by for a quick visit then?"

"Alright. I'll wait 'til then. Last night was a lot of fun. It was good to see you dance."

It had felt good. When she had entered the barn, she'd vowed to enjoy herself. For a short while, she'd shrugged off her worries and had fun. Then, she'd screwed everything up with Ryan. Maybe she saved herself a lot of heartache. She couldn't be mad at him for setting boundaries. Doing so was healthy and an exercise in protection.

She'd do better to learn from his example than rail against him. Starting now, she'd respect the distance between her house and the ranch. "I'll see you later. Bye, Hank."

CHAPTER
14

Ryan ripped the sheets off the mattress, balling up the bedding and tossing it on the floor. He wasn't usually so quick to housekeeping. Changing linen and cleaning toilets wasn't his favorite task. Today, he made an exception.

Once the guest checked out of the yurt, he wasted no time turning over the room. A last-minute booking scheduled for tomorrow meant Eric couldn't extend his stay. If Ryan stayed busy with the cleaning, he avoided confronting Meg with the inevitable frank conversation.

He shook the pillows out of the cases. He had been tricked by the feel of her in his arms. She was strong and small at the same time. Her skin had been softer than the worn quilt at the foot of his bed. He had liked holding her. Hank was spot-on to push them together. His heart had jumped into his throat, and he had opened his mouth to speak.

Then she had told him nothing would change.

She wanted to remain status quo? He had spun her through the rest of the song. He did his best to move and operate like a normal person. By the end, the dance floor had been packed.

Ted had approached him with a problem.

Eric had strode onto the floor, heading straight to her.

Ryan had left, and she didn't stop him. He had spent the rest of the night on his normal tasks of cleaning up and helping guests. In the chaos, he had lost track of her.

He had stayed at the barn until late into the night, sweeping, mopping, and thinking. After everyone had left, he strode around the back and unplugged the lights. A light rain had started, preventing him from lingering at the site.

He loved Hank. The meddling cowboy wasn't infallible. He was an opinionated rascal with too much time on his hands.

Ryan twisted the sheets around his hands, wringing the cotton. More than anyone, he blamed himself. He listened to Hank when he should focus on work. How could he take on one more problem? As much as Hank might argue otherwise, he couldn't deny what Ryan witnessed with his own eyes.

While it lasted, love was great. Once it was gone, the loss was devastating. Grandma's passing nearly killed Hank. If the worst had happened, and his grandfather succumbed to his broken heart, where would Ryan have been? Struggling with a business he couldn't handle on his own. How long could he have lasted?

Luckily, Meg figured out she needed to draw a line between them and stated her decision. Before he let his guard down and put himself out there for her rejection, he knew the truth. He had walked away unscathed, unlike the torn apart yurt.

"What happened in here?"

He turned toward the door.

Ted strolled in, frowning. "Did that city guy leave it like this? Should we run up a charge for extra housekeeping?"

"I'm cleaning." Ryan bent and grabbed the bedding off the ground.

"Oh, that's what you're doing?" Ted scrubbed a hand over his face. "I wanted to ask about the bison. Any more word?"

"Oh, right." Tightening his grip on the bundle in his arms, Ryan rocked back to his heels. "I have to follow up with the town council. I forgot."

"Not like you. Any particular reason why?"

None that I care to discuss. Ryan never backed down from a confrontation, but he had no good reason for his distraction lately. Hank might argue the point. "Nothing out of the ordinary. First week is always an adjustment. I owe the mayor another call."

"You've been busy." Ted grabbed the bundle from his arms. "Let's leave the rest for the professional crew."

Ryan rolled his eyes but didn't correct his ranch hand. The cleaning crew was scheduled to stop by in an hour. He'd barely finish dusting at that point. He knew his skill set. While he could manage the house at his own pace, he didn't have enough time for the guest rooms. "Fine. Go out, and I can lock up."

Ted left.

Ryan scanned the room once more. The circular space felt expansive and welcoming. With a slim bathroom and closet set in the outer band, the inner sanctum focused on a comfy bed. What more could a guest need? *A companion.*

He shook his head, flipped off the lights, and locked the room. He jogged to the gator.

Ted had dropped the linens into a basket on the back of the vehicle.

Ryan secured the basket with bungee cords, looping over the handles to create an x and prevent the sheets and towels from escaping. Chasing after bedding as it blew across his land wasn't how he wanted to spend his day.

With his luck, the sheets would blow into her yard, and he'd have to head there. Was she home? Would she want to chat? She made a concerted effort to explain she wouldn't be stopping by all week. What if she turned him away?

Ted secured the last cord. "Are you heading back to the house?"

Ryan shook his head. "Opposite direction. I figured I'd follow Joe."

"Why? You don't trust him?" Ted crossed his arms over his chest.

"Of course, I trust him." Ryan scrubbed a hand over his face. "Don't start now."

"Guess I'm not sure who I'm dealing with some days."

Ryan frowned. "And that means?"

Ted shrugged. "Nothing. I've got to head back to the barn. Repairs on the outdoor lights. I'm on the radio if you need me."

Ryan nodded.

The ranch hand headed toward a pickup parked on the dirt road past the three yurts.

Had Hank put Ted up to the controversial remark? Ryan didn't have time for nonsense today. He'd focus on work, redoubling his efforts where he was wanted and needed. He'd avoid drama.

Climbing into the gator, he drove toward the cabins. Joe scheduled a group of first-timers fishing at the pond. Ted was right to question why Ryan would micromanage the seasoned adventure guide on a basic outing.

Because he'd take any excuse for space. The wind whistled past as he sped along on the gravel road. He knew the blind spots of every dip in the narrow one-lane road. He'd rather not deal with a head-on collision with one of his guests. An accident would be too much distraction from his everyday duties.

He reached the top of the last hill and cruised down the slope toward the cabins. In front of number five, third from the right corner, he spotted the Claytons at the trunk of their beige, mid-sized sedan. Ryan slowed his vehicle and stopped off the road. "Good morning." He called and hopped out of the vehicle.

"Hello, Ryan," Marcia said. "I've got to run inside." She pointed at the cabin and bolted.

Ryan smiled and approached the trunk. "Are you checking out today? Need any help?"

Ford lifted a suitcase off the ground and dropped it in the trunk. He exhaled. "We are heading home. I've got the packing under control." He shifted the suitcase into position next to several others and slammed the trunk. Dusting his hands on his jeans, he extended a palm. "Wanted to thank you for a memorable trip. Marcia doesn't want to leave."

Ryan shook the man's hand. "Glad to hear it. You'll definitely want to return next year. The property will have some major changes on your next visit."

Ford dropped his hand. "Really? Anything to do with your dance partner?"

Was Ryan that obvious? He nearly gaped as his throat swelled shut.

"Sorry, I shouldn't have overstepped. I wasn't the one who made the observation. After Marcia pointed it out, though, I couldn't shake it."

Ryan coughed. This was the most uncomfortable encounter he'd ever had with a guest. Meeting up on the trail ride, he'd nearly growled at Eric. Somehow this exchange topped that moment. "Pointed out what?"

"Well, you and the young lady had a very opposites-attract vibe. You couldn't keep your eyes off each other. Reminded Marcia of us."

"Meg is my neighbor. I've known her forever." Ryan said the words by rote. His brain processed the action of his speech, but he no longer connected with the sentiment. She meant a lot to him. He had to accept the feelings might not be mutual. Why else would she push him away at the exact moment he wanted to bare his heart?

"In that case." Ford wiggled his brows. "Maybe you're even more like us than we realized. Marcia and I were next-door neighbors. She was my best friend's kid sister. She followed us everywhere and drove us crazy with her incessant talking. She ratted us out to her parents more often than not." He sniggered.

Ryan nodded. As kids, when Meg wasn't involving him in trouble, she was setting him up to take the fall. The corner of his mouth lifted. Her heavy-handed attempts were pretty funny now. At the time, he didn't appreciate the little girl with the chocolate covered face blaming him for eating all the cookies. Or how Hank's scowl slipped at the obvious lie. "What changed?"

"I went off to college and got a good job. I came home for the holidays but never stayed. I didn't realize she was avoiding me, too. While she was the annoying kid, she had a crush on me and tried to spend time together whenever she could. When my best friend got sick, I came home. I finally saw what was there the whole time. How funny and smart and amazing she is, and how much she lights up my life. I wasn't smart enough to hold onto her then. I almost lost her. We broke up for a few months.

She found someone else." Ford lifted a hand and snapped his fingers in mid-air. "Like that. She'd be fine without me. I can't live without her. Don't be like me. Don't wait for a life-or-death scenario to spur you. I saw you two dancing. Don't miss your chance."

What if I already have? How could he trust his heart when his brain so clearly told him to slam on the brakes? He wasn't the type to ignore someone else's feelings. Last night, he'd decided against honesty by not showing her the deck. Had he let them both down?

"I have to thank you. Our trip has been our most memorable vacation."

"I'm glad. You'll have to try a yurt next year."

Ford grinned. "Marcia is ready to book now."

Rusty hinges squealed, and a screen door slammed shut, snapping into the metal frame.

Ryan glanced up.

Marcia strode toward the car, stopping a few feet away. "Ah. Much better. Thank you for a lovely trip, Ryan. I'll have to try my luck gold panning again next year."

Ford rolled his eyes. "Not me. Thanks again." He strode around the car and hopped in behind the wheel.

Marcia leaned forward. "Did he speak to you?"

Ryan nodded.

"Good." She flashed a self-satisfied smile, striding to the passenger side.

Ryan stepped back and waved as the Claytons drove off. They were right. He didn't want to wait for the worst to happen to spur him to change. If Meg didn't feel the same as he did, what happened next? She'd always been there. What if she was gone? Or what if she remained? Would his heart break a little more with each hello?

He needed time. A couple days to get his work in order. He'd dropped the ball on his bison project and needed to follow up with the mayor and town council about setting up some meetings.

He had another new round of tourists to settle in. He could wait until later to discuss his feelings. It wasn't life or death.

CHAPTER 15

L ounging around the house got old, fast. Meg finished the laundry, cleaned the bathrooms, and started supper in the slow cooker before noon. If she stayed home much longer, she'd launch a full-scale renovation. Adding to her physical exhaustion did nothing to alleviate her emotional strain. She couldn't avoid Ryan forever.

By one o'clock, she stalled long enough. She loaded Colby in the little white SUV and headed to the ranch. The front of the house was quiet. Ryan's pickup was gone. She exhaled a heavy sigh. She wasn't a coward. She wouldn't be afraid to face someone because a situation hadn't worked in her favor.

Hopping to the ground, she followed the dog around the house to the shed.

The door was open. The interior was dimly lit.

With a woof, the dog brushed past and raced inside.

Stepping over the threshold, Meg scanned the nearly emptied interior. Without boxes stacked to the ceiling, the building didn't have the claustrophobic atmosphere she'd first encountered.

Hank continued to make progress without her. Her heart squeezed. Had she disappointed him? Had he overexerted himself?

"Hi, Meg. Thanks for coming," Hank said, his voice carrying from the back.

She strode forward.

Hank sat with his back against a wall.

Colby laid on the floor at his feet.

Twisting her neck, Meg surveyed the room. Without stacks of cardboard, she glimpsed the uninsulated plank walls. A few knots had dried and fallen out of the wood. Crumpled up newspaper filled the holes, duct tape securing the make-do patches in silver crosses. With the unconventional patches, the exposed-to-the-elements building would be unbearably icy in the winter. Could the building be repaired and insulated?

She shivered. "You're almost finished. I can't believe it."

"I'm motivated." He pointed to one side of the room. "Only that stack left to go through." He sighed and met her gaze. "I'm sorry to tell you I haven't found anything else of interest. It was boxes of broken knick-knacks and old paperwork."

She nibbled her lip. She wished he'd waited. One man's trash could most definitely be another's treasure.

"You're disappointed. I promise we aren't talking anything older than the nineteen eighties." He crossed a finger over his heart. "On my honor. I wanted to finish, and Ted helped load the truck since he needs to run an errand in Miles City. It was all donation. We might hit pay dirt in that stack."

She nodded and pulled up a chair at the table. "I'm happy to help finish."

"Good." He smiled. "I remember boxes of old, hardcover books. Some are leatherbound." He wrinkled his brow. "I'm not sure how those will fare at an antique store."

She straightened. Maybe she hadn't missed a chance after all. "Actually, I'm starting an online store front, too. Books can definitely spark interest from the right crowd."

"I'm not talking first editions here."

She shook her head. "You don't need to. A lot of books are purchased for their looks. Designers use them to decorate shelves in high-end homes."

He chuckled. "We were happy to have something to read. Never cared what the spines looked like. I probably have some of Susie's paperbacks, too. Early in my marriage, I boxed up most of my books in our library to accommodate hers. She needed space for all her romance books. Some boxes of paperbacks are here somewhere."

"Romance books will definitely fly off the shelves inside my store." Meg grinned.

"Some summers, we had our power knocked out by storms once a week. She used to read to me."

Meg propped her elbows on the table, resting her chin in her palms. She couldn't dream of a better way to spend a rainy afternoon. During her childhood, she remembered a handful of such nights. Her summer days were filled with reading as much as she could. "I remember. On a few rainy days, she read to me, too. Susie had a great voice. I loved her accents."

"She was happy to have such a captive audience. What did she read?"

"*Anne of Green Gables* and all the books that followed. She gave Marilla a raspy voice." Meg smiled. "What did she read to you?"

"Her romance books. Everything from Jane Austen to Danielle Steele."

Reminiscing, Meg didn't feel the ache of missing one of the most important people in her life. More than a neighbor, Susie Kincaid poured love into everyone she cared about. Meg warmed at the shared memories. She and Hank hadn't spoken of his wife since her funeral. Why the change? Meg straightened. "Is missing Susie the reason for cleaning the shed?"

He shook his head. "Trying to get you to sort out your feelings for my grandson is the impetus."

She dropped her jaw. Over the years, she'd had her suspicions. Convincing herself she was mistaken; she'd shoved aside her concerns every time Ryan appeared instead of Hank. She never imagined confronting Hank or that he'd so readily admit to his matchmaking.

"I've seen how you look at him." Hank leaned back in his chair. "Just like me and Susie. You're so confused at his silence and overwhelmed by his speech."

Her skin burned.

Hank chuckled and bent, scratching Colby behind the ears. "Getting to spend time with this little lady and helping your business is the icing on the cake."

Meg coughed. "Am I so obvious?"

"Only to a trained eye." Hank winked. "You've got to make him see sense, or he will never be honest."

She frowned. "With me?"

"No, worse. With himself. You've always been his conscience."

She wasn't sure she agreed with the assessment. For as long as she could, she had happily lurked in status quo as Ryan's frenemy. Progress couldn't be held back indefinitely. Herd and the community were changing. Did she have a role in town? Or worse, could she only stay if she was connected to the Kincaids?

She had plenty of reasons not to ask hard questions. She couldn't put off what she knew was true, but she needed a plan. "Let's finish things up. You have the makings of a nice man-cave here."

"You can change the subject, because I know you'll take my words to heart." He sat back. "I'll admit to you, because it's going no further, I'm a little stiff today. Do you mind bringing the boxes to me?"

She smiled. Admitting weakness wasn't standard protocol for the cowboy. She appreciated his confidence in her and owed him the same in reverse. "Of course, I don't mind."

One at a time, she carried the boxes over for Hank's inspection. At his direction, she divided the piles into donate, sell, and throw away. By the end of the hour, she acquired a tidy stack of boxes full of vintage romance novels and old hardcover books. She started trekking the pile around the house from shed to SUV and back again.

She should have parked closer. The parking lot at the barn was empty and half the distance to the shed. But she didn't want to potentially sneak up on Ryan. Her parking spot on the circle drive in front of the house would alert him to her presence.

On her fifth trip, she paused to help Hank into the house.

The shed felt like a never-ending project, like excavating London with centuries of history layered on top of each other. Hank promised to leave the haul-away to Ted and to wait on the final boxes until she had time later in the week. She hated noticing how he slowed down but couldn't ignore worrisome signs that the stubborn man had overtaxed him in recent weeks. While she believed his confession of matchmaking was truthful, she didn't think that summed up his entire purpose in the endeavor.

On her final trip, she whistled to Colby and set the box down outside the shed, shutting the door. She rolled her shoulders and her neck, her upper back aching from a day of manual labor. Bending, she groaned as she grabbed the box. Why had she saved the heaviest for last?

Colby woofed.

Frowning, Meg followed the dog's gaze, pointing toward the barn.

Ryan stood in the doorway of the big, red building. His hat shaded his face. She couldn't be sure he was looking at her. Tiny hairs stood on end on her skin. She felt his gaze. She couldn't move or speak, her throat closing. She wanted to shout. Her heart skipped a beat as she willed her heavy limbs into locomotion.

What would she say? *I think we're a match. Hank agrees. I might not stay. Maybe I should leave?* She hated the ultimatum implication. Staying was about more than him, but she was honest enough for the admission leaving wouldn't be. She could fight her feelings for only so long.

He lifted his head, changing the angle.

Meeting his gaze, she smiled.

He turned away, striding back inside the barn.

Hank was wrong. She was a fool who talked herself into a fantasy. She was Ryan's neighbor and sometime burden. Every exchange had been heightened by her overactive imagination.

"Come on, Colby. Let's get to the store," she murmured.

The dog spun around and raced to the SUV.

Meg followed at her own pace weighed by the heavy burden of disappointment. She'd let down herself more than anyone. Any effort on his part must have been fueled by pity. She didn't need to come back and subject herself to that again. She'd stay in town, or on her property, for as long as she could.

CHAPTER 16

"Welcome to Finders-Keepers," Meg greeted an older couple entering her store less than thirty minutes later.

The woman lifted her gaze and smiled. "Good afternoon." She turned to her companion and handed him her purse.

With a sigh, the man kissed her on the cheek and walked to the wall kitty-corner the front window, and leaned against it.

The woman hustled toward the front counter. "I promised I wouldn't take too long." She tilted her head to her companion. "He's been a good sport for a long lunch at the saloon and a costumed photo session. I've delayed our departure long enough. I'll come out and ask."

The no-nonsense manner raised her hackles. Was Meg being put on the spot or her merchandise?

"Do you have any ice cream molds?"

Releasing the pent-up breath, Meg dropped her shoulders and rounded the counter. "Yes, ma'am. Right this way." She strode toward an Eastlake vitrine and opened the center doors, stepping back, to reveal two glass shelves of pewter ice cream molds. From flowers to animals to holiday emblems, she loved the whimsical shapes. Popularized in the U.S. around the turn of the twentieth century, the molds hinted at the luxury of the upper classes. To have the ingredients, refrigeration, and time to produce and shape ice cream suggested above average means. Her family never had any. The Kincaids owned several.

"What is that?" The woman pointed at one on the top shelf.

Carefully reaching inside, Meg grinned and grabbed the most talked about item she'd ever listed for sale. She wasn't sure she could post it for sale online without having the listing flagged for indecency. Opening her palm, she rested the five-inch object in the center. "What do you think it is?"

"A topless, pregnant woman's torso," the woman replied.

Meg shook her head and opened the mold. "I did too, until I tested it. This makes a Thanksgiving turkey."

The woman chuckled. "Oh, I have to get that. I have every other holiday in my collection."

Meg extended the mold. "How many George Washington busts?"

"Too many."

Meg smiled. In her excursions for inventory, she came across many commemorative molds of the first president.

The woman closed her fist around the turkey breast. "I haven't been surprised in a long time. Before the internet, I had a lot more fun discovering different pieces."

Meg nodded. "My mom says the same. She used to visit flea markets and estate sales for Depression glass. Once stores started posting their goods on websites and online auctions, it changed the dynamics. But..." She pressed together her lips.

"What?" The woman tipped her head to the side. "Is something wrong?"

"I suppose you'll think I'm a hypocrite. I am in the process of opening an online store myself."

The woman grinned. "Then I'll look forward to checking in on your site every so often." She held up her hand. "This piece is perfect. A unique souvenir from a special vacation. We stayed on the outskirts of town."

"Oh, you were guests at the ranch?" She inflected a hint of surprise, like the Kincaid ranch wasn't the only lodging within forty miles for out of towners.

"Yes. We had a marvelous time. I can only imagine what you might find on that property."

The stranger had no idea. In the last few weeks, Meg discovered valuable objects and painful truths. She wouldn't trouble the customer with either.

"Where did you find this? I haven't seen one like it."

"I picked it out of a box at a garage sale in Chicago. I was visiting my mom and dragged her along one Saturday."

"Chicago?" The woman whistled. "That's a long way from Montana. What made you leave a big city? Did you grow up here?"

Meg shook her head. "No, ma'am. My mother did. I spent summers here as a child. My family owned the Hawke ranch, next door to the Kinkaid's place."

"I'm sure you must have had a lot of family heirlooms, too." The woman turned toward her companion, raising on tiptoe. "Ford, I need my wallet. See? Record time."

Ford pushed off the wall.

Meg hustled behind the counter and rang up the mold, accepting and swiping the extended credit card before handing it back with the receipt. She grabbed a stack of tissue paper, setting it on the glass.

The woman placed the mold in the center.

"What is *that*?" Ford asked.

Meg suppressed a smirk at the incredulous tone and wrapped the mold. She grabbed a paper bag emblazoned with the Finders-Keepers logo and placed the mold inside.

"Get your head out of the gutter, dear. It's a turkey." The woman grabbed the bag by the handles and pressed it into his chest. "I'll meet you outside."

Ford shrugged and tipped his head toward Meg.

"Can I help you with anything else?" Meg asked.

"Do you have a mailing list? Any way I can follow your store before your website is up? I'll be back to visit Ryan next summer of course."

The guest was on a first-name basis at the ranch? Meg grabbed a card from the holder next to the register.

"I think I saw you dancing at the barn last night."

Meg couldn't escape from public view at her store? Was her house the only remaining refuge? She wasn't sure where the bossy stranger would direct the conversation. She wanted it to stop here. She flipped over the business card and jotted down the website address she'd secured in pencil on the smooth back, extending it with a tight smile.

"You make a nice pair." The woman grabbed the card. "Good bye, and thank you again." Without a backward glance, the customers left.

The overhead bell jingled as the door opened and shut.

A loud yawn echoed in the silent room.

Meg stared at her dog.

Stretching, Colby got to her feet and pressed against Meg's thigh.

Absentmindedly, Meg stroked the dog's head. If she couldn't escape her feelings at her store, how would she find peace in Herd? She had an inkling but wasn't ready. Because once she laid her heart at his feet, he'd either trample it or embrace her.

She wasn't sure which scared her more.

Instead, she reached into her purse and pulled out her laptop. Powering on the device, she clicked on her blog and hit compose on a new post. She stared at the blinking cursor against the bright, white digital background.

If she penned her letter to the town, poured her hopes and fears into a searchable document, she wouldn't be able to shy away from the problem. "I can't hide from myself."

Colby woofed.

With a smile at her dog, Meg rolled her heavy head and focused on the screen. Lifting her fingers to the keyboard, she dashed her hands across the keys, the rapid clicking not quite keeping pace with her thoughts.

"History is messy, and small-town living is complicated.

"Herd isn't uniquely immune to real-world problems. Perhaps, to visitors, we are a picture-perfect Old West town trapped in time. Locals and transplants, however, know we chose this place and reaffirm our commitment to it every day.

"Not every mistake can be fixed. I'm starting to think that's the point. We can't unsay hurtful things yelled in ignorance, but we can strive to do better. I'm not sure how many people actually read this blog besides my mother and my favorite cowboy. If you are a regular visitor here, you're used to getting stories of some of the unique objects I sell in my store. This post is different.

"Recently, I've learned some history about our town that is hard to process. Full details are not my story to tell, but I can share the following. Under the tourist friendly image is a legacy of loss and betrayal. During the early years, neighbors treated each other with a cutthroat ruthlessness and did the same to the greater landscape.

"Today, our Herd is a kinder place, and we are blessed to live during easier times. The town wouldn't exist without the founders, but reconciling their actions for our positive outcome is difficult. As the last Hawke in town, my presence has never been questioned. I have struggled to fit into the community.

"I have doubts about how I connect. Am I here because of name alone? I've loved this place from my earliest memories and am grateful for the ability to try to build a life for myself here. I strive to do my best to honor the people who came before and the promise of those to follow.

"Herd was founded for a new chance. Under the greed and pain, the initial premise was good. I want to carry that spirit into the future. One person is presenting the community as a whole with an opportunity to pay retribution. It's not my place to tell. When the news comes out, I hope you'll listen. I want us all to lean into everything that makes us great as we repair past hurts."

Colby snored and swatted the ground with her paws, scratching the pine floor.

Meg hit publish, closed the laptop, and returned the computer to her purse. If she determined to be brave, she couldn't back down from her words now. Of course, she had no guarantee the person she wanted to read the words would. "I have hope," she murmured.

Ryan spent the remainder of his day in a rush. From one request to another emergency, he stumbled into the busy pattern of his normal life. He usually liked it.

Guests had questions, comments, and concerns. He was the ultimate authority on the land. Some might find the process too cyclical with the constant turnover of the rooms. Not him. He'd rather have work than endless time on his hands. This was one of the reasons why he started the enterprise.

He locked up the barn and headed toward the shed. After ripping apart the yurt, he almost banished thoughts of the historical expert from his mind. He couldn't shake Meg.

She said she wouldn't leave but that didn't mean her life wouldn't change. She was alone. If he didn't have Hank, he would be, too. He couldn't bear it any more than he could watching her with someone else. He was jealous and foolish.

He cut through the yard, close to where she had been earlier. When she had turned, the sunlight had dappled on her profile and shimmered on her copper strands. She had waited. For a declaration? He had had no idea what came next. Like a coward, he had escaped.

Sniggering, he shook his head. The truth was always a sound starting point. He needed more time. If he could secure the ranch's future, he'd focus on personal matters. He sniffed and caught a phantom hint of her lavender scent on the breeze. He was right to put distance between them.

He had his life, and she had hers. Besides Hank, they had no reason to interact. He opened the shed door and squinted in the dark interior. The building was nearly empty. He sighed and kicked a box left on the ground. She'd written donate on the cardboard in loopy letters.

He rolled his eyes. She always had to be noticed. *Not fair. I can't help but stop everything and watch her.*

"Hey," a voice called.

With a jerk, he twisted around and pinched a nerve in his lower back.

Ted frowned. "Sorry, should have knocked. You okay?"

Ryan winced, rubbing a hand on his back. "How can I help?"

"I'm finishing for the day. Wanted to give you a heads up. I'll take those boxes into town tomorrow. Then the project is done. Just in time for Hank's birthday. Who would have thought?" Ted shook his head.

Definitely not me. Ryan couldn't shake the ominous feeling. He was missing something important.

Hank wouldn't have cleaned up without a purpose. What was it? Really just matchmaking, like he implied?

Or a fear of his mortality? At almost eighty-nine, Hank was the longest living member of the Kincaid family tree. If Ryan had any say, he'd keep his grandfather around forever. One day, he'd have to let go.

"I'm heading home for supper. Thanks, Ted. See you tomorrow."

Ted strode out of the shed.

Ryan followed, shutting the door.

With a wave, Ted set off for his cabin. For nine months for the year, he ruled over the opposite side of the pond by himself. His two-bedroom abode was a recent build next to the renovated bunk house, now a co-ed dorm for summer spa staff, facing the guest quarters. Change was inevitable.

Ryan dragged his gaze to the darkened house and frowned. For years, Hank teased Ryan about Meg driving him crazy.

But Hank never conducted such sloppy setups. Was he worried about running out of time?

Jogging up the back steps, Ryan opened the door to the kitchen. The house was silent, dark, and still. No hint of cut herbs and simmering spices curled in the air. No snoring greeted him. Twisting his neck from one side to the next, he squinted but saw nothing. He stepped forward, letting the door slam shut and cupping his hands around his mouth. "Hank!? Hank!?"

The kitchen was empty.

He strode across the slate floor, pushed open the swinging door, and blinked rapidly. The lights in the front of the house were on. He darted his gaze through the family room turned lobby, and his heart dropped to his knees.

"Hank?!" The name ripped from his throat was more guttural than enunciated.

Sitting in a spindle back armchair near the stone fireplace, Hank slumped. He was ghostly pale.

"Hank! Hank!" Ryan leaped across the room, narrowing the gap in seconds with one big jump.

Hank's head lolled against his chest, spittle dripping from the corner of his mouth. His chest barely moved with shallow inhalations.

"Don't worry, Hank. I'm getting you help. You'll be fine." Ryan pulled the phone out of his pocket and texted Ted *9-1-1*. Then he called the paramedics.

Within seconds, the front door opened and crashed against the wall.

Ted raced into the room. "Let's get him into the truck. Maybe we can meet the ambulance at the end of the road."

Ryan nodded. He lifted his grandfather under the armpits, hoisting him to his feet. In his hold, the once strong bull of a cowboy was slight and shrunken. *You can't go anywhere now. I won't let you.*

Ted grabbed Hank's legs. Together, they carried Hank out the front door. By the time they reached the gravel drive, flashing lights and blaring sirens stopped them in their tracks.

Ryan tightened his grip. He couldn't let go. Readjusting his hold until his knuckles whitened, he clutched the one person who had been his constant in life. *I need more time.* How much did he need to learn about life from Hank? His work wasn't done. If Ryan had to fight or bargain with a higher power, he'd do exactly that.

In slow motion, the ambulance parked. An EMT jumped from the driver's side, leaving the door ajar and racing to the back. After an interminable few seconds' pause, the EMT reappeared wheeling a gurney opposite another uniformed person.

Holding up Hank offered Ryan the only tangible, physical support. He locked his knees and stood as straight and motionless as possible.

The EMTs stopped inches away and motioned for Hank.

For a second, Ryan pulled back. This was all wrong. None of this was supposed to be happening. Hank shouldn't die alone in a hospital, forgotten and scared. Tears stung the back of Ryan's throat.

With a reassuring word from the paramedics, Ryan, Ted, and the two professionals lowered Hank onto a gurney. One EMT fastened an oxygen mask, covering Hank's nose and mouth. The other explained instructions.

A low buzzing filled Ryan's ears. What started low increased in volume like someone playing with a dial on a car radio. What were the EMTs saying? He couldn't make sense of the words as he stared at their moving lips.

Thankfully, Ted remained. He listened and nodded.

Ryan stood in place, having difficulty in processing information and senses.

Ted was mobile. Taking the front steps two at a time, he raced up and locked the house. His heavy footfall, as he jogged back down, registered somewhere in Ryan's mind.

Ted loaded Ryan into the truck and drove to the hospital, following the flashing lights.

Was the siren blaring? Ryan took a deep breath, straining for any sound outside of his body. He heard nothing.

The paramedics didn't need to blare the emergency alert. In the middle of nowhere, they didn't need to stop traffic. Neither would they need to draw attention to the sad news. Without a doubt, everyone in Herd would know within twelve hours.

But would she?

He turned toward the window, biting his nail. Why hadn't she been there? Where was Colby? Weren't dogs supposed to alert others to danger and get help? Blaming her didn't ease his guilt about avoiding the house after letting down his grandfather the night before. Forcing her to be the scapegoat was his only option.

If Hank succumbed, he'd abandon Ryan. On his own, he'd be alone all over again. The prospect shouldn't be as terrifying as an adult as it had been in his childhood. His primal fear gripped him tight. He hated the fate he couldn't seem to escape. At least, this time, he had a villain. This was Meg's fault.

CHAPTER 17

After Meg sold the ice cream mold, she helped another customer. She smiled and chatted, selling a pair of boots and a hat. She rang up the purchase and followed the woman from the store. She was ready to lock up for the evening and start inventorying the books. Standing in the open doorway, she waved goodbye.

"Meg!" a feminine voice called from down the block.

She turned toward the sound, cheeks burning. The voice was crisp and commanding, like a teacher correcting a naughty student. When she spotted the blonde in the colorful dress barreling down the sidewalk, she widened her gaze. "Stephanie?"

"Hi," Stephanie said, slightly breathless, and stopped a few feet away. "Glad I caught you. How are you?"

Meg pressed a hand to her collarbone. "I'm fine." She scanned the other woman. In a dress, she was a little too put together for a regular day. Had she been at a meeting for the school? "Do you need something?"

Stephanie held up a finger and slowed her breathing, taking several big gulps of air. "Yes, I do." She drew in another deep breath. "By any chance, could you be the master of ceremonies for the auction and dinner at Frontier Days?"

Meg twisted her neck but spotted no one else on the stretch of wooden sidewalk. "Are you sure you mean me?"

"Yes, you would be doing me a huge favor."

"I don't know if I'm qualified. It's a big role."

Stephanie nodded. "We need a good storyteller. That's you."

Me? Meg shook her head. She wasn't a writer and couldn't spin a yarn, not like Hank Kincaid. Neither was she the town historian like Joe. Where had Stephanie gotten the impression Meg had any qualifications? She hated to miss the opportunity to participate, but she couldn't lead Stephanie on. "Are you certain you mean me?"

"Of course. I love reading the Finders-Keepers blog. My colleagues first told me about the site. You tell some great stories about the town. Not lately, though."

Meg stiffened. "I've been busy."

Stephanie shook her blonde hair behind her back. "I was touched by what you just posted. I get alerts on my phone."

Meg cringed.

"No, don't be embarrassed. You were real and vulnerable. I don't think I could be so staggeringly self-aware in such a public way." Stephanie smiled.

The friendly expression softened the sting. If she thought she had an audience, she would never have shared such a vulnerable entry. She wasn't sure why she turned to the internet instead of a notebook. Next time, she'd do better.

"I relate a lot to the sentiment. It's tough to take pleasure in what our town has to offer when we know more of the pain in the past," Stephanie said.

We all have the opportunity to make some amends. Yet another gift Ryan bestowed on the town.

"In fact, I'd love to have you come in to speak to my class next year," Stephanie continued. "History is complicated, but untangling memories piece by piece is illuminating."

What could Meg say to a bunch of kindergartners? Why not ask Joe? He was the go-to resource for the town's past. Wasn't he writing a book and interviewing everyone he could?

If you want a friend, be a friend. A chance to participate in the community, to be someone others leaned on, might never come again if she turned Stephanie down. "I'd love to help with Frontier Days. I'm not sure about presenting to five-year-olds."

Stephanie chuckled. "You'd be great at both. I'm ecstatic to have you involved in this year's event. Thank you so much."

"I don't know what to do. How should I begin? What are your expectations?"

"We can meet and go over the whole thing. I'll help. It'll be fun." The beaming smile brightened Stephanie's whole face.

Would it? Meg had wished for an opening to participate. The last time she had graced the town stage, she hadn't been alone. Ryan couldn't be lured to her aid again. If she wasted her chance, she squandered an opportunity at a friendship, too. She couldn't remember her last interaction with a peer in a social setting. "Okay, I'm in. I'll look forward to it."

"Great. Can we meet tomorrow at The Golden Crown? Let's meet for supper at six. I'm running late for an appointment. I've got to run now." Stephanie waved, spun on her heel, and jogged down the wooden sidewalk.

Turning, Meg stepped inside her store. She felt lighter than she had in years, since first deciding to move. Her dreams stood a chance.

Ryan included? She strode to the back and gathered her things and her dog. She'd rather do the work of inventorying from the comfort of her home. She couldn't handle another person acknowledging what happened last night or what she'd just posted on her blog. Locking for the night, she and Colby hopped into the SUV and drove home.

She opened the trunk and grabbed one box of books, leaving the rest for the morning. If only she could push aside her thoughts for a few hours, too, she might have peace. Shutting the trunk, she followed Colby, jostling the heavy box in her arms and leaning against the siding as she fiddled with the keys.

She couldn't shake the worry she'd let down Hank. He'd been one of the constants in her life. From her early childhood, she knew she could count on Hank Kincaid. He had never asked her for anything before showing up at the store and inquiring about the project. She shut the front door and dropped the box on the kitchen table, next to stacks of library books and a legal pad filled with more questions than answers.

Why had Hank asked for her help now? What was she missing?

While she'd turned to him for assistance with everything from a skinned knee riding her bike between the ranches to repairing the leaky faucet in the kitchen, she couldn't remember him every doing the same in return. He showed up with a smile and a friendly word. He was the closest she'd ever had to a grandfather.

As she served Colby dinner and ate leftovers over the kitchen sink, she mentally drafted another blog post about the discovery. She wouldn't divulge the particulars of the value but rather how the experience changed her. Without the unexpected shake-up in her routine, she would have been locked into one perspective her whole life.

No, she couldn't do the fun part. She had to put in the real work for her business. Pulling up a chair, she sat at the kitchen table. Covered with books about website building and the basics of coding, she'd ignored the work for too long. She grabbed the legal pad and found her laptop in the purse on top of the box. She grabbed the slim device and powered on the computer. Her to-do list grew every day. She uncapped a pen and added another: list books online ASAP.

With a sigh, she pulled up her website. She could only learn so much from reading and worrying. She needed practical experience. For several hours, she focused on the work, her vision blurring as she typed code and attempted to fix flaws in the long strings of letters, numbers, and characters. Her handiwork might have improved or ruined her website but at least she made progress. She stretched her arms over head and arched her back, adjusting on the chair behind her kitchen table.

In the corner of the room, Colby snored. She earned her snooze.

Meg dropped her arms and rolled her neck. She wished she could say the same. Had Hank wanted her to take charge of her destiny? She owed him a call and a thanks for the push. She scanned the room, where was her cell phone? Had she left it in her purse? Shortly after moving in, she gave up on the house line. The cost was excessive for one person who was usually in town.

Rifling through her bag, she came up empty. She swallowed the groan at the mental slip. Leaving her phone in her vehicle was dangerous and irresponsible.

She grabbed the keys and raced outside. In the cupholder, the phone screen flashed bright. She frowned. A call? She must have turned the device onto silent at some point. She opened the door and grabbed the phone, frowning at the screen. She'd missed calls and texts for the last three hours.

In her clammy hands, her grip loosened, and the phone clattered to the ground under the car. She shut the door and laid on the ground, reaching for the phone. With her fingertips, she brushed the device's edge. Scooting under the car, she grabbed the cell, pinching the nerves in her neck. Wincing, she uncoiled her body and straightened.

She unlocked the phone and stared at the list of calls. All from Ryan? Her heart skipped a beat. As much as she wished he sought her out to apologize for the day's snubbing, she feared the worst. He wasn't the type to call nonstop. On a good day, he was an uneasy conversationalist.

She called back, and the other line rang and rang.

She bit her bottom lip. Did he think she'd been purposefully avoiding him? Was he trying to give her in-kind treatment?

"Hello?" Ryan said.

She scrunched her nose at the gruff tone. "Ryan, hi. I'm so sorry. I got busy and left my phone in the car."

"Meg, stop. You need to come to the hospital. Hank passed out. I don't know what happened."

She sucked in a sharp breath, tears stinging her eyes. "I'm on my way."

She hung up the phone and raced inside, grabbing her purse, kissing Colby on the head, and locking up the house. She hopped behind the wheel, turned over the engine, and prayed hard. She had to make it to Hank. She had to do what he asked her and be honest with Ryan. Or, harder, be truthful with herself.

CHAPTER
18

Ryan hated hospitals ever since, as a young child, he had woken up in a bed with Grandma stroking his hair and Grandpa explaining what had happened. A car accident. No one's fault. A tragedy.

Ryan had lost his memory of that night, and he'd never regained it. He accepted it as a small mercy. While he couldn't remember his parents' final moments, he could hold on to every other piece of his life before and be grateful for everything that came after.

Loss never defined his life. He'd grown up surrounded by love. He'd put all his faith in his grandparents and was never steered wrong. Now he sat on a hard chair in the lobby, waiting for word and fearing what came next.

Shortly after arrival, he'd flagged down the paramedics and was given the news. Hank had been rushed straight into emergency. They couldn't share more and told Ryan to wait. In the lobby, he paced back and forth. Meg should be here.

He'd put distance between them. She waved, and he turned away. Because he couldn't do more without being absolutely vulnerable. He'd never wanted to be so scared and out of control as he'd been at five, the only survivor in a car accident. Controlling every variable kept him safe.

Today, his need for sameness endangered everything that mattered. He'd pushed her away. She'd left, and Hank had been unattended.

Because he refused to be honest and accepted her announcement as pushback against any change to his comfort level, he was alone. It was his fault.

A call from the ranch sent Ted back after twenty minutes. Alone, Ryan started calling her. With each hit to her voice mail, his blood pressure rose. After a few terse words, he'd hang up and start the process again. He couldn't stop. Because doing so meant giving up or accepting she didn't care or worse was in danger. He couldn't lose her, too. For hours, he tortured himself with unanswered calls. Until finally, she had called him.

She's never been mine. The phone call was brief. He couldn't say more without breaking down. Resting his face in his hands, he stared at the tile floor and breathed in the smell of industrial cleaner. He wanted to leave this place as soon as he could.

"Mr. Kincaid?"

He snapped up his head and frowned at a young doctor, scrubs peeking out from under the white coat. Ryan stood, dusting his palms on his jeans. "Yes, hello. I'm Ryan. Hank's grandson. How is he?"

The doctor, a man probably a few years younger than Ryan, nodded. "I'd like to keep him overnight. Possibly for two nights. I want to monitor him, but he didn't have a heart attack."

"What happened?"

The doctor frowned. "We are still running tests. The best guess is a panic attack."

"Panic?" Ryan drew back his chin. Hank the big strong cowboy was overwhelmed and incapacitated by panic? How?

"It can mimic a heart attack. Given his age, I'd like to observe him for a couple nights to be sure we aren't missing something else."

Ryan couldn't argue with that but had trouble connecting the pieces. Had he been the source of anxiety for Hank? "He'll be here for his birthday on Thursday?"

"Not necessarily. He's awake. Would you like to come back and see him?"

"Sure." Ryan rubbed together his clammy palms, turning toward the door. She wasn't here yet. He faced the doctor again. "A family fr..." He coughed. "I have more family coming. Can I leave her name with someone so she's allowed to visit?"

"Is her last name Kincaid?"

Ryan shook his head.

The doctor pulled a piece of paper and pen from his pocket. "Write it down, and I'll let the front desk know."

Ryan scribbled the name and handed both back to the doctor.

"Mr. Kincaid, your grandfather is a healthy man. We are being cautious. I want to assuage your fears about why we are keeping him."

"Thank you. I appreciate that."

The doctor turned and pushed through a swinging door, leading the way down the corridor.

The bright, white space was blinding. Florescent lights bounced off every surface.

Ryan's vision blurred. He blinked back the tears, overcoming the emotion he'd buried so deep in his efforts to be every bit the cowboy Hank was. Had he missed the biggest hurdle? Love? Hank had Susie. His strength was wound so tightly with his faith and respect for his wife. She remained his guiding force years after her death. What did Ryan have besides work? *A woman I've loved and kept on the sidelines.*

The doctor stopped and twisted a doorknob, opening the door. "I'll leave you two alone."

Ryan entered the room. Stuffing his hands in his pockets, he dragged in a shaky breath and inhaled the cleaner smell again. Past the bathroom, a bed faced a TV and window.

Dressed in a gown with a blanket over his lap, Hank pushed the buttons on the remote.

He looked too human for Ryan's lifelong image of the man as a superhero.

"Oh good. You're here. Can you fix this thing?" Hank dropped the remote on the bed and folded his arms over his chest. "Stuck in a hospital for my eighty-ninth birthday, and I can't even find the game."

Ryan frowned and approached the bed, grabbing the remote and powering off the TV. "What game?"

"Any game. I'd settle for golf at this point."

Ryan rolled his eyes. "It's late, and you need to rest so you can celebrate your eighty-ninth birthday. Do you remember what happened?"

Hank shook his head, pursing his lips.

"Were you alone and overexerting yourself in the shed?"

"No, after Meg left, I went into the kitchen. I felt a little dizzy, and my gut burned." Hank rubbed a hand along his breastbone. "I sat down. I woke up here."

Exhaling a pent-up breath, Ryan relaxed. He didn't want to blame her but struggled with his default setting. Trouble and Meg were synonymous. "Any tightness in your chest? Pain in your arm?"

"It wasn't a heart attack." Hank rolled his eyes. "I don't know how else to describe what happened, but I know it wasn't my chest."

"What did you feel?"

"I was starting supper. Suddenly, I felt weak like all my energy drained. My head started spinning so I sat down."

"I'm so mad at Meg." Ryan gritted his molars, rubbing his jaw. "She should have been there."

"Boy, what are you talking about?" Hank pushed himself up on the hospital bed. In the thin, blue-patterned gown, with a blanket draped over his lap, he couldn't assure his usual, stern expression. "Did you hire me a babysitter while I wasn't looking?"

"No, of course not."

"Pardon?" Hank folded his arms over his chest. "Am I mistaken then? Did you give her another reason to hang around?"

Ryan strode to the window and gazed at the parking lot. Meg was her own person and had reasons for her actions. Answering Hank's question would only push the man's buttons.

Had Ryan somehow caused Hank's episode? With his stresses mounting, Ryan hadn't paid attention to his grandfather. He'd disappointed his grandmother's memory. He was supposed to take care of the older man, and instead he neglected him. While Ryan was distracted, had he missed obvious signs of poor health?

Turning around, he leaned against the windowsill. "Can I ask…" He pinched the bridge of his nose. Pressure built behind his eyes, his temples throbbing. "What was the real reason you started cleaning out the shed?" He dropped his hand to the side and met his grandfather's gaze. "Were you trying to set me up with Meg? Or settling your affairs in case you…"

"In case I died?"

Ryan pushed off the window, folded his arms over his chest, and broadened his stance. He hated saying that word. As the silence stretched, he nodded.

"I'm not afraid of dying, boy. When it's my time, it's my time. I wouldn't mind seeing my Susie again." A wistful smile lifted the corners of Hank's mouth. "I worry about you."

I know. Ryan frowned and gripped his upper arms. "The reason?"

"If I say both, will you be mad?"

Ryan shook his head. Years ago, he and Hank reached an agreement that neither would hold a grudge if the other was being honest.

"Then that's my answer. I'm tired of waiting on you and Meg to figure out what is right in front of you. I thought maybe I could get you two together and clean out my shed in one go. Now I'm done, and I can't enjoy the new space. I'm not going anywhere anytime soon. At least not according to the doctor." He sighed. "I can't have cake."

The words were so bitter, Ryan lifted the corner of his mouth. He couldn't stop the smile.

"They told me I'm here for at least two nights, and I'm on a salt free, sugar free, fun free diet." Hank held up his hands. "And I didn't have a heart attack! This place is the worst."

"Hank, it's one birthday. You'll be okay."

"When you get to eighty-nine you don't skimp on any celebration."

"We'll have cake when you get home. If you do as the nurses say, maybe you can go home on your special day. Two nights counts tonight."

"I better get to leave. The wish only works if you blow out a candle on the actual day and eat the cake."

"Why are you so feisty? Did you have a wish lined up?"

Hank lifted his chin. "I always do."

A knock sounded on the door, saving Ryan from formulating whatever response he could muster. He hated for Hank to waste any wishes on him.

The knock sounded again.

Ryan stepped around the end of the bed. "Come in."

The door opened.

Meg poked her head around the side of the panel. "Hi," she murmured.

"Come in, come in, he's decent." Ryan turned to his grandfather and arched a brow. "Or as decent as he's going to get."

Hank narrowed his gaze. "Don't listen to him."

Meg passed Ryan, approaching the bed and hugging Hank.

Her light, lavender scent saved Ryan from the overpowering aroma of hopelessness the walls of the building contained. She grounded him. Why hadn't he understood until his grandfather's life was endangered? *Don't wait for life or death*. Marcia and Ford had warned him.

"Hank, are you feeling alright?" She stepped back, out of the hug, but remained at the bedside.

Hank held her hands. "I am, darling. I'm disappointed about my birthday. I wanted to celebrate at the ranch."

She turned to Ryan, tilting her head. "He won't?"

"We don't know yet. Maybe. I promise, with a witness, your ninetieth will be a celebration Herd has never seen."

Hank's grin lit up his entire face, his color brightening. "You swear, boy?"

With one finger, Ryan crossed his heart. He'd do anything to keep his grandfather hale and hearty, including the probable disruption of his ranch for the better part of next summer. He lifted his gaze to Meg.

She nodded.

Their unspoken communication remained operational. What would happen if he was frank with his feelings? *Now or never.* "Can I talk to you? In the hall?"

She widened her gaze, her cheeks pinking.

Hank patted her hands. "Go with him. I'll be fine. Just a little scare, but they want to keep me for a few days."

"Better safe than sorry. Have a good rest, Hank." She kissed his forehead and strode to the door, biting her lip as she passed. The door shut behind her.

"Don't mess this up, boy," Hank said.

Ryan hoped he wouldn't. He exited the room and spotted Meg leaning against the opposite wall.

She met his gaze and stepped forward. "Please understand I wasn't avoiding your phone calls and texts. I legitimately forgot my phone in the car. I was working on the website and lost track of time."

"I didn't think you were."

"You didn't?" Her voice cracked. "There were so many messages and voice mails. I haven't checked them all. I didn't want you to think I was trying to play a game with you because you didn't acknowledge me today."

He swallowed pushing down the horseshoe sized lump stuck on his Adam's apple. He had snubbed her. "I know you aren't petty. I didn't think you were playing tit for tat."

"So...why?"

Her words were so soft. *Because you're the only person who would understand what I was feeling.* She slipped between his defenses like a knife slicing between his ribs and lodging straight in his heart. He spent his time wrapped up in worrying about tomorrow. In doing so, he ignored today.

When he got home from the hospital, he realized what he pushed away—happily ever after. Was he ready now? He hated his vulnerability. "I needed you to know."

"About Hank?" She tiptoed toward him, cutting the distance between them from feet to inches. "Is there anything else I need to know?"

"I...can't talk about..." He scrubbed both hands over his face. Why was this so hard? He didn't need another pep talk about honesty. He'd had his fill. He felt raw and exposed.

Was it the location? The subject matter? The brush with death? Hank never let him live in fear. Any time Ryan hesitated ever, his grandfather jumped in to encourage him to try. What if Hank's words at the dinner last night had been the last piece of advice?

The doctors only wanted to keep him for a short period but what if something else happened? Ryan learned to focus on the future so he could manage his daily expectations. No living soul was guaranteed a tomorrow. He stopped worrying about the next day and looked a year or three into the future, constantly moving the target. The advice was to live in the moment. He'd never figured out how.

"I wanted to talk earlier today," she said, her chin trembling. "After a discussion I had with Hank. I've disappointed him."

"No more than I have, I'm sure." Ryan shook his head.

She sniffed and swiped at her glistening eyes.

His gut clenched, and he set his jaw. He could handle anything but tears.

"When I thought he was gone?" Her voice cracked.

"Shh." He closed the distance between them and reached out, brushing hair behind her ears. He only touched her with the very tip of his fingers. Any more and he'd crumble.

Under the fluorescent lights, against the stark white of the sterile space, she was beautiful. Her hair shimmered with red catching in the artificial light. She stood before him with no artifice.

Holding his gaze, she dragged in a breath and looked straight through him. "I promised Hank."

Ryan removed his hand and stepped back. "Please, not..." He wasn't even sure how he intended to finish. Not now? Not here? Not ever?

"Okay." She nodded and dusted her hands on her jeans. "I'm heading home. Please make sure Hank knows if he needs anything, I'm around." She spun on her heel, her shoes clacking against the tile.

The door at the end of the hall opened and shut, the swinging creating a breeze that blew away her lavender smell and left him with pain. He had himself to thank.

CHAPTER 19

The next evening, Meg pushed through the swinging front door of The Golden Crown. Her senses were assaulted from every direction. Animal mounts loomed overhead, staring at the occupants with beady eyes brightened by the rows of electrified kerosene-style hanging fixtures. Underfoot, sawdust covered the floor in a thin layer, muffling heavy steps. Though no longer required to soak up the tobacco spit, the sweet sawdust smell covered the scent of spilled beer.

The saloon was the only official restaurant in town and welcomed families as well as regulars. Along one wall, the impressive walnut bar spanned the length of the building. In the back corner, the poker club held court. The low rumble of masculine laughter from the card players mixed with the buzz of conversations and occasional high-pitched squeal of laughter.

Twisting her neck, she scanned the crowded space. She should have called and canceled the meeting with Stephanie. In light of last evening's events, the kind-hearted teacher would understand. Hank's hospitalization was a convenient excuse for her inner turmoil.

Ryan asked her to talk later. But did he really want to have the conversation? Or had he pushed her away and, for once and for all, rejected her? Meg spent the day feeling useless. She wasn't sure she could handle company but at least the meeting promised her a distraction from her pain.

At a table near the center of the room, Stephanie sat with sheets of paper strewn across the circular, oak top.

Meg navigated through the maze of tables and stopped at the seat opposite. "Hi, Stephanie." She pulled out a chair, the feet scraping the ground.

Stephanie glanced up.

For a second, her stare was as blank as Big Barry, the massive, stuffed bison head mount centered on the back wall.

"Oh, hi, Meg." Stephanie gathered the papers into a messy stack, clearing the table. "Sorry, just going over some details for Frontier Days. Please sit. Thanks for meeting me. I wasn't sure..."

Word traveled fast, as Meg expected. She scooted her chair closer to the table, moving her purse into her lap and retrieving a small notepad and pen. "Yeah, I wasn't sure either."

She still wasn't. Her closest confidantes were Mom and Hank. With one in the hospital and the other over a thousand miles away, she had no one to commiserate with about the Ryan situation. Instead, she spent her night replaying the whole scene. "I need to feel useful today."

"Will he be alright?" Stephanie asked.

"He's getting great care." Meg forced a smile. He was. The scare shook her to her core. She knew the fragility of life. No one could live forever. Hank almost convinced her otherwise. "Persuading him to take things easy when he gets home will be the real challenge."

"How are you?"

Meg rubbed a hand over her itchy nose. Did Stephanie mean about Hank or Ryan? In small towns, everyone knew everyone else's business. The hospital hallway discussion was probably overheard. Meg anticipated the question. The genuine caring in the teacher's delivery pierced Meg in the heart. "I'm a little shaken."

"Of course you are. He's pretty much your grandfather, too. You must have some amazing stories about growing up here."

Meg shook her head. "Not as many as Ryan. I only spent my summers here. We did manage a certain amount of good-hearted mischief."

"I don't think I've ever heard Ryan in anything less than a professional capacity, and I've definitely never heard any personal anecdotes."

"He takes his responsibilities to town very seriously. He's always been stoic. Even as a kid." Meg lifted the corner of her mouth as a memory tickled the back of her brain. "Once, he did prank Hank. I helped. Hank had been giving Ryan a hard time about being too responsible. Ryan did his chores and then some. If he wasn't working at the ranch, he was reading and studying. He always wanted to make Hank and Susie proud."

"I'm confused. Where's the trouble?"

"Hank wanted Ryan to be a kid and not act like a small adult. Hank used to say all the time, we'd have years of being grown-ups." *He was so right.* Hank was as stubborn as he was talkative and charming. Shaking him off an idea was nigh impossible for anyone but Susie.

The problem with always having a lot to say was others had trouble knowing when to listen. Everything Hank said had value. How could anyone absorb each piece of advice?

Stephanie leaned forward.

"Ryan decided to give Hank what Hank claimed he wanted. I lured him to the stables, and he tripped a wire. A bucket of corn syrup upended onto his head. Ryan popped out with a fan and blew a bag of feathers on his grandpa. I've never seen Hank so angry or Ryan run so fast. After getting punished, Ryan went back to being his industrious self, and Hank never said a word to discourage him again."

Stephanie chuckled. "I can't even imagine those two acting like that. Ryan goofing and Hank yelling is so out of character for both." She propped her other elbow on the table, interlacing her hands. "What was town like?"

"Quiet. For me, it was such a welcome, restful change from living in the city. All the space and fresh air rejuvenated me. As an adult, I can think back and understand how strained the economy was and the toll on folks. The turnaround has been wonderful."

"I'm glad for it. I can't imagine living anywhere else," Stephanie said. "I'd love if you could include tidbits about your experiences into your master of ceremonies role."

I'm not sure how much I can include when it mostly involves Ryan. If he pushed back against Meg last night, he wouldn't want her implying they had a connection on stage. Was he interested in someone else in town? The thought burned like the old Kincaid ranch branding iron. "How much do I need to prepare? Is this like a monologue?"

Stephanie shook her head. "Don't worry, you need an oratory. You'll welcome the guests and give a run-down of the evening's events. You'll run the auction and introduce the band. Any point where you can add a personal point of reference or anecdote is what we're looking for."

Like the time I tricked Ryan into partnering me on stage? Heat crept up her face.

Stephanie riffled through her stack of papers. "I should have something to guide you in here. Let me look."

With her head down, she was hopefully oblivious to Meg's burning cheeks. Pressing a cool hand to her hot skin, she darted her gaze through the room. In the corner, she met Ted's steady stare.

He nodded and pushed back his chair, striding toward her.

Her heart stuck in her throat. Was he about to deliver bad news? Why else cut short a round of cards with his friends?

"Here is a timetable and a list of auction prizes so far." Stephanie slid a paperclipped bundle across the table. "If you want to get started, you can keep this and make your notes. We can meet up again whenever you're free. I'm not teaching summer school this year, and my classes at the ranch finish before noon. I have a lot of availability an—"

Booted steps cut off the rest of her speech.

Ted stopped at the side of the table, between Stephanie and Meg. "Evening, ladies." He reached for the brim of his hat and tugged it off.

Meg's chest tightened. "Hello, Ted. Are you here for poker?"

For a second, he frowned then scrubbed a hand over his face. "Yes, ma'am. Every week if I get the chance."

Good, he'd taken her lead on public niceties and nothing serious. "Will you participate in the tournament in September?" Meg persisted with questions she knew the answers to. *How is*

Ryan? She couldn't think the words without a lump clogging her throat.

Ted opened his mouth.

"Oh, I'm sorry. I'm being so rude. You know Stephanie, of course." Meg cut him off. If she gave him the opportunity to speak, would she like what she heard? She wasn't sure she could take the chance. "She's in charge of the poker tournament among so many other things."

"Good evening." He tipped his head to the other woman. "I've had positive comments from the first round of guests about your yoga classes."

In response, Stephanie stared, slack jawed.

"I'm participating in Frontier Days." Meg barreled through the half second of awkward silence. Any lapse could provide an opening for bad news. "Stephanie has asked me to be the master of ceremonies. Seeing as I love to talk, feels like a natural fit."

"You'll be great." He turned to smile at Stephanie. "You've made an excellent choice."

Stephanie might have said "uh huh" or pushed back her chair. A squeak sounded but her face didn't move. The reaction was strange given Ted's bland grin.

"We're reviewing the responsibilities of the role." Meg shuffled the papers. "Good to see you, Ted. Please don't let us keep you from your game."

Ted shook his head. "Sorry to interrupt your work. Could I have a word, Meg?"

Meg sucked in a breath. He wasn't letting her escape the conversation. She glanced at Stephanie. The frozen woman turned beet red. Who knew embarrassment was so contagious. "I'll be a second, Stephanie. Should we get dinner? Maybe you can flag down a server and get a couple menus?"

"Okay," Stephanie croaked and covered her mouth.

Meg pushed back her chair and stood. "Can we speak outside?" she asked Ted.

He nodded and waved her ahead.

Retracing her earlier route, Meg wound through the other diners and pushed the door outside. She strode toward the replica hitching posts in front and leaned back against the wooden rail. If she needed solid support for the conversation, and the churn in her stomach told her so, she couldn't do much better.

Ted stood opposite. "I'm not good with small talk so I'm coming straight out with it." He crossed his arms over his chest. "You need to come to the ranch."

Her chest tightened. Ted was a good man and a solid friend. He never made demands or requests. His tone was unequivocal. She wanted to do what he asked. She couldn't. "Ryan doesn't want me there."

"He's upset. Whatever was said ... whatever happened ... doesn't matter. You're his family. Come to the ranch."

I'm not. She could have been but Ryan pushed against change. Was there more to Ted's speech? If Ryan felt like this, and shared his concerns, why didn't he come out and address her directly? Why was Ted a mouthpiece? She narrowed her gaze. "How much did he tell you? Did he put you up to this conversation?"

"To answer your questions in order, nothing, and no. He doesn't know what he wants. I have eyes and a brain. I can make sense of other people's relationships. He's hurting."

"How would I know what's best? My appearance might set him off."

Ted held her stare.

She understood Ted's sentiment with startling clarity. She'd known Ryan the longest, second only to Hank. If anyone knew him, it was her. No matter how he felt about her, they'd always have their shared memories. They were connected. He'd flounder when the time eventually came for Hank and Susie's heavenly reunion.

Meg owed Hank and Ryan her undying loyalty even if Ryan would never want her heart. After he pushed her away, however, she couldn't show up unannounced. "I'm sorry, Ted. I can't help. If he invited me, sure. I can't show up. He'll consider it an ambush."

With a slow nod, Ted released a heavy breath and put his hat on his head. "Have a good night."

Unlikely. "Good night." She pushed off the post and strode back inside the saloon. She'd have to swallow her pride for the sake of friendship. But not yet. Her heart throbbed. Eventually, the pain would lessen, and she'd accept the return to their previous roles. Not tonight.

Rinsing the bowl under the kitchen sink faucet, Ryan stared through the window and across the lawn toward the shed. He had so much left to tackle before Hank came home. He didn't wish for more time. He hated the house without his grandpa's booming voice bouncing off the walls.

He couldn't trust himself around the few remaining guests from last weekend and wasn't ready to check-in the new arrivals. Instead, he sequestered inside the shed. Alone with his thoughts and his pain, he started the final push to complete the shed.

He had patched and repaired worn plywood. He'd insulated and added drywall. Electricity would have to wait for a few weeks until the scheduled appointment with the electrician to power the shed with lights and a mini-split to keep the climate comfortable. He needed to paint and lay a proper floor.

With so many tasks remaining, he might stay awake all night to last another painfully silent morning on the ranch. He was so bone-tired from a sleepless night, a full workday, and an evening on the project, his knees almost buckled under his weight. If he went to bed now, however, he'd end up staring at the ceiling on a second night of replaying all the ways he screwed up with Meg. Should he call? Show up? Let her say words he wasn't ready to hear?

The backdoor slammed.

Ryan frowned, meeting Joe's gaze. Why was he here? It was almost nine.

"Are you going to get that?" Joe called, cupping his hands around his mouth.

"Huh?" Ryan moved the bowl to the dish rack and turned off the faucet. He stared at his prune textured fingers.

"The oven," Joe yelled. He jogged across the tile floor, grabbed a pot holder, and opened the door.

Smoke poured out, curling in the air.

Oh no, the cake. With a jolt, Ryan snapped to the present and shut off the timer and oven. Grabbing a thick dish towel, he reached for the rectangular cake pan in Joe's hands. He raced back across the room, throwing the blackened cake in the sink and opening the window.

Blinking through the haze, Ryan batted at the smoke-filled air.

With a fist covering his mouth, Joe coughed and shut the oven door.

He hadn't noticed he ruined the birthday cake. Oblivious to the blaring timer, the pungent burning stench, or how long he'd been rinsing the same bowl, he was trapped in place as he argued with himself. If Joe hadn't alerted him, what would have happened?

Opening the back door, he tilted his head to the exit.

Joe raised his arm, covering his mouth and nose with his inner elbow, and jogged outside.

Ryan followed, leaving the door ajar.

"I hope that wasn't your dinner." Joe coughed into his elbow.

"It was Hank's birthday cake." Ryan leaned against the siding. "I did a pretty good job, too."

"Scratch or mix?"

Ryan shot him a look. His grandfather cooked his meals. On his own, Ryan survived on canned foods and cold sandwiches.

Joe sighed. "I can pick up another box for you tomorrow. Or, better yet, let me call in an order to the General Store."

"I'll get the cake. I'll order it."

"You promise no more unsupervised cooking?"

Ryan rolled his eyes. Under normal circumstances, he could handle light teasing. Joe picked the wrong moment. Nothing was typical today. "Why are you here late? I don't need babysitting."

"I lost track of time." Joe raised a hand to the back of his neck.

Ryan didn't believe him for a second. Ted would be playing poker in town tonight. Had he and Joe come up with a plan to make sure Ryan wasn't unsupervised? He wanted to be right-eously indignant. Since he almost charred his home, however, he couldn't argue in his defense.

"I stopped by because I wanted to see if you needed anything. I wasn't checking up on you. I was worried. I'm trying to be a friend."

Ryan snorted. Joe was a good friend. Ryan didn't have a good track with other people in the last twenty-four hours.

"Are you pushing me away, too?"

"What does that mean?" Ryan drew together his brows, his upper lip curling. Anger bubbled under the surface like a hot spring. What did Joe know? Had Ryan's hospital conversation been overheard and recounted? He hadn't said much but managed enough to hurt someone he cared about deeply.

"It means why isn't Meg here? Why are you alone? You had a huge scare. You shouldn't be by yourself. It's not typical for her to mind her own business as far as you and Hank are concerned. I'm pretty good at putting two and two together." Joe shrugged. "I was a kid detective."

The comment was almost enough to lighten Ryan's mood. He could picture a kid version of Joe holding an oversized magnifying glass and snooping around. Ryan didn't want to be so transparent. It hurt too much. He scrubbed a hand along his jaw, unshaven whiskers scraping against his skin. At least Joe wasn't well-informed enough to know specifics and start refuting Ryan's arguments. "I'm better like this."

"No, you're not." Joe shook his head. "I'm worried you believe your lies."

The soft sincerity threatened Ryan. He couldn't be weak. Everyone—an entire economy—depended on his strength. "Isn't that what we all do?" He croaked and coughed, clearing his scratchy throat. "Don't we tell ourselves what we need to make every day bearable?"

Joe stepped closer, wrinkling his brow. "Hey, are you okay? Should I stay? I'm very worried right now."

I am too. Under the close inspection, Ryan almost caved. He slid down the wall and sat on the porch, legs extending in front of him. Without Hank and Meg, he was trapped in a house and a life haunted by memories and regrets, exactly what his grandpa worried about. In the moment, yesterday, he'd been too terrified for truth. Letting them continue status quo was meant to save them from pain. Neither happened. He still lost, and he got hurt.

If he let her speak or—better—told her the truth about his changed feelings, how suddenly he realized he'd taken for granted the person he needed more than anyone else, would he be out on a covered porch utterly dejected and nearly burning down the legacy he fought so hard to modernize for the chance of a future?

Maybe, maybe not. Fear stole his options. He ended up with no one, like he always feared. Once upon a time, his problems were solved easily. Either a conversation and bear hug from his grandfather, or an apology and ice cream cone with Meg fixed everything. He was desperately unprepared to navigate life alone.

"Do you want me to call her?" Joe sat. "Ask her to stop by?"

Ryan lifted his gaze and stared, unseeing. His next move had to be the opposite of his last. The call to action couldn't be spurred by someone else. He needed a plan, courage, and strength. At the moment, he was an empty shell. He'd finish the shed, seeing a project to completion, clean himself up, and head over to her place after Hank came home. "I know what I need to do. And I promise no more cooking."

Joe chuckled. "I'm glad I stopped you from setting the whole place ablaze. It's been a solid start to the summer. A lot of great tours so far. Guests are very interested in history. I'd hate for everything to go up in smoke."

Ryan smiled. "Thanks for the heads up about Stephanie. She's a nice fit for the job."

Joe nodded. "She's a sweetheart."

Ryan widened his gaze.

Joe held up both hands. "Not for me. She's too young. I talk pop culture in the teacher's lounge, and I can see her eyes glaze over from the door."

"I wouldn't hold that against her."

Joe scowled.

Ryan chuckled. "I did want to mention. I promised Hank a huge celebration for his birthday next year. I'm anticipating an all-hands-on deck scenario. Be ready."

"I look forward to it. You sure you're alright?"

Ryan nodded and got to his feet. At the door, he sniffed. While smoke lingered, the haze cleared from the kitchen. "I will be. Thanks for being a good friend and stopping by."

Joe stood and tipped his head, jogging down the stairs. "I'll see you tomorrow."

Ryan nodded and walked inside, shutting the door. He had a lot to squeeze into a short time. He could do it. When life shoved him against a wall, he pushed back harder.

CHAPTER 20

Meg tightened her grip on the steering wheel and shifted forward in the driver's seat. She'd only been to the hospital once and wasn't sure where to go. Until a couple nights ago, she hadn't appreciated her luck with good health.

In the shotgun seat, Colby whined.

"Shh." She reached out a hand and petted the dog, never taking her gaze off the road and the signs. "We're picking up your cowboy. I promise."

Slowing, she turned into the circle drive in front of the medical building. She parked and turned on her hazards, swiveling in her seat to face the automatic doors. For two nights, she'd done nothing but stew. If Ryan hadn't cut her off, she would have put everything out there for him. She'd have done as Hank asked.

Ryan's scared face haunted her. While the small mercy of stopping the conversation ripped her heart in half, she had no other choice. Instead of honesty, she vowed distance. Time healed all things. She'd keep to her land and her house, inviting Hank over to her turf. Maybe one day she could stand to look at Ryan again.

While she waited for any word, she spent her time creating her online store from behind the register of her physical branch. Once she stopped asking questions, she started learning the answers. Why had she been so scared and intimidated to start? Was it her fear of failure? She'd had enough falling flat on her face in recent weeks to forever abolish any such hang-ups.

Slowly but surely, she began to list the books from Hank's consignment. She hit publish on the site only an hour ago and already her phone pinged with sold notifications.

She could do this. She could stay. Grandma thrived on the ranch for years on her own. Meg would be as strong and independent.

A knock sounded at the window.

She turned and lowered the window a crack.

"Are you picking up Hank Kincaid?" A fresh-faced, pony-tailed, twenty-something woman in nurse's scrubs asked.

"I am. Should he sit in the front or the back?"

"Back."

Meg nodded. "I'll hold the dog so you can help him."

"Is this Colby?" The nurse smiled.

Colby woofed and wagged her tail, thumping the uphol-stered seat.

"Mr. Kincaid has been talking about you all morning, little girl. We'll be right out." The nurse walked away.

Meg rolled up the window and reached for the dog's collar, holding her around the shoulders with both arms. "Shh, shh."

Excitement radiated off the dog's body. Her pants came fast and furious.

The back door opened.

Hank grunted, reached for the door handle, and pulled himself inside.

The nurse helped him with his seat belt and shut the door. She waved at Hank and flashed Meg a thumbs-up.

Colby howled.

Hank chuckled. "Well don't stand on ceremony for me, pup. I won't break. Get back here."

"You sure?" Meg frowned.

Hank nodded and grinned.

Meg let go of Colby.

The dog vaulted over the center console and into the back seat. She landed with a thud and launched into licking Hank's face. The loud slurping sounds were greeted with warm laughter.

Meg turned in her seat, put the SUV into gear, and drove through the parking lot. She navigated onto the highway. For most of the ride, only the sounds of Hank's laughter and Colby's tongue filled the SUV. Meg was glad for the silence. She feared telling Hank the truth. She'd ultimately disappointed him. She couldn't feel worse if she was confessing to her own family.

When the sounds of joy quieted, she studied him in the rearview mirror and smiled, meeting his gaze. "Happy Birthday."

"Not much of one." He sighed.

"I double checked. You'll have a cake." Although sending a quick text to Ted was the coward's way out of dealing with the ranch. He'd replied and asked her to pick up Hank.

"Ryan promises a big celebration next year, and I'm holding him to it. I already have a few ideas."

I'm sure you do. Hank's plans and schemes kept him active. If meddling in her life helped him, she was glad to have been a pawn as long as not sticking to his script wouldn't pain him. She wanted to be part of the birthday. A beautiful summer evening under the stars would be the perfect backdrop for Hank.

She needed distance. For Ryan's sake and hers, she had to stay away. How did she explain? She lifted her gaze to the rearview mirror.

Hank scratched the underside of Colby's neck.

Colby licked the side of his face.

At least Meg wouldn't have to break up this pair. "I started the online store. I silenced my phone before I came to pick you up. Your collection of hardcover books are the first items up for sale, and they are flying. Within seconds of publishing the first few listings, the books were sold."

"Oh, that's good. Not that I'm surprised. I don't work with amateurs." He winked. "You planning on staying in town then?"

She nodded. "As long as I can."

"Good, you're a little piece of sunshine."

She peeked at him again and smiled.

With both hands petting Colby, he focused on the dog with adoration. He could have been speaking to the dog.

"I don't drive you crazy with my chatter. Or my dog?" she asked.

He chuckled. "This dog is special. Not a lot like her."

There are plenty more that need a chance. Colby was a rescue, but, following the unspoken code of dogs, she saved everyone around her. Given a chance, every dog astounded the humans in their orbit with their limitless capacity for love and forgiveness.

Meg turned onto the dirt road leading to the ranches. She passed her house and eventually pulled in front of the Kincaid ranch house.

The drive was full. Three pickup trucks occupied most of the gravel.

The full cavalry? She steered her SUV to the end of the drive and parked, twisting the key in the ignition. At least she wouldn't need to go too far for assistance. "Stay here, Hank. I'm sure I can get you help."

Opening her door, she hopped to the ground and raised a hand to shield her gaze against the bright sunshine. Crunching the gravel under her heels, she had never felt more conspicuous or unsure. She'd approached this house countless times. Did she have a right to walk onto the property without an invitation?

On the porch, Ted and Joe stood shoulder to shoulder.

The full-time cowboy and part-time adventurer were lanky. Neither man was as broad-shouldered as Ryan. Between them, they had enough muscle to accomplish the task.

Her stomach clenched. She wasn't sure what she would say if she did see Ryan. Blurt her feelings before he could cut her off? At least then she wouldn't walk around with the nagging tickle of unsettled business. A smarter person would accept that he'd already turned her down. She whistled and waved.

Ted and Joe descended the steps.

"Thanks for getting, Hank," Ted said. "We were on decoration duty."

She widened her gaze and twisted her neck from one to the other.

Joe held up both his hands. "Not our idea. Luckily, I had some input from the other teachers on what to buy."

Where's Ryan? She didn't ask. He made his stance pretty clear two days ago. She hadn't thought that he'd avoid her. He could, conceivably, be preparing for a new round of guests. It was Thursday. He probably had a full booking. *He should be here.* "I have the birthday boy in the SUV. He's in the back seat with Colby. Can you help him?"

"Of course," Joe said.

Ted nodded.

The pair approached the SUV. She followed a few paces behind.

Ted reached the vehicle first and opened the back door. The men helped Hank to the ground.

"Don't coddle me. I'm not an invalid." Hank shook off the men.

Meg nibbled her lip. The doctor and nurses might have a better response to his declaration. Letting him get worked up would only set Hank back.

Colby jumped down to the ground.

Meg closed the door behind her pet.

"Just help me inside to the kitchen. Then you two can go," Hank said and turned toward her. "Do you mind if Colby sticks around for a little bit?"

Meg shrugged. "Of course not, if that's what you want."

"It is. I left something in the shed. Do you mind getting it for me?" Hank asked.

Now? She wanted to sing the birthday song, stay for a slice of cake, and then go home. With enough of a crowd, she wouldn't feel awkward. She could handle the new normal as long as she knew what to expect.

Heading to the shed wasn't in her plan. How could she say no to Hank? She'd pop over, find whatever he needed, grab it, and head out. Maybe she didn't need any cake. Her stomach growled. She cleared her throat, covering the treacherous sound. "Sure. What am I looking for?"

"You'll know it when you see it." Hank winked.

Joe and Ted led Hank toward the house, Colby excitedly barking at their heels.

She scrunched her nose against the tickle and burn of coming tears. She had an idea what she would find behind the house. She wasn't sure she was up for a formal rejection. Was he about to finish his "I can't?"

Well, fine. He'd have to tell her to her face. She sniffed and rubbed her eyes dry. Crunching the gravel under her shoes, she strode around the side of the house. At least she would know where she stood. For better or worse.

Ryan had never been more grateful for the community than during the two nights Hank remained in the hospital. He required assistance with the resort operations. Driving back and forth from the hospital, he counted on others.

Stephanie sat behind the front desk, answering questions from guests after her yoga classes. The members of the bluegrass band, all teachers at Joe's school, similarly stepped up to interact with guests, filling the void left by Hank, arguably the biggest draw to the property. Joe and Ted helped shuttle Ryan back and forth.

He found the drive impossible alone. He wasn't scared of much, but every fear resided within the hospital's four walls. If he hadn't been such a coward, would he have found the courage for honesty with Meg? He knew what she was getting at. Maybe if he'd have let her kill his hopes for a future at the place that terrified him, he wouldn't be prepared to ruin his ranch with her rejection.

Scanning the interior of the shed, he studied the two-nights' handiwork. Late into the night, he painted and laid laminate flooring over the subfloor. In the attic, he found a rug to warm up the space and added an armchair and ottoman. The room wasn't perfect. Luckily, his grandfather valued effort.

He told his grandfather to come down the minute he got out of the SUV. He couldn't wait to show the space to its owner. He wanted to reward Hank for finally fixing up the mess. *If only I could do the same.*

Ted had informed him of Meg's text. Ryan had dictated the reply. He needed a moment. If he raced from his grandfather's return into the big romantic gesture he had planned, he'd crash.

On his trip into town, he'd purchased a cake and ordered something special for her. Will at the General Store had shot him a curious look. Ryan had ignored his peer, thanking him for the two-tier chocolate frosted cake and leaving before he had bumped into anyone else.

A knock sounded on the shed door.

He turned toward the entrance, watching the panel slowly open.

Meg stood on the other side, twisting her neck as she took in the transformed space. "Wow." She stepped inside, leaving the door ajar. "When did you do all this?"

He shut his eyes, her lavender scent wafted in the air and tickled his nose.

A rain storm was predicted before sundown. If he stayed in the shed with her, he knew the electrical surge between them would cause a lightning strike. He opened his eyes and met her gaze.

Lifting a shoulder, he shrugged. "I didn't sleep much the past couple nights."

She rubbed her palms. "Me, too."

Because of Hank or me?

A cold breeze snaked through the entry.

She scanned the shed. "It looks nice." She rubbed her hands together. "Very cozy."

"It will be. I'll add heating and a/c and lights."

"Maybe a dog bed? I'm sure Colby will love to be here with him." She lifted the corner of her mouth.

The smile was hesitant and shy.

"Where's Hank?" He frowned. This wasn't the plan. He wanted to ride over to her house later with the roses he ordered. After he was certain Hank liked the room, Ryan wanted to apologize and explain.

"He told me to get him something down here." She nibbled her lip and crossed her arms low over her belly. "I think he meant you." Her cheeks flushed, and she stared at the ground.

Tell her. Now or never. This moment wasn't what he planned or—more accurately—rehearsed. He'd meant to catch her off-guard and leave her in no doubt of his intentions. Instead, every word caught on his Adam's apple, choking him.

With a sigh, she turned. "I can go."

"No, please stay." He cleared his throat. "I'm sorry about..."

"Giving me the wrong impression?" She shook her head. "Don't be. Hank had all sorts of ideas. You were right to stop me the other night." She met his gaze and sniffed. "Let's not make this any harder or more awkward than it already is."

"Too late."

She stiffened. "I want to help with your events. Let's be careful to keep our relationship civil."

In a handful of steps, he reached her.

She shuddered. "Don't push me away for good."

His heart slammed into his ribcage. "Is that what you think I want?" he murmured. "For you to leave?"

She lifted a shoulder. "To leave you alone, yes. That's what I think."

Joe was right. Hank was right. Everyone in town was probably of the same mind. Ryan should have listened. He'd let his misconceptions and fears take her for granted and then push her away. "Meg, you drive me crazy." His words tumbled out, more growl than speech. "Your constant need for chatter bugs me. Every time you walk into a room, you demand my attention. You've been this way your whole life. You're never growing out of the behavior."

Wrinkling her brow, she pressed together her lips but kept her attention on the floor.

This is all wrong. How had he gotten so off-script? He meant to flatter her with pretty words and entice her to take a chance. Who would waste a second on a jerk like him?

She didn't move.

Had he struck the right balance? If he was lucky, his impromptu honesty would mean more than any practiced compliment. She'd see through smooth lines anyway.

"No comment?" He arched a brow. "Good, I need to finish. Because I realized I don't like it any better when you are quiet. When you don't speak, I have to. I end up saying way more to you than I've ever said to any other person living or dead."

She shrugged. "I'm sorry I'm such a bother."

"No, you're not, and you never have been." He stood a few feet away now. If he extended his arm, he could graze her cheek with his fingertips. "I was foolish. You challenge me. No one else ever has. And the most surprising thing is? I like it."

She rolled her eyes.

"Fine. Don't listen to my words. Look at my actions. At sixteen, I vowed to never dance with you again in public." He reached for her hand. "I was foolis—"

Squeezing his hand, she lifted her quivering chin, her eyes glittering with unshed tears. "I love you."

"You stole my line!" He gaped. What was the point in preparing a speech and ordering a bouquet if she was going to do all the work? Was this his lurking in the bottom of a muddy creek future like his guests, the Claytons? He could only be so lucky.

She stuck out her lower lip.

In another second, she would turn pink and launch into some speech. He chuckled. The laugh shook loose the last bits of tension stiffening his spine. He knew every expression and could anticipate every rebuttal. Still, she surprised him in the most unlikely ways.

She could find someone else in a second. He'd be miserable for the rest of his life. Ford's advice was also a warning. Thank goodness Ryan heeded both in time.

Wrinkling her brow, she pursed her lips. "What's so funny?"

The corner of her mouth twitched. She was barely suppressing a smile.

Gently, holding her fingers with a light touch, he tugged her close. He reached for her waist and pulled her against his chest, wrapping her in both his arms. He would never let go as long as he breathed. Without her in his embrace, his world made no sense.

"I guess, since I love you, what's mine is yours."

She widened her eyes. "You really love me? Or you sort of love me? Or you l—"

He lowered his mouth to hers and kissed her like she was the tall glass of water after the dusty ride through the ranch in

August. She was more than the past or the future. She was his present.

If he could focus on one day at a time, he'd have all he needed in the world. The trouble would be keeping her occupied so she didn't start her chaos without him.

CHAPTER 21

A week later, Meg raced up the front steps of the ranch house at six thirty. Without knocking, she twisted the doorknob and strode through the front entrance, shutting the door behind her. She inhaled the scent of roasting meat and buttery bread. Her stomach growled. Strolling to the door at the end of the hall, she pushed inside.

At the stove, Hank stirred a pot.

Colby sat at his feet, tail wagging.

Joe, Ted, and Ryan sat around the big table, laughing and smiling.

She lifted the corner of her mouth, feeling the contagious, happy spirit in the room. "Did I miss dinner?"

Hank turned and glanced over his shoulder. "You're right on time. Go and wash up."

At the sink, she scrubbed her hands under the faucet. Turning off the water, she grabbed a paper towel, dried her hands, and turned. "Oooff!" She spun straight into Ryan's arms, hitting her forehead on his chin.

He dropped his arms and stepped back, rubbing his jaw. "Might need a bit of work on my timing."

She smiled and stepped forward, reaching on tiptoe and draping her arms around his neck. "Let's try again."

He lowered his head and kissed her.

Warmth spread from her heart to her toes. The gentle press of his soft lips on hers and his strong hands on her waist reassured her. They might have taken the scenic route, but they ended up where they belonged.

He dropped his hands and stepped back.

"Hank? Can I help?" she asked.

"No, I made those three set the table. Just get a good seat." He turned and winked. "Come grab the pot, Ted."

Ted nodded and pushed back from the table.

She slid onto the bench, next to Ryan.

Hank sat at the head.

Ted set the pot in the center of the table and motioned for the bowls, filling each to the rim.

When she grabbed hers, she breathed deep. Beef stew was Hank's specialty and the ultimate comfort food for the ranch.

Ryan passed the bread basket.

She bit her lip, grabbing two.

He arched a brow and turned, extending the basket across the table to Ted.

She liked having inside jokes. For so long, she felt like he laughed at her. Sharing humor together brightened her day. "Did you get the email from Eric?" she asked Hank, leaning around Ryan. "He cc'd me."

Hank nodded. "I did. Do you think those prices are real?"

"For a signed souvenir photograph card, apparently yes." She shrugged.

"I wish you sold the collection for me," Hank murmured.

"I don't regret anything." She shook her head. "You'll get five figures from the auction house, and the consignment is already sold out both online and in my store."

"Really?" Ryan turned. "Wonderful news. You're on a roll."

"Speaking of. How's your Frontier Days speech coming?" Joe asked. "Stephanie is pleased you agreed at the last minute."

Ted grunted and raised the bowl to his mouth.

Meg wasn't sure what to make of that sound. She was thrilled to be involved. "I think I have a good start. I'll be meeting her at the end of the week to go over what I have so far."

"You've got plenty of town stories to share," Hank said.

"I'm not sure how many I'll be allowed to divulge." She bumped Ryan with her shoulder.

"As long as I'm not the bad guy or the punchline of every joke, I'll be fine," Ryan said.

"Okay, cowboy." He might play rough and tough for others, but she'd only just begun to understand how marshmallow soft he was on the inside. Their strengths and weaknesses complimented each other. They were far better together than they'd ever been apart.

Under the table, Ryan reached for her knee and squeezed.

"I wish you'd taken a cut from the sale," Hank repeated.

"I'm doing fine." She smiled. "I set aside enough profit from selling the entire collection of Susie's books for a special order for the corner of my store."

"What's that?" Joe asked, stuffing the last bite of a roll in his mouth.

"A photo booth," she said. "I got tired of shooing away customers. I'll keep a selection of cheap props. The good stuff is on display in a locked cabinet. Hank, do you think you'd be up for a trip to San Francisco in the autumn? Might be fun to go to the sale."

Hank rubbed his jaw. "I could be interested. I have plans for the proceeds."

"You do?" Joe asked. "I never think of you as a spending money before you have it type."

"I'm not, and we don't know how much we'll get. Ryan's yurts just about covered the loan on the Hawke land. I'd like to invest in the future, too. I'd like to buy into the events side of the business." Hank smiled at Meg. "If you two will have me?"

She nodded, tears stinging her eyes. She could think of nothing better.

"I'll join you in the city," Ryan said.

"We're going for business, boy," Hank replied.

Meg's cheeks heated. Was it wrong she'd merge her professional and personal lives at the first chance? With any luck, her future became part of the Kincaid legacy.

"I have professional reasons," Ryan said. "The zoo has one of the oldest American Buffalo herds in the nation. The zoologists and caretakers have a wealth of knowledge. When my forebears were rounding them up, a park superintendent bought a couple bison and started conservation efforts in the nineteenth century. Thought they might have a few tips to share. I'm always interested to learn what I can." Under the table, he squeezed her knee.

"A good idea." Ted nodded. "The herd will be a big adjustment to operation next summer." He turned to Joe. "How are your town education efforts?"

Joe covered his mouth with a hand and held up a finger. Swallowing, he dabbed his face with a napkin. "I have an informal, educational night planned at the end of the month. The school gave us permission to use the building. I should have a booth up and running at Frontier Days, too. I'll be happy to answer questions and dispel any rumors."

Ted raised his bowl to his mouth and slurped.

Meg widened her eyes but didn't comment. Her exposure to life on the ranch had always been restricted. Now she had the full experience. *If this is the worst I see today, it's a good day.*

"Sorry, ma'am," Ted said. "I'll dust off my manners soon enough. Don't forget, Ryan, I should have a quote for the deck build next week."

She bit her lip to keep from crowing.

Under the table, Ryan squeezed her knee. "You'll get your big celebration for ninety, Hank. Meg had an idea for expansion, and you're our test run."

Hank leaned back. "As long as I am thoroughly feted with catering, balloons, and fireworks, I'll be your guinea pig."

Ryan shuddered. "I knew agreeing to your demands was risky."

"Demands?" Hank asked. "You mean strongly worded suggestions, and I have my first one. Joe, I want you and Abby in charge of the entire event."

"Entire event?" Ryan murmured. "What does that mean?"

Meg elbowed him in the ribs. It wasn't a time to tease.

"Are you sure you need both of us?" Joe asked. "Don't you think it's better to have one person in charge?"

Hank shook his head. "Teamwork makes the dream work."

Ryan leaned close to Meg. "He's not even trying for subtlety."

"Boy, hush." Hank waved a hand. "I know what I want and it's a two-person job."

Joe nodded.

"Might have to be in town if we get an early snow or a late thaw. I can't start construction until the summer tourist season is over," Ryan said. "Other projects and repairs come first."

Meg bumped her shoulder into his. "Don't worry. I'll be here the whole time to oversee the building project."

"I'm counting on it," Hank and Ryan said in unison.

Meg chuckled and the others joined in. "Full steam ahead," she said. She liked being part of life on the ranch. The changes were significant and exciting. She was thrilled to be included in the conversations, even if she agreed to helm the biggest celebration in the town's hundred plus year history.

"Hank, thank you for dinner," Ted said. "I better go do my rounds."

"I have to get going, too," Joe said. "Last staff meeting in the morning and then summer vacation officially starts. You'll get me and Stephanie full-time." He pushed back from the table, grabbing his empty bowl and plate.

She widened her gaze and glanced at her full bowl of stew. From the corner of her gaze, she spotted Ryan's almost finished dinner. She'd have to eat faster to keep up with the others in the future.

"Have a good night," she said.

"You too," Joe said.

Ted grunted.

Hank crossed his arms over his chest and slowly nodded, acknowledging the goodbye.

With boots clicking against the tile floor, Ted and Joe left through the back door.

Ryan pushed back from the table, carrying his bowl to the stove, and ladling in another hearty serving.

Meg turned to Hank. "What was that look about?"

Hank shrugged and leaned back, scratching the dog behind the ears. "Just thinking."

She shook her head. She knew better than to attempt to discourage him. Once he set his mind on a path, stubborn Hank wouldn't quit. His focus wasn't a bad thing. She could personally attest to the success.

Ryan set his steaming bowl of stew on the table, stepped over the bench, and settled next to her.

She leaned against his shoulder, and he scooted closer. Draping an arm over her leg, he squeezed her knee. Warmth spread from his palm to her heart. She belonged here with these Kincaid men. She didn't have much more figured out about them but had the rest of her life to learn.

Their bond was deeper than blood, strengthened by choice and time. Every day, she was more grateful for the catalyst that finally launched her into her role in this house. Family had each other's back. In Herd, everyone was Hank's family.

CHECK OUT
THE REST OF THE SERIES!

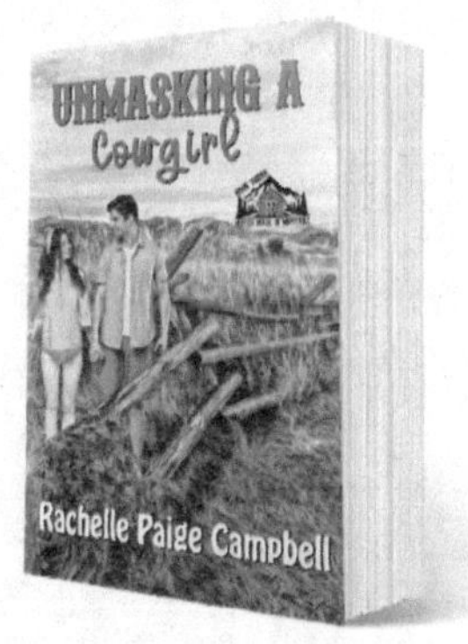

Find more great romance reads from
Rowan Prose Publishing!

Rachelle Paige Campbell writes contemporary romance novels filled with heart and hope. She believes love and laughter can change lives, and every story needs a happily-ever-after. Check out her blog for updates on current projects, and sign-up for her newsletter to learn about upcoming releases and announcements: rachellepaigecampbell.com

9 781961 967267